# LAKE VIEW HOUSE

# BOOKS BY HELEN PHIFER

HELEN PHIFER

# LAKE VIEW HOUSE

Bookouture

Published by Bookouture in 2022

An imprint of Storyfire Ltd.
Carmelite House
50 Victoria Embankment
London EC4Y oDZ

www.bookouture.com

ISBN: 978-1-80314-407-8
eBook ISBN: 978-1-80314-406-1

*In Loving Memory of Dorothy Patterson*

# PROLOGUE

The summerhouse had once been a glorious affair, built into the side of the Lakeland fell above the magnificent, now dilapidated, Lakeview House. Unused and unloved for decades, the stone walls were crumbling, the cracked windows covered in rich, green moss, making it impossible to see through them. The slate roof sagged in the middle under the weight of the sycamore tree that had grown against it at a strange angle, the leaves on the branches covering the building in the summer, shielding it from the prying eyes of anyone who walked the fells looking for adventure. This made it the perfect hiding place for what he needed.

Brambles and knee-high weeds covered the front entrance; he used a small gap at the rear of the building, which was hidden from view, to get in and out. Animals and birds no longer nested in the eaves or took shelter in there because they sensed it was dead inside. The damp walls, earthy soil, and smell of death reeked from it on the warmest of days – a warning to any passing walker to steer clear. It wasn't a place to take shelter from a sudden thunderstorm or the rays of the burning sun. It was a house of death, where he took the bodies of the injured or dying he found on the fells, and left them there until it was time to take them to the lake.

He'd known about this place since he'd been little, left to wander around the village and fells. Exploring every nook and cranny, the House – as the locals called it – had been his playground. The legends of the ghosts that wandered the vast corridors scared people enough to keep them far away. But he wasn't afraid of the dead; he liked them. A lot. He wasn't afraid of the living either. There really wasn't anything that got under his skin enough to scare him – except for maybe himself. When he looked in the mirror, he didn't see what others did. He saw a monster, and sometimes it was hard to live with.

Stopping to take a breather, he wiped his brow with the handkerchief he kept tucked in his back pocket. The sun hadn't risen, and the air was clammy. Picking up the ends of the sleeping bag, he began to drag it once more, the muscles in his arms screaming in protest. This one was heavy, much heavier than he'd have preferred, but he wouldn't turn an opportunity away, and this one had been too good to be true.

While the Mountain Rescue Team had been searching one side of the fell, he'd scaled it from the other direction and found the injured walker first. Smashing him over the head repeatedly with a rock, he'd watched as the semi-conscious man had slipped away.

His fascination with the process of dying keeping him enthralled, he'd watched the slow rise and fall of the man's chest taking shallow breaths, until it stopped completely. Then he'd had to work fast to move his body before the rescuers came and found him. He grinned. They were too late to rescue anyone this time.

It was a squeeze getting the body through the narrow gap, and he had to push and shove to make it fit. He tugged, straining so much he could feel a muscle in the side of his head begin to twitch. Then finally it was through. His breath labouring hard with the exertion, he sat on the broken chair he'd found in a skip when they'd refitted the village pub.

He was hot. Hotter than he'd ever known. Thunder was forecast and he wished it would start to rain now. He would stand on the fell in the rain and relish the huge drops of water as they fell onto his skin, cooling him down and washing away the smell of sweat and death that was clinging to him like an invisible cloak.

He looked at the sleeping bag and wondered if he should have just taken it straight to the lake; he was going to have a hard time dragging this one back down the hillside. It was always easier tugging them back down, though. Sometimes he kicked them with his boot and watched them roll. They didn't always roll far, but sometimes they would pick up speed and he would have to run to keep up with them.

Hopefully, this one would roll all the way back down, or he was going to be too exhausted to enjoy watching it take its final journey.

# ONE

Sitting behind the fold-up camping table, which was shoehorned into the space between the bed and the wardrobe, Madison Hart stared out of the tiny window. The lack of air circulating around the cramped box room that was now her temporary bedroom made it hard to breathe, and her armpits were damp despite showering an hour ago. At least this council estate had been given a nice name: Windermere. Only it didn't look anything like the Windermere she'd visited once as a kid. Memories of the huge lake and the grand houses that edged the Lake District beauty spot were of a much nicer view than this.

A group of rowdy teenage boys were kicking a football at some home-made goalposts on the patchy, worn-out piece of grass below, their shouts and jeers distracting her from her work. Tearing her gaze away from them, she looked down at the blank page on the computer screen. That was a lie; it wasn't completely blank. It had two words typed on it. *Chapter One*. She was learning that such a thing as second-book syndrome did exist, and it was a terrifying state to be living in.

The six-month deadline had seemed like an age away three months ago, but now it didn't. Looking down at the handwritten notes in her journal, she put her thumb in her mouth and began to bite at the corner of the nail. A loud ping alerted her to the latest email to hit her inbox, giving her a welcome excuse to click away from the offending, almost-blank page.

Hey, hope you're good. I've found you the perfect hideaway. You can get away from the city, like you keep talking about, and it's as far away from that arsehole Connor that I can think of without you having to emigrate. It will also be the perfect place for you to write that damn book. I can't wait forever to read the follow-up. I need to know what happens. Like now. Not in twelve months' time. I've included the details on the attachment, along with the owner's email. Do it now, Madison Hart. See, I used your Sunday name to get your attention. I swear to God, if I was you, I'd be on it right now. It's perfect. Don't hang around or someone else will snap it up. You don't need to tell the creep where you're going. Get your mail forwarded on to me and I can send it to you. It will be our secret.

Love always, Stella x

She read it again, hovering the mouse over the attachment, wondering if she was brave enough to even consider whatever it was that her best friend had sent her. Double-clicking, she waited for the attachment to download, sucking in her breath at the picture of the house and gardens that appeared on her screen. It was breathtaking. She glanced quickly around her room, at the magnolia-coloured woodchip walls, then back at the laptop. This room would be lost a million times over inside of that house, because it was huge.

It was a bloody mansion, set in acres of lush, green country-side, and there was even a lake below it. Hadn't she just been thinking about those grand houses by the edge of a lake?

Zooming in on the picture, she sighed. She knew it had been too good to be true. Many of the windows were boarded up, and it didn't look as if it had been lived in for years. It was a wreck.

She blew out her cheeks, wondering if Stella had been joking. Switching back to her blank page, she continued to stare at it for a few more minutes, before opening the email once more. This time, she read the text below the photograph and felt her heart skip a beat.

> The owners of Lakeview House are looking for a long-term house sitter to oversee renovations on the property. The position is live-in and pays well; to be discussed if you meet the required criteria. The right applicant will have free rein of the house and grounds. Contact with the owners will be through email, as they live in France. The House is situated in Armboth Valley in the Lake District. There is a small village nearby, where supplies can be obtained. If you like your own company and are not afraid of living in the middle of the beautiful Lakeland fells, this could be the perfect opportunity.

Madison blew out her cheeks. It was more than perfect. Her stomach was doing tiny somersaults the way it did when she got excited by one of her plans.

She could get out of London, and if she couldn't find inspiration to get this book written in that place, then she had no hope. And it was true, she wouldn't have to worry about Connor finding out where she was. Her gran could have her spare room back, while she would get paid for strolling around the house and gardens of a mansion, pretending to be the lady of the manor. It didn't matter if it was a bit of a wreck; she could make it cosy.

Before she could talk herself out of it, she began typing an email, then hit the send button. Standing up, she decided to go for a walk to Tesco nearby and get the ingredients to make something nice for tea. She might even splurge on a bottle of wine, because she was feeling epic. Even if the house owners weren't interested in her, she'd taken a huge leap. It felt as if she might be on the right road to getting her crappy life back on track.

# TWO

Seth Taylor slid back the bolts on the heavy double doors of the Horse and Cart. Pushing them open, he stepped out onto the cobbled street. The warmth from the rays of the early morning sun felt good on his face. It was always cool inside the pub, even on the hottest of days. Rubbing his eyes and yawning, he wondered if he should give today a miss; he wasn't feeling the love.

Last night, he'd spent more time tossing and turning, trying to shut off his busy mind, than he had sleeping. The last thing he felt like doing was helping the lads out with a practice rescue off the Lakeland fells that surrounded the village. He always tried to help them prepare for practices since his ankle injury had forced him to withdraw from actively taking part himself, but he had a lot on at the moment.

The pub wasn't doing as well as it needed to, and his dad's latest test results were the worst they could have been. His cancer was terminal, and it was a matter of time; there was nothing that could be done. Yet the stubborn old bugger was still insisting on opening every day and working until closing. It was very noble of him, but it meant that Seth was too scared to go far in case he was needed.

As he looked around the sleepy village, a sharp tug on his trouser leg startled him. Whipping his head around, he saw Alfie standing next to him, grinning.

'Bloody hell, Alfie, what are you doing sneaking up on people like that? One of these days someone might turn around and knock your lights out. It's not funny.' He gave the teenager his sternest look, which made no difference at all judging by the laughter that erupted from the youngster's mouth.

'Sorry, Seth. Got you good this time.'

Seth nodded. 'Yes, you did. But I'm serious, Alfie. If you do that to Mrs Grant from the post office or my dad, you might give them a heart attack. What would you do if they were lying on the floor, unable to breathe because you scared them to death?'

'Come get you to save them. You know how to save people.' Alfie handed him a flyer.

Seth accepted it, pushing it into his jeans pocket. He couldn't be angry with the lad even if he wanted to. Alfie was fifteen, going on ten. Bright enough to be let out on his own to wander around, but with a childlike manner that was far too innocent. It was lucky he lived in the village and not in one of the busier towns.

He was safe here even when he was left to his own devices, which he often was. When she wasn't drinking or reading people's palms, his mother ran the gift shop on the main street, which sold all sorts of junk that the villagers referred to as kooky, but the tourists loved.

Alfie turned and walked off in the direction of the playground. Seth envied him; the lad's life was pretty uncomplicated compared to his.

He went back into the pub, squinting to adjust to the darkness. The loud footsteps, vibrating on the wooden floorboards above him signalled that his dad was up and about, ready to fight another day. He sighed. If his seventy-year-old dad could cope with the crap life was throwing at him, then so could he.

Seth's phone began to vibrate, and he pulled it out of his pocket. Maybe he should go and help set up the practice after all. His dad would soon get fed up of him acting like his babysitter, and it would be a welcome distraction. Not to mention tiring enough to make him collapse into bed tonight and sleep right through.

# THREE

Connor Wood slowed his car until it was crawling along Camden High Street. The bookshop he was searching for was off one of the side streets. His knuckles clenched the steering wheel so tight they were white; he should have taken more notice the time he'd dropped Maddy off to go and see her interfering friend. But that day, the traffic had been bad, and she'd jumped out at a set of traffic lights.

*Damn.* He slammed the palm of one hand against the steering wheel, catching the horn, which blared for no apparent reason, making him look like an idiot. Feeling the hot flush as blood rushed up his neck, making his cheeks burn, he thought he might actually combust into flames his anger was so intense. She'd made a complete fool of him. Well, she wasn't getting away with it.

He didn't even know what the shop was called, or her friend's name, come to think of it. It was something like Sam, or maybe Della. Then it came to him: Stella, that was it. Stella with the huge head of ginger curls, an arse one of the Kardashians would be proud of, and the most annoying, loud cackle of a laugh that he'd ever heard in his entire life.

She was the complete opposite to Maddy. Not that he'd say no if the chance came around, because he'd sleep with anything if it was half-decent. Suddenly an idea occurred to him. Instead of showing Stella how angry he was about the whole situation, as he'd intended, maybe he needed to play it cool. Be nice to her, flirt with her a little. Ask her out for a drink after work, tell her he felt bad how things had ended between him and Maddy, and how he needs to talk to someone about it all. He didn't think she was likely to be inundated with offers from blokes, and if he played her right, he might be able to get Maddy's new address without letting her know what he really wanted it for.

A car behind him sounded its horn. Connor glared in his rear-view mirror at the elderly woman and continued driving. If he had to spend the next three hours hunting for Stella's book-shop, he would. His pride wouldn't let this one go without a fight.

Turning off at the next junction, he pulled into a loading bay and took out his phone. Maddy had had the cheek to block him on Facebook, but she hadn't blocked him on Messenger. He began typing another message to go with the other two hundred unread messages that he'd sent to her.

His blood was boiling that she'd walked out on him when it was his brother's wedding in three weeks. She'd promised faith-fully that she'd go with him, and he'd bragged about how much in love he was with the new publishing sensation, bestselling writer Madison Hart. How they were head over heels with each other, and he couldn't wait to introduce her to his family. In truth, he despised his family, and hadn't thought he'd ever feel so angry and bitter about anyone as he did about them. But then he'd come home from work and found that she'd gone. Packed her bags and left him.

Well, it wasn't happening. He wasn't having it. When he'd finished breaking her fingers, one by one, she'd be lucky if she'd ever be able to use them to type another word again.

If he'd carried on driving along the high street, instead of turning off, he'd have seen the woman who was causing him so much frustration. Maddy had come out of Tesco and decided to pay Stella a visit, turning the corner into the narrow side street and walking towards the quirky bookshop halfway along. She stepped through the door of the shop, just as Connor lifted his head from his phone and began to drive off towards the opposite end of the high street, ready to start his search from the beginning again.

# FOUR

Stella was serving the guy with the black man bun who came in every Thursday at 15:15 without fail. The overpowering smell of sweet caramelised onions clung to his clothes, and always made her want a hot dog with the full works. Stella had a bet with Aden that the guy either worked in a greasy spoon or was unfortunate enough to live above one. He was a nice bloke, though. He bought a book each time he came in, and never left empty-handed. He was an excellent customer, and right now Stella would put up with him coming in smelling of anything.

Aden liked to tease her that onion guy fancied her, but she hoped to God that he didn't. She might not have much going on in the love department at the minute, but he wasn't her type at all. Not unless he got rid of the long hair and asked the fire department to hose him down and make him smell a lot better than he usually did.

She took the book from him and stared down at the title: *Serial Killers of the Eighties*.

'Oh, you like this kind of stuff, then?'

His cheeks flushed and he stammered, 'Well, yes and no. I'm fascinated with them, but I don't actually like them. It's more of a morbid interest. It's not like I agree with them, or anything like that.'

'It's okay, I'm not judging you. I love it. I watch all the documentaries on Sky and Netflix. Although I shouldn't. I live on my own and freak myself out every time I hear a noise.' She started laughing and he joined in.

'Yeah, me too. Although obviously I'm far too much of a man to admit that in public.'

'You just did.' She noticed Maddy hovering at the back of the shop and waved before turning back to her customer. 'Hey, have you read that bestselling thriller *Death Wish* that's taken the charts by storm? I think you'd like that. It's brilliant, and it's got a really creepy killer in it.'

He shook his head. 'No, sorry. I like true crime; I don't like the made-up stuff.'

Maddy turned away, but not before giving Stella a death stare. She shrugged and carried on talking.

'Seriously, you should. The author happens to be a very good friend of mine, so I can vouch for her. In fact, she's standing over there. Pretending to ignore me and not doing a very good job of it.'

Maddy lifted her hand and waved. Onion guy turned to stare at her.

'I'm sure it's a very good book,' he said. 'I'll make sure I buy it next week.'

'Oh, you don't have to do that.' Maddy smiled, embarrassed. 'Ignore her. She thinks she's my agent on commission.'

'I am, it's a bookshop. I'm supposed to sell books to people, it's what I love. There's nothing better than recommending a book to someone and them coming back to tell me how much they loved it. You don't think I do this for the money, do you? Because there's not much in it, to be honest.'

Onion guy held out his hand to Maddy. 'I'm Joe Thomas, I work down the street at the new burger place. If you ever need a place to hang out and write, you're welcome to come in and sit there.'

Maddy smiled. 'Thank you, Joe, I'm Madison Hart. That's very kind of you.'

'And I'm Stella Sykes, owner of this fine establishment.'

Joe took his book from Stella. Pushing it into his backpack, he took her hand as well, giving it a shake. 'Nice to meet you both. I'll see you next week, Stella.'

As he began to walk away, Maddy shouted, 'If you go to the library, you can get a copy without having to buy it, in case you don't like it.'

He laughed, then walked out of the shop.

'I hate it when you do that, Stella. It's all very embarrassing and he seems nice. You'll put him off coming in if you try to force him to buy my book.'

'I'm trying to help you. He is nice, isn't he? Apart from the smell of onions that lingers around him.'

'What smell?' Madison asked.

'You didn't smell him?'

'Not really, and there are worse things to smell of. He could be the guy for you, Stella, and he must like you if he keeps coming in every week. Why don't you give him a chance? Ask him out for a coffee?'

'Why don't you mind your own business? Every time he comes in, I want to go eat my body weight in hot dogs. If he works in that fancy burger joint, which, by the way, is supposed to be very good, I'd be screwed. I'd end up that big, I wouldn't fit through the front door.'

'You know, I have no idea why you don't write books. Your imagination is far better than mine. Anyway, I only popped in to tell you I sent an email about that house. It's amazing, creepy, probably scary as hell at night in the dark on its own in the middle of nowhere, but it would be the perfect escape. So, thank you for sending it to me.'

'Yeah, it's bound to be haunted. They usually have the odd ghost knocking around that the owners can't get shot of, everyone knows that. Even more inspiration for your book. Aden reckons onion guy likes me.'

'He probably does, a lot. Aden is never wrong. If I hear back about the house, I'll let you know. I just wanted to let you know that I'd done it, and if I get the chance, I'll take it.'

A customer came over to speak to Stella, so Maddy left them to it.

# FIVE

Seth climbed out of his ancient Land Rover, groaning louder than the driver's door's badly rusted hinges. Every part of him was aching, and he wondered if he was coming down with something

He spotted Alfie come running out of the kooky shop. When the boy saw Seth, he headed his way, just as the door burst open and his mother, Glenys, ran out.

'Alfie, get back here now or you're going to be sorry for the rest of your life!' she screamed.

The boy ran past Seth, his eyes wide, breathing heavy. 'She's gonna kill me this time. She's flipped.'

Seth watched the big lad pump his legs even harder as he pushed himself to gain some distance from his banshee of a mother. As she caught up to Seth, he put out his arm to slow her down.

'Calm down, Glenys, he can't have been that bad that you want to kill him in public. What's he done now?'

Glenys stared at him. Struggling to breathe from only running a short distance, she was sucking in gulps of air. Putting her hands on her hips, she bent forwards to try to calm herself down. Finally, able to breathe, she shook her head.

'It's not easy, you know.'

Seth smiled. 'I can't imagine it is, and I never said that it was.'

'Yeah, well. I see the looks you lot give me when you think I'm not watching. I'm not a crazy kook, like you all refer to me. I have gifts, and I use them the best way I can to make a living to keep me and Alfie. You know I like a drink, but if I didn't try to relax with the help of a couple of glasses of cider, I'd be in the madhouse for sure. He's not easy to live with. God knows I love him, I really do, but he's hard work. I spent hours setting up a new booking system on my desktop computer for clients to book appointments, and it drove me mad. But Alfie's just gone and deleted the entire thing, along with my contact numbers, so I can't even phone them to rearrange. The whole lot has gone because the flipping icon was in the wrong place on the screen and he didn't like where it was.'

'I can understand you being mad, but battering him isn't going to help, is it? Haven't you got a Facebook page?'

She nodded.

'Well, just write a post explaining you've had a technical glitch and ask everyone to get in contact with you to confirm their appointments. Most people our age spend more time on Facebook than they do anything else.'

She stared in the direction her son had headed, then looked at Seth. 'You know, that's not a bad idea. Why didn't I think of that?'

'I'm sure you would have once the anger had subsided. Why don't you come in the pub for a nice cold glass of cider on the house? You can use the Wi-Fi to get on Facebook and everything will be okay,' Seth offered. 'It will all work out.'

'You do know that one day you'll make someone a great husband, don't you?'

He laughed. 'Is that Mystic Meg speaking, or an observation?'

'Cheeky.' Glenys laughed. 'It's both, if you need to know. Thanks, Seth, for calming me down. I shouldn't get so wound up, and I know he doesn't mean it.'

'You're welcome. Now, come on, I could do with a drink. You go in and I'll go and tell Alfie he doesn't have to sleep under a bush on the fells. Last thing I need is to hear Mountain Rescue has been called out because he's been reported missing.'

Glenys smiled and walked towards the pub, while Seth went in search of Alfie. He knew the boy would be hiding in the playground, because he'd seen him there many a time, crouched down in the tunnel that ran through a grassy hill.

Letting himself in the gate, he called, 'Alfie, it's okay, it's me, Seth. Your mum has agreed she isn't going to kill you.'

He waited and heard the shuffling as Alfie emerged on his hands and knees. His huge eyes looked up at Seth, who nodded at him.

'Come on, lad, have you had any tea?'

He shook his head.

'Right, well, your mum is at the pub having a quick drink, and I'm starving. You can come and help me make some sausage sandwiches.'

'I like sausages.'

'I know you do.'

Alfie stood up and they walked back to the pub in a comfortable silence.

# SIX

Maddy hauled the last of her bags out of the tower block lift, dragging it to her car where her gran was sitting in the passenger seat, guarding the contents with her life. She grinned at the sight of her tiny grandmother, who scared even the toughest of teenagers because she shouted louder than an army drill sergeant.

Pushing the bag into the back seat of her VW Beetle, Maddy slammed the door shut and her gran stepped out of the car. There was no mistaking the tears in her eyes. She was a tough cookie and would never cry in public or in front of Maddy, which made her granddaughter realise how much she loved her.

Scooping the elderly woman into her arms, she squeezed tight, then rocked her back and forth. 'Thank you for letting me stay with you. I'm going to miss you so much.'

'Honey, you're always welcome here, you know that. Are you sure you want to do this? I know you want to get away, and I understand that. But that house is far too big for one person to live in and look after. Are you any good with a hammer? It's in the middle of nowhere. What if you need a pizza at two in the morning?'

Maddy laughed. 'Aw, you're funny, Gran. I'm just going to have to make sure I keep plenty of pizzas in the freezer and make my own.'

Her gran arched an eyebrow at her. 'Now who's funny? Last time you cooked pizza the whole block had to be evacuated because you set off the smoke alarms. I'm being serious, Maddy, it's going to be lonely out there. I worry about you.'

'You don't have to worry. I promise I won't try to burn the building down.'

'You better not, it's been standing for hundreds of years. I don't think the owners would be too happy if you did.'

Kissing her gran's wrinkled cheek, Maddy let go and stepped back. 'It's what I need. I have to write this book. I can go for walks in the fresh air or swim in the lake, then I can spend the rest of the day writing. It's perfect. I don't have to worry about bumping into Connor, and it will be like being on holiday for six months and getting paid for it. As soon as I'm settled and the place is liveable, you can come and stop for a couple of weeks. You can have a holiday as well. Get some fresh air in your lungs.'

'Maddy, I love you, girl. I do. But I don't want to be stopping in no haunted mansion in the middle of a mountain. I bet they don't even have Netflix out there.'

Maddy giggled. 'You're not selling it to me.'

'I'm not trying to.'

She got into the car, putting the window down. 'I love you and I'll ring you as soon as I can. I don't know what the phone signal will be like, so don't worry. I promise it's all good. I'm excited to escape for some peace and quiet.'

Lifting her hand to her mouth, the elderly woman kissed her fingertips and blew the kiss in Maddy's direction, then she turned and headed back into the block of flats.

Maddy's heart felt as if it was tearing in two; she hated upsetting her gran. It wasn't as if she was moving to New York, although that was on her bucket list. It was the English Lake District, where she was going to be living in a house on her own, surrounded by sheep. It would probably be an added bonus if she couldn't get Netflix, because then she wouldn't be likely to binge watch every episode of *Stranger Things* and *The Killing*. No, this was a once in a lifetime opportunity which had come along at the right time, and she was grateful that the owners had said yes to her email.

She had one last person to say goodbye to: Stella.

# SEVEN

Connor stared out of the wall of windows overlooking the Thames. When he'd asked for a few days off work, his concerned boss had actually left his office to come and see if everything was okay. The miserable old sod had been impressed when Conor had explained that he wanted to spend some time with his girlfriend. He hadn't told him that the spending time with her involved beating her to within an inch of her life and breaking her fingers.

Connor knew he worked too much, but it was his choice. He wanted to be the best he possibly could. At school he'd been an overachiever, and he harboured a dream to write a book one day. Maddy had appealed to him because she was already on her way to being published when they met. He'd thought he'd be able to use her to further himself, maybe even get her to help him write his book. But that wasn't going to happen now, was it? She had taken herself, her success, and her contacts in the industry away from him, leaving him with nothing of value from their relationship and a bad taste in his mouth. Not to mention a burning rage inside of him he hadn't realised could send him over the edge.

He knew he was a complete control freak – or so his many previous girlfriends had told him. Even if he could change, he wouldn't. He didn't want to. He liked knowing exactly how things were going to be, how much money he was earning, and what he was going to do with it. But he had never expected Maddy to pack her stuff and leave him, after the time they'd spent together. It wasn't right. *He* finished relationships; it wasn't the other way around.

Connor pressed his forehead against the glass. It was hot outside. The kind of heat that was perfectly acceptable if you were sat around a pool in the Maldives sipping cocktails, but not in the city. Today, he was going to track down that bitch, come hell or high water. He would find out where she was, then stalk her until he knew he could get her alone. He wasn't going to let her know it was him; she would get the shock of her life when someone jumped her down a dark alley. He'd pay some cheap whore to give him an alibi, and all would be good. Maybe when he'd paid her back and she couldn't write for months he would be able to move on with his life. Until that happened, this burning anger was going to fester away inside of him until it exploded.

He knew Stella was his best way to find her, but yesterday's search of Camden High Street for her bookshop hadn't been successful as he'd hoped. He moved to sit at his computer and googled Stella's name, then waited for the articles to load. Various pictures of her standing outside her poky shop filled his screen. He grinned. Why hadn't he done this yesterday?

A picture of Maddy with her arm around Stella, holding a copy of her book outside the front of the bookshop, brought the red mist down over his eyes. He saved the image, then printed it out, but not before punching the screen and cracking the glass across her smug face. A sliver of glass sliced his knuckle and he watched as a trickle of bright red began to drip down his finger.

Red was such a pretty colour; Maddy only ever wore black or grey. He couldn't wait to turn her skin into a bright, red explosion of marks.

He licked the blood from his finger and picked the picture off the printer, which was still spewing out paper. He only needed one for now – a little reminder of what his goal for today was.

* * *

He strolled into Stella's bookshop thirty minutes later. Instead of marching up to the counter and demanding to know where Maddy was, he knew he would have to play things a little cooler. Instead, he began browsing a stand of travel books, while at the same time keeping an eye on the man behind the counter who was chatting loudly on the phone. There was no sign of Stella and he'd never seen this bloke before in his life, but that might work in his favour. When the man ended his phone call, Connor sauntered over to the counter.

'Hi, is Stella around?'

The man shook his head. 'No, sorry. She's nipped out for lunch, then taking the afternoon off. Can I help you?'

'Not really. I needed to speak to her about a mutual friend of ours. I'll try to catch her at home.' Connor didn't have a clue where she lived, but it sounded good.

The man shrugged. 'Well, she's not home now, or I'd have heard her size eights stomping around the flat. You wouldn't believe how much noise one woman can make, it's enough to give you a migraine.' The man winked at him and Connor took a step back.

'Thanks, not to worry. Bye.'

He turned and left, pleased that at least now he knew where Stella lived, and he hadn't even had to ask. She wasn't going to be very happy that her employees were so careless with her personal information.

He'd come back later when it was darker, and the shops were closed. It would be better if there were no witnesses.

# EIGHT

Stella poured the last of the wine into her glass; she'd already had a couple at lunch with Maddy. Now that her friend had set off to drive to the mansion in the Lakes, Stella was starting to regret sending her the email. She hadn't really thought that Maddy would actually land the job; she'd had just been trying to cheer her up.

Smooth FM was playing through the Alexa that Maddy had bought her for her birthday, and Stella began singing along with Sade in her sexiest voice when a knock at the door stopped her in full flow. She jumped, spilling red wine down the front of her top. *Shit, who is knocking this time of night?*

Putting the glass down on the kitchen worktop, she went to the front door and peered through the spyhole. It was dark out there; her security light needed a new bulb, so all she could see was a shadowy figure. Too nosy for her own good, and against her better judgement, she opened the door and stared at the man standing on the other side until the silence became uncomfortable. He was smiling at her, his eyes cast down, not meeting her stony gaze.

'Connor,' she managed eventually. 'What are you doing here?'

'I'm sorry to bother you, Stella, but I needed to talk to someone about Maddy and you're the only person I could think of.'

She didn't know whether to shut the door and phone the police, or let him in, but she'd always been a pushover. She didn't know what she could actually say if she phoned the police, anyway; as far as she knew, asking to chat wasn't a criminal offence. The wine she'd consumed clouding her better instinct, she opened the door and stepped to one side.

'You better come in then.'

'Thank you. I really appreciate you letting me in. I know we didn't get on too well, but I think we got off on the wrong foot. I'm not the ogre she made me out to be.'

Stella pointed to a stool at the breakfast bar. When he sat down, she walked around the other side, keeping her distance from him.

'Would you like a glass of wine?'

'Maybe a small one. I'm driving.'

She took another bottle from the rack and opened it, passing him a glass. 'So, to what do I owe this pleasure?'

He sighed. 'I miss her so much. I really thought that she was the one, that we had something very special. I don't know what she's told you about me, though I can imagine it's not good. But it was the shock of finding her gone; it totally screwed with my head. I've been walking around in a daze. I can't eat or sleep for worrying about her.'

'Maddy said you were too controlling, she felt suffocated by you, and that your temper was getting worse by the day. She doesn't lie; she never has as long as we've been friends, and I have no reason not to believe her.'

Stella watched him carefully, wondering if she'd said too

much. He stared down at the floor and shrugged, then lifted the glass, taking a large gulp of the red wine.

'I'm guilty of all those things and I'm not making excuses, apart from the fact that I loved her so much I wanted to keep her to myself. I know now that it's wrong and I shouldn't have treated her like that. Only it's too late now to do anything about it. I don't know where she is or if she's okay. I just wanted to tell her how sorry I was for screwing everything up.'

He looked so miserable that Stella found herself wanting to pat his arm and comfort him. Instead, she finished the last of her wine and refilled her glass.

'I don't know where she is. Last I heard, she was stopping with her gran. Then she rang me today and told me she'd found a job and was moving away.'

He looked up in surprise. 'What? Where? What sort of job, and where has she moved to?'

She shook her head. 'Sorry, I don't know. She said she'd let me know when she was settled. I can talk to her next time she rings, though, and ask her if you can contact her? I can't give you any more than that and you shouldn't expect me to.'

The loud sob which escaped his mouth completely threw her off guard. She'd expected him to fly off the handle and go mental. Instead, there were tears falling from his eyes and he seemed to have shrunk in front of her. This time she did step forward and patted his hand.

He clasped hold of hers, then lifted his sleeve to wipe his eyes. 'Oh God, I'm sorry. I'm a mess. I shouldn't have come here. You've been so kind, thank you. I'll be so grateful if you could ask her if we can just talk. That's all I want. To say sorry.'

Stella smiled, tugging her hand away. The tingling sensation of his skin on hers wasn't supposed to happen; she was supposed to feel revulsion at him even having the audacity to touch her. Yet she didn't. It was as if there was some kind of static electricity running through them, and it had left her wanting him to do more than hold his hand.

He stood up. 'Thank you for being so kind and understanding.'

She nodded, unable to find the right words. He crossed the room, and before she could move, he bent down and kissed her cheek, leaving that tingling as well. Then he walked towards the door.

Speechless, Stella lifted a finger to the spot where he'd kissed her cheek. Oh God! In the space of five minutes, she'd gone from hating him to wanting to drag him into her bedroom. Maddy would go mad! She needed to snap out of it, because if this was the other way around, she would feel betrayed, hurt, and so angry with her friend that she'd probably never speak to her again.

'Bye, Stella. Thank you.'

She shut her front door, locked it, and slid the safety chains across. Not to keep anyone from getting inside; more to keep *her* from getting out, chasing after Connor, and making another huge mistake in her disastrous love life.

# NINE

The Beetle was making a funny, grating noise whenever she changed gear, but thankfully –according to the satnav – she was almost there. *Please make it to the house before you blow up.* She patted the steering wheel.

It had been the most breathtaking, glorious drive of her life. At least, it had when she'd finally got off the motorway and onto the A591. She'd never seen so many green hills, mountains, and amazing houses. She'd stopped for a break in Grasmere, grabbing a coffee and a few pieces of gingerbread from the tiny shop at the entrance to the churchyard. Spying a bookshop, her heart had soared, and she'd wandered inside Sam Read Bookseller and been instantly reminded of Stella's pride and joy. Picking up a couple of books, she paid for them and told the assistant behind the counter she would definitely be visiting them again once she'd got settled.

When Lake Thirlmere finally came into view, she breathed a sigh of relief. She was hot, sticky, tired, and needed a cool shower. If she was brave enough, and there was no one around, she might strip off and dive into the lake for a swim once she'd found the house. The blue waters in the photograph had looked so inviting.

Maddy had always loved swimming. That and writing stories had been her two favourite pastimes when she'd been in junior school. As she'd got older and started to develop, she'd fallen out of love with the swimming, too self-conscious about her body to be able to just pull on a costume and enjoy herself in the way a carefree nine-year-old can.

She missed the turn-off, which – she only realised as she'd driven past – was overgrown and very ordinary, with two broken gateposts and no gate. Finding a wide enough place on the narrow road to do the most spectacular eight-point turn of her life, Maddy prayed a coach full of tourists wouldn't come around a bend and plough into her. That was the thing with being a writer – she had an overactive imagination at the best of times.

This time, she slowed down and turned onto the bumpy, gravel drive; it didn't look as if anyone had been down here in years. The car wasn't doing too well, judging by the sound the engine was making, but at least she was here. If the Beetle broke down, she could leave it and walk the rest of the way, dragging her stuff behind her. But as she drove along the endless, winding track, she was glad the car was still crawling along. It was so much farther than she could ever have imagined.

Rounding a sharp bend, the lake and house came into view and she felt her heart race at the sight. It was beautiful and desolate at the same time. For a fleeting moment, fear filled her heart: What had she done? She was a city girl, used to the noise, the smells, and the life that went on around her twenty-four hours a day.

Pausing, she took out her phone and snapped a photograph to send to Stella later. On the way here, she'd decided to photograph every opportunity to write a blog about the place and her life while living here.

The drive skirted past the lake, which now looked an inky shade of blue due to the looming clouds. It was almost eight, so she needed to get inside and as settled as she could before it got dark. She didn't know if she was brave enough to go inside when the sun began to set; the Gothic mansion looked like somewhere Count Dracula could have made his home, instead of Whitby Abbey.

Parking as close to the imposing building as possible, she got out of the car and groaned, stretching her legs and arms. The email from the owners said the key would be under the terra-cotta plant pot nearest to the door. There were at least twelve plant pots. All of them had dead, withered plants inside, and were no doubt full of woodlice. That was something else she hadn't thought about. Insects were not her thing. What if the house was full of them and rats?

She shuddered, walked towards the plant pot that was nearest the stone steps, and lifted it. A couple of woodlice scurried away from the plastic bag underneath it. *Bingo!* She grabbed the bag, shaking it just to be safe, and opened it to pull out a large, iron key.

Approaching the front door which wouldn't have looked out of place on St Paul's Cathedral, she put the key in the lock and turned. The door opened without so much as a creak or groan, much to Maddy's relief. Her imagination was already in over-drive. She stepped inside the vast entrance and heard her own voice whisper, *Wow.*

The entrance hall was empty apart from a long sideboard, which was covered with a dustsheet. On top of it was a wicker picnic hamper with an envelope tucked into the corner, along with three huge torches. Maddy picked up the envelope and lifted the hamper lid. Inside, it was filled with a selection of tea, coffee, biscuits, bread, jam, and a slab of what looked like home-made fruit cake. All it needed was a couple of bottles of ginger beer and she'd be inside a *Famous Five* adventure and living out one of her childhood fantasies.

She laughed to herself, then stopped as her voice echoed around the empty walls, sounding too high-pitched. Sliding her finger along the envelope, she opened the letter.

Dear Madison,

Welcome to Lakeview House. In the kitchen is a fridge-freezer, which has been stocked with an assortment of food to keep you going until you can get into the village. I trust it is acceptable, and hope you like at least some of it. The builders aren't due for another three weeks, as the plans are still being finalised. There has been a bit of a hiccup with the planning department, who are being very strict about the renovations, so you will have the house all to yourself for some time. It will give you the chance to settle down and make the place your own.

If you need anything at all, you can email the owners direct or you can email or telephone myself at Corkill & Sons Solicitors. The numbers and email addresses are all on the noticeboard in the kitchen. The electricity is a little erratic; this is one of the first jobs the builders will be working on. The sockets seem to work fine, but the lights are temperamental. There are candles, matches, and more torches in the pantry.

Yours sincerely,

Gordon Corkill

'Well, thank you, Gordon, I'm sure everything is perfectly acceptable. Except for maybe the lighting situation.' She found a light switch and pressed it down. Nothing happened. The hall was beginning to get gloomy, and Maddy didn't know how she felt about being on her own in a house this size with only candles and a bloody torch to see with. She made up her mind: if it was too scary, she would sleep in the car tonight and then move her stuff in at daylight.

Picking up one of the torches, she pressed the button and the powerful beam flooded the hallway with bright light. She shone it around; there were so many doors to choose from. She decided to open each one, take a cursory look around, then move on to the next. All she needed to know tonight was where the kitchen, bathroom, and bedroom were. The rest could wait until tomorrow.

Trying to imagine where the kitchen would be in a house this size, she realised that it could well be downstairs in the cellar. The thought of having to go downstairs where it might be pitch-black made her stomach flip over, so instead she walked to the door farthest away, held her breath, and pushed it open. Relief flooded her entire body to see a kitchen straight out of a sixties' bad dream.

Stepping inside the room, she walked over to the old fridge-freezer, which was the size of a small mountain, and opened the door. The interior light came on and she was pleasantly surprised to see a bottle of champagne, two bottles of white wine, milk, eggs, cheese, and various cold cuts of meat. Her stomach groaned, and she decided to find the bathroom and a suitable bedroom, then come down and grab herself a selection of food and a glass of wine before retiring to her bedroom for the night.

It was too late to be exploring on her own, and for a fleeting moment she wished she had someone here to share this adventure with. Stella would be so freaked out; Connor would have loved it. Such a shame that he'd turned into a complete psycho without a good reason.

A loud sigh escaped her lips. If she didn't finish this sequel, she could write a book about a crazy writer who decided to live on her own in the middle of nowhere inside a haunted house.

# TEN

Seth walked Glenys, who was a little worse for wear, down to the shop at the bottom of the main street. Upstairs was a deceivingly large flat, where she and Alfie lived.

'You're all right, you know, for a local,' she told him. 'I always liked you. Some of them are stuck-up arseholes who look down their noses at anyone who isn't from around here.'

Seth grimaced. 'Thanks, that's good to know.'

'Where's Alf? The little shit. I suppose he'll want feeding.'

'He's already gone on ahead to open the front door and get the kettle on for you, and he's been fed. I gave him his tea. You need a strong coffee and something to eat as well.'

'I could eat you.'

Seth couldn't imagine anything worse than being eaten by Glenys, but he laughed. 'Whoa. Not tonight, you're not. Enough of that kind of talk. You'll have everyone gossiping.'

They reached the side door to the flat and he let go of her arm. 'Get yourself inside and lock the door. I'll see you tomorrow.'

She blew him a kiss, tried to step across the threshold and

fell forwards, letting out a screech. Seth grabbed the front door and quickly shut it behind her, then turned to walk away.

He needed some fresh air and began to walk towards the path that led down to the lake, his favourite place. The sound of the water lapping at the edge soothed him more than a double whisky ever could. As he reached the lakeside, he looked along to where the old Lakeview House was; he could make out its huge outline even in the dark. It looked so desolate, he felt sorry for it. No one in the village acknowledged its existence. Partly because they were a superstitious lot who thought it was a house of death, and second because they loved to tell tales of how it was haunted.

Seth didn't believe in that rubbish; he did, though, believe that old buildings could somehow store memories of significant events that had occurred in them. The limestone and slate, which had been used to build a lot of the houses around this part of the Lake District, was said to be like a conduit for that kind of thing. If he had the money, he'd love to buy it and turn it into his home, and imagined being able to sit at one of the large windows and stare at the lake all day long.

As he turned away, out of the corner of his eye he saw a flash of light moving along the first floor. Whipping his head back around, he stared intently. There it was again; it was a torch. Someone was inside the house snooping around, and at this time of night it had to be a burglar; no one in their right mind would be in there this late.

He watched the beam as it moved from room to room, briefly shining in one before moving onto the next. It stopped in the room with the two huge full-length French windows that opened out onto a balcony overlooking the gardens and lake.

Seth was unsure what to do. He didn't know if he should ring the police who would probably take hours to turn up – that was if they could find the place to begin with. Or he could go there himself and see what was going on and if the house was being burgled. He didn't think there was much in there of any value to take, to be honest, but the thought of someone trespassing and maybe damaging the already sad, old house, filled him with horror.

He couldn't exactly sneak up on whoever it was in his noisy heap of a car. Pulling out his phone, he dialled the police on 101, to hear an automated voice tell him he was ninth in the queue.

Seth looked again; the light seemed to have stopped. What should he do? He could get a few of the blokes from the pub to go with him to check it out, but they'd probably all be a bit worse for wear by now. And if there was still someone inside when they got there, it could all get a bit out of hand.

He cursed Glenys. If she hadn't drunk half the barrel of Strongbow and needed walking home, this wouldn't have been his decision to make. It wasn't that he was afraid of coming face to face with whoever was in the house – he just didn't want to. He didn't need any more hassle than he already had going on in his life. Ending the call, he pressed 999, and this time a voice answered immediately.

'Oh, hello. I'm sorry to bother you, but I'd like to report a break-in at the old Lakeview House near Armboth Village.'

He gave his details and began to explain the best way to reach the house. The operator wanted to know if he was nearby.

'Sort of. I'm a couple of miles away, farther down the lake. I can just see the light from a torch moving around in the house.'

'Can you wait and direct officers if they need it?' the operator asked.

'Well yes, but then they'd have to come and find me first, and I'm in the village. Wouldn't it alert the burglar that the police were on their way if they fly through the village to find me?'

'God knows. Okay. Thanks, I'll recontact you if we need further directions.'

Seth, who wasn't a betting man, didn't know if he would be brave enough to place a wager on the police getting to the house and catching whoever it was red-handed.

He walked along to the wooden memorial bench that the regulars had bought in honour of his mum when she'd died ten years ago and sat down. He might as well wait and see if he could see the blue lights when they reached the long drive up to the house.

At least it would be more entertaining than cleaning tables back at the pub.

# ELEVEN

Maddy had opened four of the doors on the second floor and found that the rooms had been emptied of everything except for dust and cobwebs. When she'd started to wonder where she was supposed to sleep, she'd opened the door to this room and her question had been answered.

This was a huge room, situated in the centre of the house with two glorious full-length doors that looked onto a small balcony overlooking the lake. There was a brand-new bed, still covered in plastic, and next to it was an assortment of pillows, duvets, blankets, and sheets. Thankfully, everywhere had been dusted and swept, and no cobwebs came into view as she shone the torch around. *Honey, you've hit the jackpot!* she whispered to herself. It was like something out of *Beauty and the Beast*; she kept waiting for the torch or the candlestick to burst into song.

She flicked the switch and the room filled with bright light, making her eyes water. Immediately, she felt her shoulders relax and she let out a huge sigh. This was a sign everything was going to be okay; she could cope if she had light up here.

Leaving the light on, she decided to leave the rest of the house to explore until the morning. A loud growl erupted from her stomach and she realised she was starving. She ran back to the staircase, out to her car, and grabbed her overnight bag with her essentials and the laptop case, then went back into the house, dragging them up to her new bedroom.

She made a second trip downstairs to the very dark kitchen, leaving the fridge door wide open to illuminate the room while she made some huge doorstep sandwiches and grabbed a bottle of white wine from the shelf. There were a couple of glasses, plates, and cutlery on the draining board. Placing her sandwich on a plate and tucking the wine under her arm, she took hold of the glass and went out into the hallway.

'Police! Stop right there.'

Maddy felt the glass slip from her hand as she screamed. It fell to the floor and shattered into pieces as the bright torch beam blinded her.

'Who are you?'

'Madison Hart, I'm the new caretaker. Christ, I'm shaking, you gave me a heart attack.'

'We had a report there was a break-in in progress,' one of the two policemen replied. 'Have you got any ID on you? And we need to confirm that you should be here.'

Maddy shook her head. 'Not really. Oh, my driving licence is in my purse. And there's a letter on the sideboard from the solicitor. Who in their right mind would be in this house at this time of night unless they had to?'

'You'd be surprised.'

Maddy walked across to the sideboard, putting her food and bottle of wine down. Picking up the letter, she passed it to the nearest officer.

'Can you get your ID for me, please?' he asked.

She went out to the car once more, took her purse from the glove compartment, and rushed back inside. The officer was speaking into his radio, asking the control room to contact Gordon Corkill to confirm she was supposed to be there. The much younger officer looked at her and shrugged, mouthing 'sorry'.

Maddy took her driving licence from her purse and held it out to him. He looked at it then smiled at her.

'You're brave. I wouldn't want to live here on my own.'

'Why?'

He looked around, a faint blush rising up his cheeks. 'Well, you know. It's huge and been empty for years. The lights don't work either.'

She tried not to roll her eyes at him, not wanting to annoy him. 'Yes, I know. It's perfect for me. I needed to get out of London. I'm a writer, so the peace and quiet will be amazing. The upstairs lights seem to work in some of the rooms. Besides, I'm a big girl, I'll be all right.'

The older officer took the licence and stared at it. 'Sorry about this. We just need to confirm you're supposed to be here. I don't suppose a burglar would be making sandwiches at this time of night, and there isn't much to burgle, is there?'

'Not really. How did you even find out there was someone here?'

'Some keen-eyed villager noticed your torchlight moving around the house and phoned up. It might be a small village, but they don't miss a trick.'

Maddy didn't know whether that was a good or a bad thing. He began talking into his radio again.

'Right,' he said eventually. 'Well, it seems that Gordon has confirmed that you're legally entitled to be here. I'm sorry to have bothered you, but you understand we have to check these things out.'

She nodded. 'Of course you do. It's your job.'

'We'll let you get on then. Are you sure you're okay here in the dark? We could take you to the village and see if the pub has any spare rooms until they've sorted the electrics out.'

Maddy shook her head. 'Thank you, but I'm good. I'm not

afraid of the dark. The bedroom light works so I'll be staying up there until the morning. I'm from a council estate in London. There are a lot worse things to be afraid of than open spaces and a few lights that don't work.'

She couldn't miss the look the two officers exchanged and wondered what the hell it was supposed to mean. If it wasn't so absurd it would be funny. She'd never been in trouble with the police, but at least they hadn't dragged her out of here in handcuffs. Imagine trying to explain that to her gran!

They turned to leave, the younger one shining his torch around for one last look. 'You want to lock the front door,' he suggested. 'We just walked straight in. We could have been anyone.'

'Thanks, I will. Am I likely to get any more visitors tonight, do you think? Are the locals going to turn up with burning torches to chase me out of the house?'

He let out a laugh so loud that it echoed around the entrance. 'I hope not, or we'll have to come back and rescue you. These bendy roads are terrible when you're driving at high speeds. I still feel queasy.'

Maddy laughed.

'We'll let whoever called it in know that the place isn't being ransacked and that you're supposed to be here. He can pass the word around the village so that we don't get any repeats of tonight. If you need any help or are worried about anything, you can always phone 101.'

'Thank you, I'm fine. I would hate to waste your time.'

They stepped outside and she closed the door behind them, this time taking their advice and locking it. She could hear their feet crunching along the gravel to get to their police car, and for a fleeting moment felt an overwhelming urge to run after them and ask them about the look they'd had exchanged. What did it mean?

Deciding ignorance might be bliss, she picked up her food

and wine. Remembering the broken glass, she skirted around it to go and get the other one from the kitchen. She better not drop this one, or she'd be drinking straight from the bottle.

The mess could wait until the morning. She wasn't going to start looking for a dustpan and brush now.

# TWELVE

Stella opened her eyes. Connor's face filled her mind, which made her immediately feel guilty, and she wondered how Maddy was. She'd not heard from her friend, which was unusual but not entirely unexpected. After all, she'd driven across the country to start a new life without her.

She grabbed her phone and tried to ring Maddy; it went straight to voicemail.

'Hey, let me know you made it there and didn't crash into some mountain, or drove into a lake and drowned. Missing you already.'

This sudden obsession with Connor was not what Stella wanted or needed. She knew he was a jerk, especially the way he'd treated Maddy. Then why was she feeling like some teenager with a new crush?

She got out of bed and forced herself to have a cold shower. If this carried on, she'd need to go to church and confess her sins. Maddy would go crazy if she thought she was even considering doing anything with Connor. Stella knew she'd flip out if it was the other way around. She needed to snap out of whatever it was that had hold of her. *Your hormones are what's got hold of you, Stella,* she told herself. *That and the fact that you need a man in your life to give you a little excitement.*

By the time she'd eaten breakfast and gone down to open the shop, she'd managed to push Connor's visit to the back of her mind. She had arranged for a local author who'd published a new book of poetry to give a reading this afternoon, which was great. Unfortunately, though, she'd so far not managed to give away a single ticket, so she needed to drum up a keen audience.

Aden rushed into the shop, late as usual. It didn't bother her now; it used to until she realised how much of a lifesaver he was. He'd helped her out of so many difficult situations these past twelve months that him being ten minutes late each morning was a small price to pay. Not to mention that he baked the best cupcakes she'd ever tasted. On more than one occasion she'd threatened to apply to *The Great British Bake Off* on his behalf. He'd told her if she did, he'd never bake again, so she'd resisted the temptation.

'Sorry I'm late.'

'It's fine. Have you brought me anything tasty to eat?' She was looking at the large bag he was holding in his right hand.

'Yes and no. Well, I thought I'd bake some salted caramel brownies for the poetry reading this afternoon. So don't go eating them this morning.'

'Pft, the cheek of it! As if I would. You could let me try one, though. It's not as if we have an audience yet for the poetry reading.'

He placed his bag on the counter, folded his arms, and stared at her. 'Tell me you've been and mustered the troops for this one and that you didn't forget.'

She grimaced. 'Well, Maddy going away kind of threw me a little. I forgot all about it.'

'It's your bloody fault she's gone, you and your bright ideas. She was always good for dragging a few people down here for an event. Well, that's it, you're going to have to go and call in a few favours from the other shopkeepers. What about onion guy? You could ask him and some of his mates from the burger shop.'

'I could, although I can't see this being their sort of thing. Still, it's a great idea. I'll take some tickets and bribe them all with the offer of free coffee and cake, that should work a treat.'

Aden shook his head. 'You'll be the death of me, Stella. You promised you'd do your best.'

She grabbed the stack of tickets off the counter by the till and shrugged on her jacket. 'Leave it with me. I'll have an attentive audience all ready for three o'clock.'

'You better had.'

She waved at him and began the walk down to the burger shop, but the door was locked. She frowned. *Shouldn't it be open at this time, serving up breakfast?* Pressing her face against the glass, she lifted her knuckles and rapped on the door. A voice behind her made her jump.

'Can I help you?'

She turned around to see onion guy and smiled. 'I thought you'd be open by now.'

'We don't do breakfasts. This is more of a lunch-onwards restaurant.'

'Oh, I didn't realise. Are you busy this afternoon at three?'

'Not normally. There's a bit of a lull between three and four.'

'Perfect.' She handed him a stack of tickets. 'Can you come to the shop and bring as many of your workmates with you for half an hour? There's free coffee and cake in it for you all.'

He looked down at the lilac-coloured card. 'I'm not really into poetry, and I don't know if any of my colleagues are either. Sorry.'

Stella let out a huge sigh. 'That's okay, it's a bit last minute. I've kind of fucked up a bit... well, not a bit. More like a lot. I was supposed to be telling all my customers about it and I totally forgot. Then Maddy moved away, and she'd normally come with a few friends, so I don't have anyone to bail me out.'

'I'll come, and I'll do my best to bring a couple of people with me. There's definitely cake?'

She grinned at him. 'Yes, you've never tasted cake like it. Aden is an amazing baker. I just want to eat everything he brings in. You'll love it. And I'll owe you one.'

He laughed. 'Really?'

'Yes, anything you want help with or need, I'll do it.'

He tucked the tickets into his pocket. 'That's great to know. I'll see you at three.'

'Thank you so much.'

She turned and rushed off towards the deli where she bought her daily sandwich. The owner, Mr Patel, owed her big time for all her loyalty. She'd blackmail him into coming along with his wife and her extended family. Hopefully it would be enough to satisfy Aden and make the very nice lady who had written the book of poems about her new-found sexual freedom feel good about her work. Judging by the book, she'd already learnt how to satisfy her other needs.

# THIRTEEN

Seth was leaning on the bar reading the paper, but not really digesting it. He had received a message on his phone from one of the Cumbria Constabulary control room operators at Penrith, explaining that Lakeview House hadn't been broken into. The person was the new caretaker, and everything was all in order, he was assured. He frowned. Who was this new caretaker at Lakeview House, and how come he hadn't heard anything about it?

'Penny for them, son?'

He jumped. His dad had crept downstairs without any of his usual banging and shuffling around on the floor above.

'Christ! You gave me a heart attack.'

His dad chuckled. 'Good to know I've still got it. Is everything okay?'

'Yes, and yes, you do still have it. You can go back upstairs. There isn't much happening in here today. I'll hold the fort.'

Hi dad shook his head. 'You can go and do whatever you want. I like it when there's only me here. It gives me time to think. On you go, son. I'm okay. I won't croak it while you're out for a couple of hours. And if I did... well, it would probably be a blessing, because it would take us all by surprise. Get yourself out, it's a glorious day.'

Seth nodded. 'You sure?'

His dad stuck his thumb up at him, poured himself a half of Guinness and lifted the paper.

'I might go for a walk,' Seth told him. 'Go check and see if Alfie is still alive. Glenys was pretty angry with him yesterday, and then she got pretty drunk on cider.'

'Yep, whatever you want. She's a strange one, isn't she?'

'A bit. She's okay, though. I think she's a bit misunderstood, and pretty stubborn to stay put here when no one makes her feel like part of the family.'

His dad frowned. 'Are you going a bit soft on her? It's nothing to do with me, but I do think she might be a bit harder work than you're used to.'

'No, I just think we sometimes judge newcomers a bit too harshly. I'm just being neighbourly.'

His dad winked at him. 'Whatever you say, son.'

Seth turned away, shaking his head. He didn't think that Glenys was attractive in any way, shape, or form. He genuinely felt sorry for her and thought that she deserved better than the way the villagers had been treating her.

What he really wanted to do was to go to Lakeview House and introduce himself to the new caretaker. Whoever had been mad or brave enough to take on that position certainly had his seal of approval. And he wanted to know why the owners, after all this time, had decided that it needed a caretaker. As far as he knew, the council planning department had turned down the plans last year for renovations. He hadn't heard anything to the contrary that they'd changed their mind.

It would give him an excuse to have a look around as well. He hadn't been inside for a very long time and he missed the days of going there exploring when he'd been younger. He grabbed his car keys from behind the bar, deciding to call in on Glenys then make his way up to the old house.

After some serious knocking on the flat door, he was about to get back into the car when he heard the old sash window above him groan and creak as it slid up.

'Bloody hell, I thought it was the bailiffs knocking like that. What's up? Is the shop on fire? Is the village being evacuated?'

Seth laughed. 'Sorry, I just wanted to check you were okay. The shop's shut and it's almost eleven.'

Glenys, who was glaring at him with one eye open, shook her head. 'What are you now, my mother? Jesus, in fact you're worse than her. She didn't give a shit what I was doing or how long I stayed in bed.'

He held his hands up. 'I'll see you later. I was being neighbourly if you must know.'

'Hang on, don't go.'

The window slammed shut and he heard thudding footsteps on the wooden stairs. She opened the door in a pair of brightly coloured pyjamas, her purple hair sticking up all over the place, and black smudges of eyeliner under her eyes.

'Thank you.'

He stared at her. 'For what?'

'For being nice, and for last night. I'm horrible in a morning. Alfie drives me mad, he's so cheerful and happy when he wakes up. I feel as if I've been dragged out of my crypt by a vampire hunter and about to have a wooden stake driven through my heart.'

Seth grinned. 'You know, if your shop isn't doing well you could consider doing stand-up comedy. You're funny.'

'Ha, bloody ha. Alfie wanted me to ask if you could come for tea one of the nights. He likes you a lot. I told him that you're probably far too busy to come and eat burnt chicken nuggets and frozen chips, but he insisted I asked you. At least you'll know what he's talking about when he asks if you're coming. Don't worry, I don't expect you to come. And it's not some kind of come-on because, believe me, I'm definitely not looking for a man to keep me warm at night.'

Horrified, Seth stepped back. *What was he getting himself into?* 'Erm, that's very kind of you. I'm glad you're not after a man. I mean, who wants one of those? I'd love to come for tea one of the nights.'

She narrowed her eyes. 'Are you being serious?'

He nodded. 'I suppose I am.'

'It's just tea, nothing else. There's no free leg-over included. Well, nothing apart from Alfie having a bit of male company.'

'Good. I don't want anything else. I'm not looking for a woman; they're too much trouble and I have my dad to look after. I like you and Alfie as friends, no strings attached.'

He climbed into his car before he dug a deeper hole and agreed to anything else he was going to regret. Her door shut, and he breathed a sigh of relief.

Next stop, Lakeview House. He hoped he didn't end up agreeing to stuff he shouldn't when he got there as well, or his life was going to become a mixed-up, crazy mess.

# FOURTEEN

Maddy opened her eyes and stared up at the ceiling. It looked so far away it could have been in another galaxy. This wasn't Connor's flat, with its low ceilings and spotlights; it definitely wasn't her gran's magnolia woodchip-covered ceiling. For a second, she felt as if she had amnesia, then she turned on her side and stared out of the huge French windows onto the most amazing view of the Lakeland fells.

Pushing herself up onto her elbows, she stared around the room. *Holy cow, she'd slept here*! On her own, in this huge, old house, and hadn't died of heart failure or been murdered in the bed which she'd dragged over to the windows so that she could look out onto the lake. Maddy didn't know whether to laugh or cry, so she jumped out of bed.

Crossing the room, she tried to throw open the balcony doors, but they were stuck with paint and were having none of it. *Bollocks!* She'd promised herself breakfast on the balcony, even if it had meant dragging the stool from the dresser out there and balancing her plate of toast on her knees. Her shoulders sagged a little. Not one to be defeated, she would search around for something to scrape away the years of paint that had sealed the gap.

Her stomach growled – a mixture of telling her it was starving to death and excited to explore the rest of the house in the daylight. She didn't even need to get dressed; it was only her, the house, and her laptop for the foreseeable future. She did, however, brush her teeth, wash her face, and scrape her hair into a loose bun.

Pulling on her knackered Ugg boots, which had seen better days, she grabbed her mobile phone to video and photograph each room, and a notepad. She was going to document everything and anything she found, all ready to turn into blog posts when the storyline wasn't flowing the way it should. Writing anything was better than nothing, and it would be a welcome distraction.

Already she had some ideas about some plot changes she could make to get the novel off with a bang, and she felt a lot better. This could possibly be the best thing she'd ever done in her entire life, next to writing a book, finding an agent, then a publisher buying her book. That was a pretty tough one to beat. She grinned to herself as she went down to make breakfast. There was no point in working on an empty stomach; her new rule was self-care. It was all over the magazines, and her favourite celebrity Instagram feeds were all about taking care of you before anyone else. After her disastrous relationship with Connor, she was looking after herself.

Her footsteps echoed around the empty halls, but it didn't matter. She was pretty sure after a couple of hours she wouldn't even notice the noise. It was a bit like a ticking clock. Once you got used to it, the sound could be pushed to the back of your mind and forgotten about, as if it never existed.

Skirting around the broken glass at the kitchen door, she pushed two thick wedges of fresh bread into the toaster and filled the kettle. She wondered what the original owners would think of this place now. It had been left abandoned for so many years that she imagined they would be glad someone was finally showing the building the love it deserved.

She stared out of the grimy kitchen window, which looked onto the overgrown back gardens. The builders would probably replace all the windows, but for now she was going to clean the ones that she was going to be staring out of the most. She wanted uninterrupted views of the mountains, fells, and the lake. The view was too beautiful not to be able to stare wistfully at it whenever she had a moment.

The smell of burning toast filled her nostrils and she screeched at the smoke that was filling the kitchen. Rushing over, she popped up the now-burnt toast and grabbed a tea towel to waft away some of the smoke. There was a door that was bolted at the far side of the room. Wrestling with the rusted bolts, she eventually managed to slide them all back and push the door open as far as it would go, which wasn't much.

*Christ, Maddy, you've only been here twelve hours and nearly burnt the place down.* She couldn't help but giggle. It was so absurd how her life had changed so drastically in the last couple of weeks. She'd gone from living in a luxury penthouse overlooking the Thames to a Gothic mansion nestled in a Lakeland valley.

Buttering the blackened toast and smothering it in the rich, strawberry jam, she carried the plate and a mug of coffee up to her bedroom. She knew that room was dust-free and liveable; she didn't want to eat in a room full of cobwebs and spiders.

As she reached the top of the stairs, she thought she heard footsteps behind her. Light, tiptoeing steps. Maddy froze as the hairs on her arms prickled, and she felt the skin turn taut as goosebumps appeared. A faint screech filled the air, and dread filled the pit of her stomach. There wasn't anyone here except for her. She'd know about it if there was.

Forcing herself to turn around, relief flooded through her.

There was no one behind her, coming up or falling down the stairs, which was what it had sounded like. *It's an old house; you're going to hear all sorts of noises, so you better get used to it.* She carried on walking towards the bedroom a little faster than before.

It was her imagination, that was all. Writers were cursed with overactive imaginations – it was on the list of job specifications; everyone and their dog knew that. Still, when she went into the bedroom, she pushed the door shut with her foot.

She felt safe in here. This was her room now, her space. She'd make it her own, and no spooks or weird noises would be acceptable under any circumstances. It wasn't until she tried to put her mug of coffee down on the dresser and the hot liquid splashed over the edge all over the wooden floorboards that she realised her hands were trembling.

# FIFTEEN

Connor parked in the busy supermarket car park, only a couple of minutes on foot from the bookshop. He wanted to pop in and surprise Stella, maybe buy a couple of paperbacks, make her drop her guard even more, hang around for a while and look like a lovesick, heartbroken husk of the man he'd once been.

He rubbed his eyes so they looked red and blotchy and she'd think he'd been crying all night. Women liked a man who was vulnerable, who showed their emotional side. He'd been very good at this kind of thing with Maddy in the beginning, but it had been hard work to keep up the pretence and she'd started to see through him. In fact, she'd seen through him a lot quicker than most other women, and he'd had to keep up the pretence for a lot longer until he'd cracked under the pressure of trying too hard to be someone he wasn't.

Life could be so difficult. Why couldn't he just be himself and find a woman who'd accept him for who he was? Maybe there was an Internet dating site for control freaks; in fact, there probably were a few. Who knows, he could meet the perfect woman on there? Some women liked to be controlled. Not all of them were feisty, go-fuck-yourself feminists.

He walked past the florists and picked up a small bouquet of hand-tied flowers. Lifting them to his nose, he inhaled and was pleasantly surprised at how fragrant they smelled.

'It's the roses. They're called David Austen and they smell divine. Buy her a bunch every couple of weeks or for special occasions and she'll love you forever.'

He turned to the older woman who was smiling at him from the shop doorway.

'You think so?'

'I know so. My husband brought me fresh flowers every pay day for thirty-five years. Such a small gesture, but it meant a lot. Even the months when we had little spare money, he'd still bring some.'

'I wish I'd known that before the love of my life left me.'

She shrugged. 'If she left you, then she wasn't the love of your life.'

He laughed. 'Maybe you have a point. It still hurts, though.'

'Of course it does, pride is painful. Now, do you want those, or am I giving away my top tips for free?'

Following her inside the shop, he pulled out a twenty-pound note and passed it to her. She took it from him, offering him five pounds back in return.

He shook his head. 'You keep that, for the top tips.'

She winked at him, and for the first time in a long time he felt better, as if a weight had lifted from his shoulders. Maybe it was time to move on, to forget about Maddy. Have a bit of fun, don't even think about a serious relationship, and see what happens. Stella was fun, even with her loud laugh. He could take her out, screw her with no strings attached.

Connor left the florists and rounded the corner to the narrow street where the bookshop was. He was surprised to see people milling around inside and out. Yesterday it hadn't looked busy at all and he'd thought bookshops were a dying trade. It looked like he was learning lots of new things today.

When he went inside, there was an entire family who he recognised from the deli he'd been in yesterday. The noise was deafening; everyone was chattering loudly, drinking coffee, and eating cake. He felt a bit stupid standing there with his bunch of flowers. Stella was nowhere to be seen.

The tall, thin guy with bleached blond hair from the other day approached him holding a tray.

'Brownie? Are you here for the poetry reading?'

Connor felt his mouth drop open. He honestly couldn't think of anything worse than having to listen to poetry.

'Erm, not really my thing, to be honest. Is Stella around by any chance?'

'Stella.' The thin guy bellowed her name; he had a voice that was louder than a foghorn.

Stella came rushing from the back of the shop, her cheeks flushed, her hair tied in a high ponytail. She took one look at Connor and stopped dead.

'Sorry,' he said, 'I had no idea you were busy. I'll pop back later. I just wanted to give you these.'

He handed her the flowers, which she took, her cheeks turning redder.

'Thank you, but what are these for?'

He wasn't sure he wanted to have a conversation like this in front of a shop full of strangers, who had all stopped talking to listen to their exchange. Connor tried to keep calm and not get angry.

'Just a thank you for last night.'

She smiled. 'I didn't do anything, but thank you, they're gorgeous. Are you busy? We have a poetry reading about to start in five minutes as soon as the burger guys arrive.'

There was more shuffling as a group of men came through the shop doorway. Connor shook his head.

'I can't, sorry. I have to get back to work. Maybe we could go for a drink later if you're not doing anything?'

'That would be nice. Thanks.'

He turned to walk out and had to squeeze past a tall man who was standing with his arms crossed glaring at him. Connor glared back; he had no idea what the guy's problem was. Any other time or place he'd have shoved him and told him to back off, but today he couldn't. He was trying to make a good impression and show Stella that he wasn't the loser Maddy had no doubt made him out to be.

# SIXTEEN

Seth turned his car onto the gravel drive, trying to manoeuvre his beast of a car around the many potholes. He was aware that technically he was trespassing, but he wouldn't settle if he didn't find out who this caretaker was and why they were there. He needed to know what was happening to his ramshackle dream house. Not that he could afford to do anything about it; he didn't have the money to buy it, nor for the major renovations it so badly needed.

When the drive finally opened out and the house was standing in front of him, he stopped the car and inhaled. He'd forgotten how captivating it was, standing tall and proud despite the boarded-up windows and shabby exterior drenched in ivy. There was a blue VW Beetle parked out the front.

He parked behind it and got out. Peering through the windows of the car, he could see an explosion of pink bags and cases, but that didn't necessarily mean it was a woman who was the caretaker. There were plenty of guys who liked pink; it was a lot more fashionable now. He couldn't imagine this would be the kind of place a woman would choose to stay, unless she was with someone else.

He walked up to the front door and knocked, the sound echoing around the hallway. He waited and waited, knocking again, but there was still no reply. He wondered if they were at the back of the house. Technically, he had no right to be there; he was just being nosy. *Neighbourly, Seth, not nosy.*

He walked around the perimeter of the house until he reached the rear garden. It was a mess around here, so overgrown and so dark. He had to stay close to the wall of the house to avoid being swallowed up by the brambles. It seemed unlikely whoever it was could be out here. Then he saw a door, which was open wide enough to squeeze through.

He desperately wanted to go inside, but was this taking being a good neighbour a little too far and turning into trespassing? He reached the door.

'Hello, is anyone home?' His voice echoed around whatever room he'd just hollered into, but there was still no response.

Turning to go back to his car, he decided to come back another time. But for some reason, he couldn't. He needed to know what was going to happen to this place. Despite his best intentions, he went against his own rules and pushed through the narrow opening and found himself inside the kitchen. It was massive and old-fashioned, and the aroma of burnt toast lingering in the air made him smile. Whoever was living here was as good a cook as him.

Seth walked towards the door and found himself in a huge corridor. He could hear bangs and a scraping noise coming from the floor above. It seemed pointless to shout, as whoever it was wouldn't hear him when they were busy doing something. Taking his time, he strolled along the corridor towards the intricate, oak-carved staircase that filled the entrance hall. It was a stunning piece of work, and he hoped that whatever plans the owners had for the building included keeping as many of the original features as possible.

Feeling like an intruder, he paused on the bottom step.

Should he go up? The person might be crazy and have a gun. They could shoot him, thinking he was a burglar. Pushing that thought out of his head, he slowly climbed the stairs towards the sound.

Suddenly he heard a woman's voice shout, 'Argh!' And as he reached the top of the stairs, someone came rushing out of one of the rooms, holding her hand up in the air. She took one look at him and screamed so loud he felt he jumped several feet in the air, his heart racing.

'I'm sorry,' he started. 'I'm Seth. Hello. I live in the pub, and I didn't mean to scare you. I've been knocking.' He cringed at his stilted explanation.

She stared back at him, and he realised she was terrified. He also noticed for the first time that there was a stream of bright red blood running down her arm.

'You're bleeding, quite a lot. Here, let me help you. I'm a first-aider; I used to be a volunteer with the local Mountain Rescue.'

She looked at the blood and her face paled. 'Oh, shit. I hate blood. You scared me to death.'

'I'm sorry about that. I did knock a lot, and I shouted.'

She looked as if she was about to pass out, and he rushed up the remaining stairs to grab hold of her arm. 'Look, I won't hurt you, I promise, but you need to let me sort that cut out. You're bleeding a lot, and the nearest hospital is thirty minutes away. I can help you. I've done it plenty of times out on the mountains.'

Nodding, she let him lead her to the stairs and down to the kitchen. He sat her on a stool with her arm raised above her head, then grabbed the only cloth he could find, folded it into a pad, and pressed it against the open cut.

'Are you here on your own?' he asked.

'Yes. Oh God, has it stopped bleeding? I'm no good with blood, especially my own.'

'Don't look at it, and not yet. If you can hold it up, I can go out to my car and get my first aid kit. We can patch it up and see if you need to go to the hospital.'

'Thank you. What's your name again?'

'Seth.'

'Thanks, Seth. I can't afford to bleed to death on my first day or get gangrene and lose my hand. It's my most valuable asset.'

He arched an eyebrow at her, wondering if she'd lost so much blood, she was going a little crazy. What on earth did she mean?

He ran towards the front door where he let himself out, retrieved the green bag with the first aid kit in it, and ran back.

'Wow, that was fast.'

'It's easy when you're on the flat.' He grinned, pulling pads and bandages out of the bag. 'You should try doing that halfway up Helvellyn. It's a lot harder then.'

He busied himself cleaning the wound, which had slowed down to a trickle, then patted it dry and put a pressure pad and wound bandage around it.

'You're good at this,' she commented. 'Are you a doctor?'

He smiled. 'I almost was. I did three years then changed my mind. It wasn't for me.'

'Well, thank you. I could have died out here on my own. You saved my life.'

'You're welcome. I think you'd have survived if you'd driven into the village. There's always someone around to help.' He looked at her curiously. 'Are you really staying here on your own?'

She nodded. 'Crazy, eh?'

'Brave, more like. Where are you from?'

'London.'

'You're a city girl and you've upped and come here to one of the most secluded places in the Lake District? There must be a pretty good reason for that.'

Maddy laughed. 'Believe me, there is. But it's a long story and I won't bore you with it. So, why did you turn up here when you did?'

Seth shifted his weight from foot to foot, looking a little sheepish. 'I'm being nosy. I tried to tell myself I was being a good neighbour, and I am – sort of. I have good intentions, I really do. It's just that I saw the torchlight moving around in here last night and thought it was being burgled.'

'Ah, so you're the mystery grass who phoned the police.'

He shook his head. 'I'm not a grass. I was worried vandals or thieves had broken in. I love this old house.'

She laughed again. 'I'm joking. You were doing exactly what I'd have done in the same situation.' She held out her good hand. 'I'm Maddy Hart, caretaker and writer. Although, if I carry on with this level of DIY, I won't have any limbs left to write with.'

He took her hand and shook it. 'Maybe you should leave the home improvements to the professionals, then. It's just a thought.'

'You're right. I wanted to get the French doors open in the bedroom so I could sit on the balcony to eat my meals and stare at the lake. The only thing is, I think they were painted shut before I was even born, and it's proved a lot harder than I imagined. I slipped with the Stanley knife.'

'You're lucky you didn't sever an artery. Those things are lethal.'

'Yes, I guess you're right. No more dangerous stuff when I'm alone. I'm glad you decided to be nosy.'

He began to pack the contents of his first aid kit back into the bag. 'Would you like me to drive you to the hospital to get it checked out? You might need a tetanus or a course of antibiotics.'

She frowned. 'Do you think so? It was a brand-new knife; I

only opened the packet about three minutes before disaster struck. Does it need stitching?'

'Probably not. I've used some Steri-Strips to seal the cut. It's up to you.'

'I'll leave it then. I don't want to spend the entire afternoon in the nearest A&E waiting room. Can I get you a drink? It's the least I can do.'

'How about I make us both a coffee and you can show me the offending doors?' he offered. 'I might be able to help you. I'm a dab hand with the old DIY; plenty of years' experience.'

'Now you're talking. That sounds like a very good idea. I think I need coffee and cake to stop me from going into shock.'

Seth grinned. He was glad he'd come inside now. He'd helped her out and she was cute, not to mention funny. She might just be the thing to brighten up his currently rather dull life.

# SEVENTEEN

When poetry lady finished her last reading, Stella jumped up, cheering and clapping, hoping everyone else would join in. They did, much to her relief, and she couldn't blame them if they were clapping because they, too, were relieved it was over.

Poor Mr Patel's mother was sitting on the stool in the corner, her eyes wide and her mouth a gaping black hole, looking as if she'd been transported to another world. Onion guy and a couple of his friends had smirked, nudging each other on more than one occasion, just about managing to hold it together.

Stella determined she would never again agree to an author doing a reading unless she first took notice of what they'd had actually written. Mr Patel waved to her, mouthing, 'You owe me a year of lunches for this one.' And she couldn't argue with him. The quiet man had stood next to his wife, mother, and daughters, his cheeks turning pinker with every word the poet had spoken. She nodded at him, mouthing back, 'Thank you', as he ushered his family towards the door, desperate to escape.

Aden was doing a very good job of telling Zara or Fara – Stella couldn't remember the poet's name – how wonderful she was. Stella decided she was also going to give him a good kick in the pants for getting her into these situations.

She needed fresh air. Her head was a mess, her nerves frayed. She walked outside, where she leaned against the window ledge and let out a loud groan.

'That was different.'

She looked around to see onion guy and tried desperately to remember his name. She was so rubbish with names; faces she never forgot.

'It was bleeding awful, is what it was.' She turned quickly to check no one was listening. Traumatised as she was, she didn't want to upset Zara/Fara. Turning back, she noticed he had one of the offending books tucked under his arm.

'Oh, no. You really didn't have to. Wait till she's left then I'll give you a refund.'

He laughed. 'No, you won't. I'll give it my sister-in-law for her birthday. She'll love it, she's into this sort of crap.'

'I'm sorry, I really am. I had no idea. And did you see poor Mr Patel's face? The poor guy will never be the same again.'

Onion guy laughed. 'At least you put a smile on his wife's face. You said you'd owe me if I turned up with some friends. Can I take my favour now?'

'Anything. I'll even give you a kidney, it was that bad.'

'Actually, I was thinking more along the lines of you coming out for a drink with me tonight.'

Stella looked more closely at him. He was cute, funny and, apart from the onions, he was nice. Any other time she'd have said yes, but Connor's face was there in the front of her mind. He'd asked her out for a drink after work and she didn't know if she wanted to let him down, despite the internal warning that was flashing inside her brain telling her not to be an idiot.

She shook her head. 'I'm so sorry, I can't tonight. Any other night would be great, though.'

He arched one eyebrow at her. 'Did the creep with the flowers beat me to it?'

Stella felt a wave of anger fill her mind. Who was this guy to judge her? He didn't know her.

'No, he's an old friend who I just happen to have agreed to meet for a drink. There's nothing going on. Not that it's any of your business if there was.'

'Sorry, you're right. It isn't. Maybe some other time.'

He strode away and she immediately felt a twinge of regret. In an ideal world, she'd steer well clear of Connor. Christ, she knew she should stay away from him; he was trouble. So what was she thinking?

Stella stared after him, racking her brains for his name; she had to stop calling him onion guy. He'd already turned the corner when it came to her: Joe. He was Joe. But it was too late to shout him back to say yes, she'd love to, and she was sorry that she'd temporarily lost her mind but it was back now. He'd gone back to the diner, and now she had to go and make small talk with Zara/Fara. Christ, could this day get any worse? And how come she'd had zero interest from the male species for the last two years, yet today she was Miss Popular?

Making her way back inside the shop, she saw Aden and made a swiping gesture across her neck with her finger. He blew her a kiss and she gave him the middle finger. He was the one who bloody owed her after this afternoon. He'd be baking her cakes every day for a year to make up for this disaster if he wanted to get back in her good books.

# EIGHTEEN

When he'd come back to visit the summerhouse, he'd got the shock of his life to see a car parked outside the steps to the house. Not only that but there were lights on in an upstairs room.

Instead of heading straight for his destination, he'd had to make a detour around the lake to investigate just what was going on. Was someone living here? He couldn't imagine it; the house had been empty for so long. Who would want to stay here when it was such a mess?

The sky was a fireball of red and burnt orange, it was beautiful and spectacular. He walked farther along to sit on a rock by the lake and think about what he was going to do. Normally, he'd walk out on the rickety, wooden jetty and sit on the edge. But whoever was in the house might be able to see him and wonder what he was doing out there.

He liked to kick off his trainers and dip his toes into the icy, cold water. There was something very satisfying in knowing that a few feet underneath the jetty was his collection of corpses. The fresh water preserved the bodies much better than salt water, and it didn't matter to him that the man-made lake was used to provide drinking water to Manchester. He didn't care about contaminating it; there must be hundreds of dead fish and God knows what else in there.

He didn't expect he was the first person to dispose of a corpse in its murky depths. The water got filtered and treated, so it wasn't as if it was a health risk. And anyway, what did he care if it was? Not a bloody thing. This was his playing field, his burial ground, his lake, and his area.

What he did care about was how he was going to get the body out of the summerhouse and into its watery resting place, without getting caught. This development was completely unexpected and a troublesome problem; it would mean waiting until the dead of the night.

With a bit of luck, whoever it was in the house wouldn't be stopping here and would leave soon. He couldn't risk killing again until he'd disposed of this body, and he couldn't risk the smell emanating from the summerhouse becoming too overpowering. One decomposing body smelled terrible enough in this heat, but it could be mistaken for a dead animal. Two might raise questions from anyone passing by as to where the stench was coming from. He wanted to repel people from this area, not draw them to it.

Number four was proving to be difficult in all aspects. The fact that he'd been a lot heavier had caused enough problems. Now, this added complication was going to make it even harder to get his body down to the lake. Supposing whoever was in the house decided to go and explore the grounds and found the summerhouse. Then what? It could all be over in a matter of hours. He might have to take care of this pesky problem before it took care of him.

His mind racing, he pulled his knees up to his chest and stared at the house. He needed to know who was inside. Not tonight, though; it was too risky. And he needed to get rid of the corpse before he got caught snooping around, just in case whoever it was called the police.

Darkness seeped through his body, flowing through his veins and swirling into his mind like a heavy fog. It made it hard to think when he got like this. It wasn't productive, and he knew that. All he could do now was try to relax, let nature's beauty fill him with peace and calm before he exploded and did something hasty he might regret a few hours later.

He was cleverer than people thought, so he knew he'd figure it out, eventually.

# NINETEEN

Seth had left hours ago, promising that he'd check on her the next morning and bring the right tools with him to get the windows open. Meeting him had been an unexpected bonus; he reminded Maddy a little of Colin Firth in the first *Bridget Jones* movie. She had a habit of comparing people to film characters. Stella would love it if she told her that she'd met her Mr Darcy on the first day of her adventure. That was what she called this whole thing now: Maddy's big adventure.

She stared down at her phone, which had no signal bars on the screen whatsoever. Seth had told her the pub had free Wi-Fi, so it looked as if she would have to venture into the village sooner rather than later to message everyone and tell them she was alive. The phone signal must be better in the village or he wouldn't have been able to phone the police to check on her last night.

Up until now, she'd been in seven large empty bedrooms; the attic she hadn't bothered with. Staring at the small door, tucked away at the end of the corridor and with a sturdy bolt across it, had sent a cold shiver down her spine. She had no reason to go up there, nor to the cellar, so she was keeping well clear of them both for obvious reasons.

Downstairs she'd found the most glorious library, or it would have been had the books still been stacked on the shelves. It had made her sad to see this room empty. Having a full library to herself was her childhood dream. *But how much writing would you do if you had a never-ending supply of books to read, Maddy?* Things happened for a reason, and she was pretty sure she wouldn't have written another word once she'd started reading.

That was the thing she missed about being a writer; reading was her first true love, and she'd been more passionate about her love of books than any lover. Now she was writing herself, she didn't seem to be able to fit in reading like she used to. The deadlines, edits, copy edits, line edits, proofreads – all ate up time and took the enjoyment out of the thrill of writing the first draft. She hadn't expected any of that. But come to think of it, she hadn't known what to expect at all. Who knew she'd have to rewrite her initial story six times before it became an acceptable first draft? She certainly hadn't. But she still loved writing, or she would once she got over the fear from the voice inside her head, which kept telling her the first one was a fluke and she couldn't possibly do it again.

She walked past the library, drawing room, and parlour; she'd photographed every room from different angles and written down notes in her journal, which was now tucked under her arm. The day had flown by so fast it had scared her a little, but this was a huge house with lots of rooms to explore. Seth had stayed for over an hour, giving her a potted history of the place and the village.

In the kitchen, she poured herself a glass of wine, then let herself out of the front door and stood on the doorstep to admire the view. The sky was alive with a myriad of orange, pink, and red. Living in the city among the high rises, she'd never really taken much notice of the sunsets. Here, it was impossible not to; the view was magnificent.

Looking around, she noticed a wooden jetty which led onto the lake and headed towards it. She hadn't noticed it before, but it looked so quaint and picturesque. She was hot, dusty, and in need of a bath. The house had no showers in any of the four bathrooms, but she could cope without one.

Kicking off her boots, she put one foot gently onto the wooden slats, slowly pressing all her weight down to check if it was rotten. She wasn't bothered about falling in, but it held her weight, so she stepped onto it properly, bouncing up and down on the balls of her feet to double-check. Satisfied it wasn't rotten and about to launch her into the lake, she walked along the jetty until she reached the edge.

Maddy put her wine glass and journal down and rolled up her pyjama trousers. Sitting down, she dangled her feet over the edge and dipped her toes into the icy water, letting out a little screech. She hadn't expected it to be quite so cold after the sun had been burning down onto it all day.

It was cold, refreshing, and wonderful, and she sipped the wine and stared around, wishing now that she wrote romance stories. This was a wonderful setting for a hauntingly beautiful love story. Maybe if she couldn't write the second in this crime series, she could try her hand at a romance instead?

Turning to look at the house behind her, she was reminded of something from one of the many ghost films she'd watched. Maybe she could write a ghost story, although that might be a bit difficult if she was having to live in the house while writing it. She'd scare herself too much. A contended sigh escaped her lips; this was certainly the life.

The phone tucked into her pocket suddenly began to vibrate as a flurry of text message alerts came through. Pulling it out, she grinned to see several messages from Stella, her gran, and her agent, who she'd forgot to tell she was coming here.

Who'd have thought she'd get a signal sat on the edge of a jetty, with her feet dangling in a lake?

She began to work her way through the messages, replying to her gran and her agent first. Stella deserved a phone call. Maddy had so much to tell her, and she'd only been here just under twenty-four hours.

But when she ended the call, Maddy was left wondering what was up with her best friend. Stella hadn't been her usual bubbly self. She was convinced there was something that Stella was keeping from her, because she was such a dreadful liar and their conversation had become strained. It shouldn't have done, because Maddy had done most of the talking, but the lack of questions from Stella had given her low mood away.

Kicking her feet gently in the water – she'd become used to the cold – she pondered why Stella might have been out of sorts. Perhaps she'd been to the accountant again and was feeling down. Every time Stella left his office, she went on a two-day binge of eating chocolate and drinking copious amounts of wine.

Maddy should have just asked her if everything was okay. She dialled the number again, but this time she didn't get through. Glancing at the screen, her signal had disappeared again. *Damn, this is going to be a nightmare.* Tomorrow she would have to go into the village and use the pub's Internet, or maybe even their payphone.

She finished the rest of her wine and pulled her feet out of the water, amazed at the shade of blue they'd turned. It must be freezing in that lake.

Grabbing her boots and journal, she walked barefoot back to the house. She needed something to eat before refilling her glass. She also needed a cool bath and to sit at her laptop and write something. Anything to get her back into the routine of working once more.

# TWENTY

Connor checked his reflection for the tenth time in his rear-view mirror then got out of the car and ran up the steps to Stella's flat. He lifted his knuckles to rap on the door, pausing for a moment to wonder if he was doing the right thing. This morning he'd decided to move on, but was moving on with his ex-girlfriend's best friend actually moving on? The voice in his head taunted him and he couldn't blame it. Despite trying to convince himself he was turning over a new leaf, he didn't quite believe it.

He knew that Maddy would find out about him taking Stella out, and that was fine by him. He wanted her to. If that was the only way to seek his revenge, it would have to do... until he caved and carried on with his quest to hunt her down. Their friendship would feel a bit strained if he was dating Stella, but he didn't care about that. All he cared about was himself. It was all he'd ever cared about, and that suited him just fine.

The door opened and he smiled. Despite his reservations and his previous feelings about the woman on the doorstep, she looked nice. In fact, she looked attractive, and he felt a stirring in his loins that he had to cover with his hands.

'You came?'

'Of course I did. Why wouldn't I?'

She shrugged. 'Oh, no particular reason. Do you want to come in, or should we go straight out?'

'Let's go, I'm hungry. Although I could be persuaded to eat you.'

Stella's mouth dropped open and he laughed. 'Sorry, that was a bit inappropriate. It was just a joke. Where do you want to go?'

Laughing, she stepped outside, pulling the door shut behind her. 'Anywhere you want, I'm not fussy. We could just go to the Magpie. They do decent food and it's not too far.'

'Sounds good to me.'

She followed him down the steps and he headed towards his car.

'We can walk if you want, it's only five minutes away. Save you messing around trying to get parked.'

He did his best not to glare at her, he really did. 'Fine.' It was hard to ignore that she'd just told him what to do. Taking orders wasn't his strong point.

They walked down the high street towards the pub where people were crowding around the outside tables smoking and laughing loudly. Connor found his fingers begin to clench into tight fists; this wasn't his kind of place at all. He preferred a nice, exclusive restaurant where there were no crowds hanging around outside.

Stella looked at him. 'It's a bit busy. I didn't realise. We can go somewhere else if you prefer.'

He shook his head. 'No, we're here now. It's fine. Should we go inside? It looks as if most of the patrons are outside, so we might get a table.'

Stella smiled and pushed her way through to the front door with Connor following, doing his best to breathe deeply and keep his rising anger levels in check.

They found a small table in a dark corner – which he was grateful for – near to the bar. Stella offered to go buy the drinks, but he shook his head and came back with an ice bucket, a bottle of Moët & Chandon, and two glasses.

'Sorry, I wasn't sure if you liked champagne. I can get you something else.'

She looked surprised. 'I don't mind at all. In fact, I'm partial to the odd glass of champagne. I just can't stretch to it on my budget at the moment. Although I can go halves with you tonight. I don't expect you to pay for everything.'

'Don't be silly. I was the one who asked you out for a drink. This is on me, and if you like it, we can have another bottle or two.'

'That's very kind of you.'

He passed her a menu, hoping she wouldn't order a huge plate of food. He didn't want to be in here any longer than he had to be.

* * *

Stella groaned, but still managed to finish her glass of champagne, which didn't surprise him. She'd been funny, much better than he'd anticipated. And although he was still angry about her choice of eatery, he was beginning to relax. All night he'd avoided the subject of Madison Hart, despite the fact that the questions were gnawing away at him.

He looked across at Stella's flushed cheeks and sparkling eyes; she'd had quite enough for one night.

'Sorry to be a bit of a party pooper,' he said, 'but I have to get up early for work. Would you mind if we left soon?'

Pushing her chair back, she stood up, shaking her head. 'Of course not. Yes, me too.'

She stumbled a little and he put his arm out to catch her.

She grabbed hold of it, pushing it through hers as she dragged him towards the door.

Outside was quieter, though the air was hot and sticky. Summer in the city was hard work when you didn't have air conditioning.

As they walked back to her flat, Stella never stopped chatting about anything and everything, except for one thing – Maddy. It angered him. He'd expected her to start blabbing on after the first bottle of champagne about what good friends they were, or how gutted she was that Maddy had upped and moved away. But her friend's name had not once crossed her lips.

In fact, she'd had managed to avoid that particular subject all night – much to his distaste.

## TWENTY-ONE

Seth did a double take as he turned the corner onto the high street. Each outside table and picnic bench was full of customers. He smiled. This sudden heatwave had brought the tourists out for a cold drink, and he wasn't complaining. A rush of guilt washed over him that he'd left his dad to cope alone.

Parking the car, he jumped out and jogged across the road, hoping his dad wasn't exhausted. But as he edged his way inside the pub, he had to look twice at the person behind the bar. Glenys was there, pulling pints and chatting with the customers. Alfie was collecting glasses, and his dad was sitting in the corner nursing a pint of what looked like draught lager.

Glenys waved and he waved back, torn between asking her what she was doing or checking on his dad. He opted to speak to his dad first and hurried to the table and sat down opposite him.

'Don't look so worried, son, I'm fine. Glenys popped in for a swift cider. In all fairness, I think she was looking for you. A coach pulled up at the town square and this lot embarked, and she kindly offered to take over so I could have a breather.'

'Sorry, I had no idea.'

'What are you sorry for? Don't be daft. Like I said, I'm not dead yet, so don't treat me as if I am.'

Seth laughed. A finger poked him in the back, and he turned around to see Alfie standing behind him holding a cold beer.

'Ma said you might need this. She said to tell you she's good. She used to be a barman before we came here.'

'A barwoman.'

Alfie shrugged. 'Don't know. She worked in a pub. Are you mad at her, Seth?'

Seth swallowed the mouthful of lager he'd just taken and shook his head. 'No way, she's a lifesaver-saver. I'm happy with her and very thankful.'

Alfie thought about what Seth had said for a few moments, then grinned and wandered off outside.

'If you ask me, she's sweet for you, is that one. She might be a bit strange but her heart's in the right place.'

'Dad, I'm not wanting to marry her. We had a chat and a laugh, and I like her as a person. In fact, I think she could be a good friend; both of them could. Just because I stopped her from battering Alfie and walked her home last night, it doesn't mean we're in a serious relationship. It is possible to be friends with someone, no strings attached.'

'Suppose so. I'm only looking out for you.'

'I know you are, but I'm forty-two. I can look out for myself.'

His dad shrugged, picked up the folded newspaper in front of him, and began to read. It was a signal that he'd had enough conversation for the time being.

Seth picked up his pint glass and walked across to the bar, propping himself on an empty stool. Glenys passed some change over to the customer she was serving and came to talk to him.

'Are you mad at me?'

He stared at her purple fringe, which she'd had tucked

behind her ear, and shook his head. 'What is it with you and Alfie? He asked me exactly the same thing. Why would I be mad at you?'

'For sticking my nose in.'

'You're a lifesaver. Like I told Alfie, I'm very thankful to you for helping out.'

'Phew! I'm not trying to get in your bed, you know, if that's what you're thinking. I genuinely stopped by to say thank you and the pub suddenly filled with people. It was as if they'd all been deposited in the town square by a UFO, they just came out of the blue.'

'Or a coach. There's one down by the car park.'

They both laughed. 'UFO sounds far more glamorous, though, it's intriguing. I wouldn't mind this lot piling into my shop when they've filled their boots in here. Oh, you're almost out of cheese and onion crisps.'

'Third World problems, eh? I guess they'll have to start on the scampi fries. I'll try to send them your way. Why don't you go and open up? They'll have to pass the shop on the way down to the car park.'

'Now that I like the sound of.' She hesitated briefly. 'You don't need me to stick around?'

He shook his head. 'No way. You need to earn enough money to buy the pizza you're going to burn or the chicken nuggets you promised me for my tea. Seriously, Glenys, thank you.'

'Ah, you're welcome. It's no bother.'

She ducked under the hatch and pushed her way through the customers, while Seth took her place with a huge smile on his face. Today had been pleasantly surprising, different, and a complete change.

He wondered how Maddy was getting on at the house; now, he did find her attractive. She was definitely his type, with her golden-blonde messy bun. Blue eyes and suntanned skin that was peppered with freckles. He preferred the natural look to Glenys's full-on, look-at-me-I'm-a-Goth kind of style.

The woman was certainly brave to be living in Lakeview House on her own, but then again, she wasn't from around here. She didn't know about any of the local legends, and if you didn't believe in ghosts or ghouls then why would a house bother you? He didn't suppose it would. In a way he was envious, because she was living in his dream home without having to worry about anything other than making sure it didn't burn to the ground, or not bleeding to death in the middle of nowhere.

He wasn't afraid to admit he was looking forward to seeing Maddy again, and he hoped it was sooner rather than later. With a bit of luck, she'd need to use the Wi-Fi to connect to the outside world. It must be tough coming from a big city like London to live here, pretty much as far from civilisation as possible.

# TWENTY-TWO

Alfie wandered away from the busy pub. Now Seth was there, he could go and do what he wanted. He didn't have to clean the tables like his ma had ordered him to. Not that he minded taking the glasses in and putting them in the dishwasher, but he didn't like the people. There were too many of them, chattering and laughing; the noise was deafening. It hurt his ears.

What he wanted to do was to go to the empty house, lie on the wooden pier, and stare down into the water. He liked to see if he could see them; some days you could and some days you couldn't. His ma told him off when she knew where he'd been, saying it was dangerous. And it might be. He wasn't a very good swimmer, which was why he never went into the water.

He would walk along the pier if the water was calm, but if it was choppy, he would crawl so he didn't lose his balance and fall in. He loved lying there and staring over the edge, but only if he was feeling brave. Some days he didn't feel brave enough and instead would press his face to one of the gaps in-between the boards, squinting his eyes to see if he could see the lake people. He hadn't told anyone about them because he knew they would think he was mad. Even worse, they might think that he'd put them in there, and he didn't want the blame for something he hadn't done. People always blamed him for everything.

Walking around the edge of the lake, he reached the drystone wall, which separated the grounds of the big, empty house from the public walkways, and clambered over. No one ever came this far along the edge of the lake. It was too near to the house, and they kept away from it.

He stared at the empty building. It was huge and looked like a hotel someone had forgotten about. He would like to live here instead of the flat above the shop. He would be able to wander the halls and not have to worry about his mam being angry with him, because she wouldn't be able to find him. There must be hundreds of hiding places inside. One day he would go inside and have a look around, just not today. It was a shame he didn't have any real friends, as they could have had a great time exploring inside it.

He picked up a handful of stones, looking for flat ones that he could skim across the lake. Every time he found one, he slipped it into his pocket. He'd forgotten his slingshot today; when he used that, he could send the stones almost to the middle of the lake. Once he'd fired a stone at the house and heard the window splinter from where he'd been standing. That had made him feel bad inside. He hadn't meant to break it, and he'd run home in case he'd got caught. That was weeks ago, and the police hadn't been to arrest him, so he had been very lucky. Now he made sure he only fired the stones into the lake, and that was how he'd found the lake people.

That day, he'd dropped his handful of pebbles onto the wooden pier and scrabbled around picking them up. As he'd looked through the gap in the wooden slats, he'd seen a face staring up at him. It proper scared him and he had screamed out loud. Leaving the stones, he'd run all the way back to his mam's shop, wanting to tell her what he'd seen. But she'd been busy and waved him away. Then he realised that it might have been his imagination playing a trick on him and he better not say anything. At least, not until he knew for sure there had been a man's face in the water, all glassy-eyed and staring up at him. He didn't want the other kids in the village to hear about it; they laughed at him anyway.

Alfie suddenly realised that the pier had wet footprints on it. They weren't very big, and for the first time since he'd been coming here Alfie felt a cold wedge of fear fill his stomach, like a lead weight. One of the lake people must have come out of the water, like in some terrible fairy tale. How had they got out? Even worse, why had they come out? Were they looking for him and, if they were, why?

He dropped the handful of stones he'd been about to throw, turned, and ran back the way he'd come. As he reached the stone wall, he risked glancing behind him to make sure they weren't following him. Doubling over to catch his breath, he noticed there was a light on in the big, empty house.

Why were they inside the house? They'd never been in it before. He launched himself at the wall, scraping his knees and elbow on a sharp stone. Not caring about the pain, he fell to the other side and began to run back home. The fear that something from the lake was going to chase him and drag him into the water to become one of them made him run faster than he'd ever run before.

# TWENTY-THREE

Connor escorted Stella to the top of the steep, rickety steps, and watched as she fumbled with the key to get into her flat. Stella knew she should have let him leave her at the bottom of the street, but he'd insisted he make sure that she got inside safely, which was a bit of a laugh. She'd staggered up and down these steps more times than she cared to remember, and only once had she fallen. Luckily, that time she'd landed on her arse and bumped down at great speed, bruising nothing but her bottom and her ego. Stella had screeched in horror, which then erupted into laughter once she'd realised that she hadn't done any serious damage. There was a lot to be said for extra padding on the derriere.

The key turned in the lock and Stella threw the door open, stepping inside. Her heart was doing this strange, out of turn, skip-a-beat thing, and her stomach was a mess of churning knots. It was now or never, and against her better judgement she gave Connor her most seductive look.

'Would you like a coffee?'

There, she'd said it. In a way she hoped he would turn

around and say no, then walk out of her life for good, because this was so screwed-up, even for her.

He smiled at her, and for a fleeting moment a look crossed his face that sobered her up; it wasn't anything she'd ever seen before, and it made her shudder. Before he could answer, she shook her head.

'Sorry, Connor, I'm being stupid. Of course you wouldn't. You have stuff to get on with and I've drunk far too much. I better get to bed. I have to be up early tomorrow, there's a big delivery.'

The words gushed out of her mouth and she stepped back and began to close the door, wanting to lock and bolt it while she recovered her senses. What the fuck had she been thinking?

Before the door could click shut, he stuck his foot into the gap, stopping it in its tracks.

'Aw, don't be so hasty, darling. I'd love a coffee. We've had such a fun night, it would be a shame to let it end here.'

Pushing the door open, he reached out and stroked her cheek. His lips smiled at her, but his eyes didn't, and cold fear began to snake up the length of her spine. Grabbing hold of the door with both hands, she shook her head and pushed it, trying to slam it shut. He snatched his foot back and she'd almost closed the door when there was an almighty crash as he kicked it with all his might, slamming it back against her.

Stella fell backwards, ripping one of her extra-long acrylic nails clean off, and screamed in pain as she landed on the floor. Connor stepped inside, shutting and bolting the door behind him, then stood over her with his arms crossed, shaking his head.

'What's wrong, Stella? We were having such a lovely evening. Why have you gone all nuts on me? I'm not a monster.'

For a moment, she wondered if she was overreacting. Had the champagne sent her into a fear-filled frenzy? Or had she come to her senses? Maddy had never lied to her the entire time they'd been friends. How stupid was she to think that he might have been telling the truth?

The pain in her finger was throbbing and she shook her hand up and down to try to ease it. Connor leaned down towards her, holding out his hand.

'Sorry, are you okay? Let me help you up and then get your finger sorted. You need to run it under the cold tap, it will numb the pain a little.'

Every nerve in Stella's body began to tingle. He looked as sincere as Buffalo Bill did in *The Silence of the Lambs*. His voice echoed in her mind: 'It rubs the lotion on its skin or else it gets the hose again.' She'd let a lunatic into her flat and now she was going to pay.

Stella decided to play along; she'd do anything to get him out of here. If she could just keep him happy until she locked herself in the bathroom and phoned the police, it might be okay. She took his hand and he pulled her up.

'There, see? What was that all about? I don't understand, Stella. I thought we were okay and that you understood me.'

'I'm sorry, it must be the champagne. I'm not used to it. I feel a bit squiffy to be honest with you. I should never have drunk so much.'

That smile again, it made her cringe inside. He tugged her towards the sink in the kitchen.

'Run your finger under the cold water, it's bleeding.'

She nodded, turning on the tap and doing as she was told. He stood to the side of her watching her every move. She knew where the kitchen knives were without even looking for them and wondered if she was going to need one.

'Seeing as this date night has turned into a bit of a terrible ending, I might as well come straight out and ask you. I suppose there's no point in waiting around much longer. Where is she?'

Stella closed her eyes, took a deep breath, and shook her head. 'I don't know, she hasn't been in touch since she left.'

He frowned. 'Are you sure about that? I would think very carefully, Stella, because first, I know she tells you every little gory detail about her life. And second, for every lie you tell me, I'm going to break one of your fingers. If you think it hurts because you broke a nail, you haven't experienced anything yet. I'll let you have a moment to think about it.'

'I don't know where she is.'

He lunged for her before she could move away. Grabbing her hand, he began to crush her fingers in his tight grip. Stella twisted away from him, lifted her foot, and slammed it straight into his balls. The shout was both terrifying and wonderful, and as he released his grip on her, she ran for the bathroom. She'd almost made it until he threw himself at her and she felt herself falling to the floor. A tight fist hit her in the face, and an explosion of blackness smattered with silver stars filled her vision. Then he hit her again and again.

Writhing and screaming as loud as she could, she was helpless as he leaned down and put his elbow against her windpipe, crushing it and stopping the air from entering.

'Last chance before I fucking kill you.'

Stella could feel her fingers and toes going numb through the lack of circulation, her lungs felt as if they were on fire. The only thing she could do was tell him and then ring the police to warn Maddy.

He released his arm, letting air flow through, and she greedily sucked it in. Her voice came out as a scratchy, hoarse whisper. 'Lakeview House, she's somewhere near Keswick.'

'All this fuss for nothing. You should have told me the first time, Stella. It would have saved you this pain. If you tell anyone what happened here, I'll come back. You know that I will, and next time I won't stop. I'll take a knife and I'll slice your throat from ear to ear, then watch you bleed to death.'

He stood up, and she watched him through the one eye that opened slightly, praying he was leaving.

He stepped back, then lifted up his foot and stamped on her head. This time, she welcomed the blackness, and let it take her away from the pain.

# TWENTY-FOUR

Maddy's eyes flew open and she had no idea where she was. Her breathing was laboured, and she was covered in a fine film of sweat. Christ, that had been a nightmare and a half! She'd been running through the halls of Lakeview House, wearing either a white wedding dress or a ball gown. Whatever it had been, it was cumbersome, and it had slowed her down. She had no idea who or what she'd been running from, but the fear had been strong enough to make her run for her life. She'd been trying to find a way to escape when she'd woken up.

There was no sun streaming through the windows. Maddy wondered if it was still night and she'd only been asleep a short time, but she reached out for her phone and was surprised to see it was almost 8 a.m. The sky was so grey and overcast she didn't think it would ever get light today. It was a huge difference from yesterday.

Her head a little tender, she glanced at the wine bottle on the table next to her laptop. It was empty; she'd finished that, and the one she'd opened the night before. No wonder her head was thudding in time with her heartbeat.

She checked her phone and was disappointed to see that

Stella hadn't been in touch. It wasn't like her, and Maddy felt a little anxious that she hadn't. Yesterday's conversation had been different, and there had been no texts or Messenger contact from her; normally she got all kinds of memes and quotes. Something was going on with her friend, and today Maddy was going to make it her mission to find out what.

Pushing herself up on her elbows, she stared at the dresser that was wedged in front of the door. *Oh crap*. Breakfast first, and then she was going to have to check every room in the entire house to see if she could find where the loud noise had come from last night.

Pushing the dresser as hard as she could, she managed to move it away from the door. She didn't remember it being so heavy last night, but that could have been the wine giving her superpowers.

It was much cooler today and she opened a drawer and pulled out the faded, navy, hooded NYPD sweatshirt she'd bought on her last trip to New York. Taking the empty wine bottles with her, she went out into the large open hallway and looked around. What a difference it was when there was no natural sunlight filtering through; it was full of dark shadows, and more than a little eerie.

Maddy made her way to the oak staircase with the ornate, hand-carved balustrades, and stared over to look down into the entrance hall. Her hand gripped tightly onto the bannister; she'd never been particularly good at heights. It was so dark down there. The entire house was gloomy today, and she didn't know if she wanted to go and investigate on her own, but her stomach letting out a loud, hungry grumble made up her mind for her. Besides, she couldn't spend the next six months living in the bedroom like a recluse, could she?

She wondered who had lived here. Had it been a vibrant family home, or the cold prison of a spinster or a widower? It didn't seem like a particularly happy or joyous house, but she supposed it wouldn't if no one had lived in it for about forty years. It was probably feeling lonely and unloved – a bit like her. The thought made Maddy smile, and she ran down the stairs and made her way to the kitchen.

There was no doubt about it – she was going to have to venture into the village today. She needed food, definitely more wine, some chocolate, and a decent Wi-Fi signal to get in touch with everyone. Surely Stella couldn't ignore her if she Face-Timed her, could she?

After a quick breakfast, she decided to wait until she'd been to the village before trying to find what had caused the loud noise last night. With a bit of luck, Seth might even offer to come back with her and help her to look. Not that she was a damsel in distress, or anything like that, but there were times when a man came in very handy. Especially when it came to checking things you were too terrified to, like empty attics and cellars.

Opening the front door, she looked down to see a sodden ream of material draped across the front steps. It was an off-white silk and lace combination. Puzzled, Maddy looked around, but there was no one that she could see in the area. She hadn't heard any vehicles, and it was doubtful that someone had carried it here, dipped it in the lake, then dumped it on the doorstep. It looked far too heavy.

Bending down, she lifted it up and realised on closer inspection that it had a shape; it was a long dress, like a wedding or ball gown. A small screech filled the air. No, it wasn't just any old dress; it looked like an antique wedding dress, something a bride would have worn a very long time ago. Similar to the one she'd been wearing in her dream. How bizarre was that? She had dreamt she was wearing a wedding dress, running through the halls, and now she'd found one on the front steps of the house – that was pretty weird.

She'd seen some strange things living in London, but

nothing like this. Was that what the bang was last night? Had someone been trying to get inside? Oh God, what if they'd needed help? Someone could have fallen into the lake, dragged themselves out, and come to knock on the door for some help, and she'd been too scared to go and see. Whoever it was might be lying dead of hyperthermia somewhere.

Dropping the dripping wet dress on the steps, she ran down them and towards the lake, scanning the grounds and grass to see if there was a body somewhere. Breathless, she looked around as best as she could, unable to see anyone. Not used to running, the stitch in her side caused her to stop and begin walking back to the house.

She pulled out her phone to ring the police. *Bloody hell, no signal!* The only thing she could do was go and see if Seth was at the pub and ask him to phone the police, then he could come back with her and help her do a search of the grounds.

She didn't need the guilt of some dead bride on her conscience. As she started the engine of her car, she hoped it would manage the short distance into the village, because right now she didn't know what to do for the best.

# TWENTY-FIVE

Joe walked down the narrow street to peer through the bookshop window, hoping to catch a glimpse of Stella. He'd been rude yesterday and it had bothered him all night. He wasn't usually that way. The guy who'd been speaking to Stella was one of those arseholes who loved themselves; Joe could spot them a mile off. He probably snorted coke, drunk-drove, and slept with anything in a skirt for the hell of it.

It had upset him, because he'd been mooning over Stella for the last five months and been too afraid to ask her out. Now he'd missed his chance and he was devastated; she was probably about to embark on an affair with the rich prick. It didn't matter. He liked her a lot and wanted to apologise. Maybe when she'd come to her senses, he might be able to pick up where they'd left off.

The shop was shut. He looked at his watch. *No wonder it's shut, you idiot, it's not even eight.* Cupping his hands to his eyes, he peered through the glass door, but it was dark inside. Wondering if he should risk going and knocking on her flat door, he heard a loud thud and a groan come from above.

Taking the stairs two at a time, he reached the front door, which was ajar.

'Stella, are you okay? It's Joe.'

A muffled reply that he couldn't make out filled him with fear, and he slowly pushed the door wider.

'Look, I'm coming in. I hope you're decent.'

Stepping into the flat, he saw her curled in a ball on the sofa, her face buried in her arms.

'Stella.'

He walked towards her, but she didn't turn to face him. He could smell the bitter tang of blood. Something was wrong, but he couldn't see what. Reaching out, he took hold of her shoulder, gently tugging her towards him.

'Stella, what's wrong?'

When she turned to face him, he gasped. Her face no longer resembled the woman it had yesterday. It was a bloodied mess of cuts and deep, blue bruises.

'Oh my God, who did this to you? Why haven't you phoned the police?'

She lifted her arm and pointed with the stub of a scabbed-up finger, missing one of her long, false nails. He looked down to see her phone smashed into pieces. He took out his phone and began to dial 999, because he didn't know what else to do. When Stella groaned 'no' at him, he stopped before pressing the call button.

He grabbed hold of her hand. Holding it gently, he knelt on the floor next to her.

'We have to get you to the hospital, Stella, your face needs sorting out. There's a deep cut by your eyebrow and it might need stitching. I'll stay with you to look after you, I promise. Who did this?'

He didn't need to hear her answer because he knew who had done it – the guy from yesterday. And Joe swore to himself that he'd get his revenge on him. You didn't hit a woman, let alone knock her senseless and leave her scared and alone, bleeding, and in pain with no way to phone for help. He was so angry he wanted to punch the wall, but he didn't want to scare her any more than she already was.

'I'm going to phone an ambulance,' he told her calmly. 'I don't have my car. It's in the garage. You have to let me phone; you need to go to hospital.'

When she bowed her head, he realised she was embarrassed, so he went outside onto the top step and rang 999, asking for an ambulance, then the police.

Back inside, he sat next to her on the sofa, holding her hand, waiting for them to arrive. It didn't take long before the sirens filled the air of the small street and he heard the heavy footsteps running up to the flat. Two police officers came in, took one look at them both, and began shouting at Joe to move away from her.

Realising they thought he'd done this, he put his hands up and shook his head. 'I didn't. I couldn't, I wouldn't. I'm her friend. I found her like this. I'm the one who called for help.'

'Step away from her, sir, and keep your hands in the air. I'm going to have to cuff you until we've established the facts of what's gone on here.'

Horrified, Joe did as he was told. One of the officers walked towards him with a pair of handcuffs. 'Hold out your hands. This is just a precaution for our safety and yours.'

Stella began to wail, 'Nooo, no, not him.'

She tried to stand up, and he watched as the colour drained from her face as she collapsed to the floor. Two paramedics ran in and Joe had never been so thankful. The coppers dragged him out of the way so they could work on Stella.

'I swear to God, I didn't do it. I came to see if she was okay and found her like this,' he told them.

The female officer – who looked around the same age as his younger sister, in her early twenties – grabbed hold of his hands and turned them around. He realised she was inspecting them for grazes.

Her much older colleague shook his head at her. 'The amount of injuries she has there would show some bruising and cuts, unless he was wearing leather gloves, then he wouldn't have any telltale signs.' He looked at Joe. 'I'm sorry, but until we can clear this up, you're going to have to come with us.'

For the first time in his life, Joe felt totally helpless. The paramedics were loading Stella onto a chair to get her down into the ambulance. She was semi-conscious, but completely out of it.

He let them cuff him and lead him down to the waiting van. The female officer jumped into the back of the ambulance, while he stepped up into the cage of the police van. He'd never been in trouble with the police, let alone been arrested. The doors slammed shut on him, blocking out all daylight.

Joe wondered how long it would take for him to convince them he hadn't hurt her. He supposed it didn't matter. As long as Stella was going to be okay, he could cope with being locked in this tiny space. He buried his head in his hands. This was not how he'd imagined his morning turning out to be; he'd been hoping to buy Stella some breakfast.

A short time later, the doors opened, and he had to blink to let his eyes adjust to the light again.

'You're off the hook. What's your name?'

'Joe Thomas. I phoned for the ambulance and you guys. I work in the diner down Camden High Street. Stella's my friend.'

'Have you got any ID?'

'My driving licence is in the wallet you took from me.'

The copper nodded. He opened the small plastic evidence bag, took the wallet out, and removed the licence. He studied it, looking from the picture to Joe.

'That's a terrible photo, mate.'

'Cheers. Any more insults you want to throw my way while you're at it?'

The officer smiled. 'No, sir, I think we've done enough for one morning. Your friend Stella has told my colleague that a Connor Wood assaulted her late last night, and that you had nothing to do with it. So, you can get in the middle of the van and I'll drop you off at the hospital to sit with your friend.'

'Thank God for that.' Joe breathed. 'Thank you.' He held his hands out for the handcuffs to be removed. 'Is Stella okay?'

The copper shrugged. 'I don't really know, but I can imagine this is going to be difficult for her. At least she's got you. I can imagine that Connor Wood won't be so okay when he's located.'

Joe nodded, hoping that they kicked the shit out of the bastard; it was the least he deserved.

As they drove to the hospital, Joe swore that if it was the last thing he did he would track down Connor Wood and give him a taste of his own medicine.

# TWENTY-SIX

Much to her shame, Maddy's car roared into the village like an army tank, announcing her arrival to every person within a two-mile radius. The engine needed looking at, and she was surprised the Beetle had made it this far.

The village consisted of one main street with some shops, a post office, and some quaint cottages. The pub stood at one end, and she was relieved it was the only one because she hadn't thought to ask Seth what it was called.

Parking outside the beer garden, she hammered on the front door, the fear that there was a dead woman somewhere in the grounds near to the house weighing heavy on her mind. A man much older than Seth, but with the same crinkly brown eyes, opened the door.

'What's the emergency?'

'Sorry, is Seth in? I need to speak to him. I'm from Lakeview House and I think there might be...' She paused. *What do you think it might be, Maddy?*

He folded his arms. 'There might be?'

'An injured person in the grounds.'

Seth appeared behind his dad and smiled at her. 'Morning, what injured person?'

Both men stepped to one side to let her in. 'This sounds crazy, but I found a soaking wet wedding dress on the front steps of the house, and I'm scared there's some half-drowned bride lying in the bushes with hypothermia.'

The older man began to laugh. He held out his hand. 'I'm Jacob, Seth's dad. And you are?'

Maddy shook his hand. 'Madison Hart, I'm a writer.'

'I'd never have guessed.' He laughed. 'Do you always have such a vivid imagination?'

She felt her already pink cheeks begin to burn.

'Dad, don't be so cheeky,' Seth interrupted. 'He's kidding. Do you want me to come and search with you?'

Nodding, she smiled. 'Yes, please. If you're not busy.'

'He's never busy is Seth, especially not for a pretty young thing with wild ideas.' Jacob began to chuckle at his own joke. Maddy didn't know whether to join in or not, seeing as his amusement was at her expense.

'Ignore him,' Seth told her. 'Come on. If that was your car making that awful racket, we'll go in mine and leave yours here. If you give the house comedian the keys, he'll get Martin the local car fixer to take a look when he comes in for his cheese sandwich and pint of bitter at lunchtime.'

Maddy passed the keys over with a grateful smile, then followed Seth towards his Land Rover. She climbed up into the passenger seat and wrinkled her nose at the odour lingering inside.

Seth shrugged. 'Sorry, it's seen better days. It's full of sweaty Mountain Rescue kit and walking boots. It's been a while since I've had a woman to give a ride to.'

Laughing, she felt her cheeks turn redder. 'Sorry, I didn't mean to be rude. It smells fine.'

It was Seth's turn to laugh. 'Err, no it doesn't. Put your window down and the fresh air will numb the senses.'

Before long they were back at Lakeview House, and she quickly jumped out of the car. The dress was where she'd left it.

Seth picked it up and studied it. 'Well, I'm no expert, but it's wet and looks like a wedding dress. You're right.'

'Do you think whoever was wearing it tried to drown herself then changed her mind?'

Shaking his head, he surveyed the grounds around him, down to the water's edge. 'No, what I think is someone has tried to play a prank to scare you.'

Puzzled, Maddy looked at him. 'What do you mean? I don't understand. How would a wet wedding dress scare me?'

'It sent you running for help, didn't it? This is a small village with its own share of idiots. Trust me, it's someone's idea of a joke.'

'Can we just have a quick search to double-check? I'll never forgive myself if someone needed help and I ignored them.'

Seth dropped the dress and began to stride in the direction of the lake, scanning the grounds from left to right as he went. Maddy followed, struggling to keep up with him.

'You check the shoreline, I'll check the grounds,' he said, and walked off in the opposite direction.

Maddy wondered if she'd annoyed him. There wasn't much she could do if she had, but she needed to know there wasn't a body out here. Walking the full length, she got to the jetty and noticed a small pile of stones scattered along it. They hadn't been there when she'd left last night, because she'd had no shoes on and she'd have stood on them. Something was going on. Who had been here, and why? She didn't know the answer, but she was determined to find out.

# TWENTY-SEVEN

Connor filled the hire car with diesel. He had a Waitrose carrier bag filled with an assortment of chocolate bars, cans of cola, and a cheap mobile phone. This was going to be fun; he'd never been to the Lake District before. He'd never heard of Keswick either, but that wouldn't stop him.

There was a good chance the police were looking for him, so he'd left his own car at home. They had those cameras on the motorways that would ping when a wanted person drove through them, so he didn't want to risk getting arrested before he'd had the chance to pay Maddy a visit.

He shouldn't have hurt Stella so bad. He knew that now, but it was too late. She'd got him angry, though, and he'd only been able to keep up the nice guy pretence for so long before he'd flipped. And she should have known better. If she was such a good friend to Maddy, she wouldn't have been so eager to jump into bed with him.

The Ford Focus wasn't flashy, so it wouldn't stand out too much. He'd googled Lakeview House and been surprised to see the run-down, boarded-up mansion where Maddy had apparently run away to. He would never in a million years have pegged her as a live-on-your-own-in-a-scary-house kind of girl. It just showed him how wrong he had been about her from the start, which made him even angrier – with himself and her.

In fact, he was furious with her for being so independent and self-sufficient. The one thing about this entire mess that made him smile was the fact that she'd chosen to live in a house that might as well be on another planet. No one was going to hear her scream for miles; when he got started on her, he could take his time. Make it last as long as he wanted.

He grinned. This was going to be such an exciting little adventure. Her success would be very short-lived... but his? Well, if he got caught, he'd be forever remembered for what he'd done to her, and he could live with that. Any form of recognition was better than living a life of anonymity.

He'd programmed Keswick into his satnav because he wanted to take his time; there was no rush. He might even book himself into a nice hotel he'd found on the Internet, called Armathwaite Hall. It had a spa, so he could book himself a massage and go for a swim, as if he was on a short holiday.

He had all the time in the world to find Maddy. Just as she thought she had all the time in the world to write that stupid, damn book. He was pretty sure that even she couldn't come up with the ending he had in store for her. She thought she was clever hiding in an abandoned house, but he would show her how clever she was.

Briefly, he wondered if the police would tell her about Stella. He'd deliberately smashed Stella's phone to pieces so she couldn't phone for help after he'd left and got out of London. She wouldn't be able to contact Maddy for a while either, so he should have at least a couple of days before she even knew he could be coming for her.

He'd never thought of himself as a killer before. But after the way he'd laid into Stella last night and the black thoughts he was having about Madison Hart, he realised that there was a very strong possibility it could end up that way. There was every likelihood that Maddy would end up dead. He could throw her body in the lake and drive back to where he came from without a second thought, then be out of the country before anyone even realised she was missing.

As he pulled onto the motorway, a broad smile spread across his lips. The last twenty-four hours had turned into a very interesting, not to mention immensely satisfying, period in his life.

# TWENTY-EIGHT

Joe walked into the hospital, flanked by the copper who had told him his name was Mark, and that he was forty-one years old and married with two kids. They'd gone from arch-enemies to friends in the space of one crazy, messed-up hour.

At the A&E waiting room, Joe sat down on one of the hard, plastic chairs while his new friend went to find out where Stella was. He heard the murmurs around the waiting room, no doubt wondering who he was or what he'd done to get preferential treatment. After a few minutes, Mark waved at him from a set of double doors, along with a nurse in a pair of blue scrubs. As he made his way towards them, Joe ignored the stares of the curious spectators and kept his eyes to the ground, slipping through the narrow gap in the doors before they clicked shut behind him.

He tried not to look at the assortment of walking wounded surrounding him. He always had a bit of a phobia about blood but thank God the shock of seeing Stella injured had propelled him into action instead of fainting, for a change. That would have looked really impressive if he'd have passed out on the floor in front of her.

His empty stomach was churning, and he didn't know if he felt sick, hungry, or a combination of both. This was not how he'd envisaged his morning going.

Mark led him to a cubicle where Stella was in the process of being patched together by a nurse. She attempted a painful smile, and he felt his heart miss a beat. Even with her bruised and bloodied face, he still found her attractive. He wanted to scoop her into his arms and hold her tight, to tell her he'd look after her and find the bastard who'd hurt her. But that was ridiculous. He barely knew her, and he doubted she would be looking for a relationship after what had just happened to her. He was more than happy to be a friend to her until she decided the time was right. He ignored the voice that whispered, *And what if the time is never right?*

The female officer stood up, passing Stella what looked like a huge mobile phone, and asked her to sign her name with a stylus.

'Right, that's everything we need for now,' she explained. 'I've asked for a wanted marker to go on the police national database for Connor Wood and we're off to make some arrest enquiries now, Stella. If you need anything, you can contact me on the number I've given to you. CID will probably want to interview you about the assault, given the seriousness of it.' She smiled kindly. 'However, they'll leave you alone for now. I've got your first account, so don't worry too much.'

Stella attempted another smile, which turned into a grimace. 'Thanks.'

As both officers made to leave, Mark turned to Joe and stuck his thumb up at him. 'Good luck, mate.' Then they were gone, and Joe wondered what the hell to say to the battered and bruised woman on the bed in front of him.

It was Stella who spoke first. 'Thank you. I didn't know what to do.'

He shrugged. 'You're welcome. If I'm honest with you, neither did I. I wimped out and panicked.'

She gave a throaty laugh. 'No, you didn't. I knew he was a wrong one. He treated Maddy like shit and I let him reel me in like a giant fish. I proper fell for his charm.' She sighed. 'I'm such a pushover.'

He watched her blink back the river of tears that were threatening to fall and reached out to take hold of her hand.

'First of all, you're not a pushover. He took advantage of you then hurt you. He's a prick, and when I get hold of him—' Joe stopped himself. The anger he felt towards that wanker was bubbling away inside his chest, but now was not the time. He didn't want to scare her.

'I wanted to shout after you yesterday and tell you I'd love to go for a drink with you,' she told him. 'I wish to God I had. I wouldn't be lying here now looking like an extra off a Rocky film.' She hesitated briefly. 'Is it really bad?'

He grimaced. 'It's quite bad, but you still look beautiful to me.'

This time, the tears did fall, and he squeezed her hand gently. Grabbing some tissues from the box on the trolley, he passed them to her.

'Sorry.'

'For what? If I was lying there, I'd be crying as well.'

'No one's ever called me beautiful before and meant it... well, apart from my mum, and she has to. It's written in the parenting rule books to call your kids beautiful, even when they're the ugliest little things you've ever set eyes on.'

Joe laughed so loud it echoed around the cubicles, and Stella and the nurse joined in.

When he finally got control of his laughter, he looked her in the eye. 'So, do you fancy coming to my place when we get out of here? It's not much, but it's clean – a bit messy. I can cook you a mean burger with all the trimmings, and he has no idea where I live.'

Stella nodded. 'I'd love to. I might not be very good company, though.'

'That's okay. You can lie on the sofa. I have a book of poems you can read if you like, while I'm making your dinner.'

'Oh God, I'd forgotten all about Zara's dreadful poetry. I'll pass on that, but I'm up for lying around on the sofa while you cook for me.'

He smiled. 'It's a date, then. How long do you think you'll have to be in here?'

The nurse looked up. 'The doctor said if your CT scan is clear, you can go home. But only if you feel up to it.'

'I'll feel up to it all right. I don't want to be in hospital too long,' Stella told her. 'I have a dinner date with a very nice man.'

The nurse stood up. 'Leave it with me, I'll see what I can do.'

# TWENTY-NINE

Maddy sat on the top step of the house, waiting for Seth to come back. When he came into view, his cheeks were red, and he was out of breath.

'I've checked as far as I can, along the perimeter of the back of the house, the grounds, and the part of the fell that I can get to. I swear there's no body or a woman with hypothermia anywhere.'

She let out a huge sigh. 'Thank you so much. I didn't want to phone the police and look like an idiot, but I couldn't not do anything. I hope you're not too mad with me for dragging you out here.'

He smiled. 'I'm not. You're new to the village, and what were you supposed to think? It must have been a bit of a shock. But I promise you, it's someone's idea of a joke, nothing more.'

'Would you like a cool drink?'

'I thought you'd never ask. Yes please.'

Standing up, she led the way inside, leaving the offending dress on the steps. For some reason, she didn't want it in the house. She wasn't superstitious or anything – she didn't believe in bad luck *per se* – but on this occasion she decided to go with her instinct and leave it out there. In fact, she would bag it up and ask Seth to drop it into the bin at the rear of the pub. She had no use for an old wedding dress, and at least whoever it was that had thought it was funny to leave it there wouldn't be able to do the same to anyone else.

Their footsteps echoed around the hall. It was still dark inside and chilly.

'It's certainly gloomy in here when the sun doesn't shine,' he commented. 'Does it really not bother you?'

Maddy shook her head. 'I don't mind. I mean, I prefer it when it's lighter. But I'm not scared, if that's what you're asking.' She felt bad. She'd dragged him out here on a wild goose chase and now she was being downright rude towards him, when all he'd done was ask her a question.

'How's the writing going? Have you managed to get much done?'

For some reason, his question grated on her more than the previous one. She found herself feeling defensive and about to bite his head off for the second time. She took a deep breath before answering.

'It's okay. I did a lot more than I expected to last night. Whether it's any good or not is a different matter. I had the help of an ice-cold bottle of Chardonnay for inspiration.'

He began to laugh. 'I'm sure it's wonderful. I've ordered a copy of your book from the village bookshop. I know she orders her stuff from Amazon because it's cheaper, then sticks a couple of quid on it. But you know, you have to shop local and support the local businesses in a small place like this.'

Maddy felt the sudden onslaught of anger subside at his confession. 'Thank you, that's really kind of you. I hope you'll like it.'

'I'm pretty sure I will, although I'm not too sure how long it will take me to read it,' he admitted. 'I'm not the book-buying or reading type.'

'Well, it's never too late to start. You might enjoy it and find yourself desperate to read another.'

'I might. But there's only one small problem with that.'

She frowned. 'What?'

'How long will I have to wait to read the next one?'

Maddy's laughter filled the entrance hall and made her feel a whole lot better about the situation. 'Now that's anyone's guess. Hopefully, not that long. What would you like to drink?'

She pushed open the kitchen door and gasped to see the floor covered in coloured shapes; confetti was sprinkled everywhere.

'How the hell did that get in here?'

Seth pushed past her and stood with his hands on his hips staring down at the floor.

'Right, that's it. Whoever did this has gone too far. It's not a joke when they've come into your house and done something like this right under your nose.'

A cold chill crept up her spine. He was right. While she'd been outside panicking, someone had come into the house to throw this everywhere then left again before she saw them.

A horrible thought filled her mind. Had they even left? They could be hiding anywhere and hadn't she thought she'd heard footsteps last night? She'd brushed it off after the loud bang, blaming her imagination. But someone had obviously been inside, and it creeped her out big style.

Who would want to do something like this? After all, so far, the only person she'd met was Seth. Surely the villagers didn't hold grudges against newcomers this much?

Connor's sneering face filled her mind. He would definitely be up for trying to scare the living daylights out of her; he was that kind of mean. But he didn't know where she was.

A cold chill settled over her like a blanket. Or did he?

# THIRTY

Seth watched Maddy. She looked petrified and he didn't blame her. This was a huge building, and he didn't like the thought that someone could be hiding in here trying to scare her.

'I think we should search the entire house from top to bottom,' he said.

'Even the attics and cellars?'

'Especially the attics and cellars. We need to make sure there is no one in here and no way anyone can sneak in here. Unless we know the house is secure, you can't stop here on your own. I don't care if it is someone's idea of a prank. You can't be too careful.'

He didn't add that you heard all kinds of horror stories on the television and in the news; it wasn't fair to freak her out if it was just someone's idea of a joke.

The only person he could think of that might do something like this was Alfie, with his childlike innocence. But would he be clever enough? Seth didn't know if he was, but right now he couldn't think of anyone else, unless there was some angry local who didn't get the job in the first place and was now trying to scare her away. That could be a possibility.

'Right, where are the torches? The sooner we do this, the sooner we know you're safe in here.'

Maddy looked at him. 'I can't believe it. I've lived in London my whole life and never experienced anything like this. I move to the country to live in solitude, and someone decides to try to scare the crap out of me. I don't understand.'

'Believe it or not, sometimes country folk are much stranger than you city dwellers. It's probably all some big joke to them. I have one suspect who could be responsible and, trust me, when I get hold of him, I'll have him by the scruff of the neck to see if it's him. For now, though, let's just check the house and see what we find. At least that way it will be secure, and it will settle your mind.'

He wondered if he should tell her about the legend of the drowned bride from Armboth House – the original Lakeview House, which was now in the underwater village, hidden in the depths of Lake Thirlmere. This house was a replica of the original, which had been submerged underwater when the water board decided to flood the valley to build a reservoir in 1894. The bride had been found floating in the lake on her wedding morning, and locals believed the culprit to have been her fiancé. No one had ever been brought to justice for her murder.

He decided against mentioning it for now. Maddy's complexion was still a lot paler than it had been yesterday, and there were fine worry lines on her forehead. He'd save that tale for later, or at least until they got to the bottom of this mystery.

Maddy opened a cupboard, took out a couple of torches, and passed one to him. 'Do we need a hammer or maybe a knife?'

'I don't think so.'

'What about the rolling pin? It's heavy enough to do some damage and won't be classed as an offensive weapon.'

He shook his head. 'I don't think we'll need any of those. I'm pretty sure we won't find anyone. It's just a precaution.'

She grabbed the rolling pin from the drawer and stuffed it into the waistband of her trousers. 'You might think it's a joke, but I don't. You can't be too careful; there are all kinds of crazy people out there. I'd rather have something to protect ourselves with than an empty hand and harsh language.'

He turned away to hide the smile that had spread across his face. She'd turned into quite the feisty woman, which made him like her even more. He crossed the room, checking the kitchen door was locked, sliding the bolt across for good measure.

'One room down, thirty to go.' He winked at her and she laughed.

'Only thirty? I hope you didn't have any plans for today, because I've well and truly spoilt them.'

He shook his head and walked out of the kitchen to what he thought might be the cellar door. 'Might as well start at the bottom and work our way up. I'd be surprised if anyone is down there, because it's bolted from this side. But I wouldn't settle if we didn't check every single room.'

He felt responsible for Maddy, although God knows he had enough with his dad to worry about without adding her onto his list. What was it with his conscience? The voice in his head whispered, *It's because you find her attractive, you fool.* He glanced across at her and realised that yes, he found her very attractive. He realised she was staring straight at him and felt his cheeks begin to burn, so he turned away from her and threw open the cellar door.

As the smell of damp and mould assaulted their nostrils, Maddy lifted her arm, holding it across her nose and mouth. 'Blimey, that smells like something from your worst nightmare.'

He couldn't disagree, although he had smelled worse, but he didn't want to upset her with tales of decomposing bodies that he'd had to carry down off the fells after days of searching for missing walkers. In fairness, the team had a good track record, and usually found their missing persons while they were still alive.

'I'll go first then.' He stood on the top step and stared down into the blackness, wondering if she'd think badly of him if he chickened out.

# THIRTY-ONE

Glenys watched Alfie fidgeting on the sofa. He had the television on with some documentary about African wildcats playing, but he wasn't watching it. Usually he'd lay there enthralled by the scenery and the raw beauty of the animals, but today he wasn't even looking at the screen. He was staring at something on the wall behind the television, and she couldn't for the life of her figure out what it was.

She walked past him, reaching out her fingers to gently brush through his hair. 'What's up, Alf?'

'Nothing.'

'You sure? You're not even watching, and it's your favourite programme.'

He shrugged. 'Can people who are alive live under the water?'

'Not really, I don't think so. I know you can stay in fancy hotels under the water, but I haven't heard of anyone living underwater. Why?'

'Didn't think so. Doesn't matter.' He turned away from her. This time, he did start watching the television, signalling the end of this particular conversation.

She walked off into the small kitchen, wondering what that had been about. He'd been a bit quiet all day; she'd ask Seth if he would talk to him. He might open up to him. As much as he was hard work and drove her mad, Alfie was her son and she loved him dearly. She didn't like to see him unsettled like this. Normally he breezed through life, not caring what was going on or taking much notice of anyone.

Switching on the kettle, she made herself a mug of tea then sat down at the small table by the window. She loved the sound of the rain, and she watched the droplets of water as they splattered against the glass, running down to land on the windowsill. The sky had turned a chalky, dirty grey and the rain had followed. That was why Alfie had come inside, and why she'd decided to close the shop early; no one came to this village in the rain unless they had to.

From here she could just see the outline of the lake, and a shudder ran down her spine. Now she was feeling off, and she didn't like it. Her senses were on high alert and she couldn't for the life of her figure out why. Something was happening in this village; the vibes were all out of sync. She didn't know exactly what, but she needed to find out why the atmosphere wasn't right. Tiny strands of invisible string seemed to be tugging her towards the lake.

It was like this sometimes. Having a bit of a sixth sense could be a complete pain in the backside. It was good for reading the customers and telling them what they needed to hear, but it wasn't so good when it descended upon her like this, out of the blue, hovering over her head like a thundercloud.

Sipping her tea, she stared out to the lake at the inky, blue water, then picked up her phone and rang the pub, waiting to see who answered.

'Yeah.'

She knew it wasn't Seth by the tone of the voice on the other end.

'Sorry to bother you, it's Glenys. Is Seth around, by any chance?'

'Haven't seen him for a couple of hours. He went up to the house.'

Was she supposed to know which house this was, because she didn't have a clue.

'Which house would that be?'

'Lakeview House. Been gone awhile. The woman came here looking all flustered and he left with her. Can I give him a message?'

'No, it wasn't important. I'll catch him again. Are you managing okay? I can give you a hand if you're busy.'

'I'm fine, thank you. Just the usual crowd of reprobates in here today. The rain put paid to any tourists, and no unexpected coach trips, thank God.' He laughed at his own joke and she smiled.

'Bye then.'

The line went dead, and she stood up. From her bedroom she could just about see the outline of the big, old Gothic house – well, it was more of a mansion. Calling it Lakeview House must have been the owner's idea of a joke. It was a place she didn't like to look at, because it gave her the shivers. She knew for a fact that something bad had gone down in that house, so she kept as far away from it as possible.

Going into her room, she pressed her face against the cold pane of glass. Staring into the distance at the darkened windows of Lakeview House, she saw an upstairs light flicker into life, and then watched as the faint beam of a torch began to move around in the room next to it. What woman was Seth's dad talking about? Surely someone wasn't living there alone? And how did Seth know her? Not that she was interested in him. She just liked to keep on top of what was going on in the village, and it seemed at the moment that she didn't know an awful lot.

What with Alfie acting all weird and the news about the house, what else was there?

# THIRTY-TWO

Connor chewed the bland sandwich he'd bought from the motorway services; God knows what it was supposed to be, but it didn't taste anything like the kind of all-day breakfast he was used to eating, that was for sure. His stomach had started grumbling an hour ago, convincing him to pull over to buy some food.

He glanced down at the cardboard coffee cup and hoped to God it tasted better than what he was chewing. He'd been driving way too slow for his taste, but he couldn't afford to get a speeding ticket or, worse, bring himself to the attention of any motorway police. He knew he was probably on a wanted list for hurting Stella, so he didn't want to give them a reason to pull him over. He needed to sneak into Cumbria and find where that bitch Maddy had gone to hide.

She was going to get the surprise of her life when he knocked on the front door. Immediately, he grinned. He liked the thought of giving her a shock, sending her into panic mode when she saw him standing there. She would know how angry he was, but would she slam the door in his face or invite him in? It didn't matter. Either way, he would get inside and teach her what happened to people who walked out on him.

The sign told him Junction 36 was thirty-one miles away, so he turned the radio up to keep his tired mind awake. Maybe he should pull over and have a rest at the next service station. After all, he was in no rush. He doubted Stella had managed to get hold of Maddy to warn her; her phone was smashed, and who remembered phone numbers these days? They were all far too long to memorise by heart.

There was also the fact that Stella had almost jumped into bed with him as soon as he'd turned up on her doorstep. How would she explain that to her best friend who she was supposed to be supporting? 'Sorry, Maddy, I wanted to sleep with Connor so badly that I let him take me out and buy me champagne. But instead of sweeping me off my feet like I wanted him to, he beat the crap out of me, and I told him where you'd run away to.' Somehow, he didn't imagine that conversation going down too well for either of them. He was relying on Stella's shame to make her keep quiet and give him the element of surprise.

He yawned. Picking up the coffee, he took a huge mouthful. It was better than he'd expected, but did they even have decent coffee shops in Cumbria? Wasn't it all grotty pubs, farmers, and tiny villages? He'd never been there, but it got mentioned on *Countryfile* a lot – not that he watched it much, but Maddy had, and that was about as much as he knew about the place.

He began to hum along to the medley of ABBA songs that was playing on the radio. He didn't like them, either, but the whole bloody world could sing a chorus of 'Mamma Mia', thanks to those films. A memory of surprising Maddy with front-row seats to the West End musical sprang to his mind. She'd loved it, he'd hated it, but it had been one of the things he'd done to try to keep her happy. In the end, it hadn't mattered, though, had it? He'd subjected himself to a couple of hours of torture just to keep her sweet. He'd remember to add that onto the list of reasons he wanted to kill her so much, when the time came.

# THIRTY-THREE

Joe's flat was much nicer than Stella had expected. After hours of waiting around in the hospital, the doctor had finally agreed she could go home, on the condition she wasn't on her own. Joe had left to work the dinnertime shift then had come straight back to the hospital.

When he'd walked into the cubicle where she'd been since being admitted, she'd caught a whiff of his aftershave and realised he'd been home and showered. There was no smell of onion lingering on him whatsoever, and that made her like him even more. The fact that he'd wanted to make an impression wasn't lost on her, and he'd phoned a friend who had collected them.

'The sofa is yours,' Joe offered, 'unless you want the bed and I'll take the sofa?'

Stella stared at the mass of squishy cushions, pillows, and the carefully arranged soft woollen throw. 'Sofa is perfect, thank you. I hope you didn't go to any trouble.'

His head shook. 'None at all, this is a bit soppy, but I love having a tidy, clean, comfy flat. I have a Pinterest board where I get ideas from.' He paused and she laughed.

'I don't think you could be any more perfect if you tried.'

'I'm not perfect, believe me, I'm not. My mates make fun of me all the time for not having my dirty socks strewn all over the place. There's one thing I'm not, though, I'm not a violent man. Especially not to women. Don't get me wrong, I've been in a fair few fights over the years, and if I ever get sixty seconds alone with the bastard who hurt you, I don't think I'll be able to stop myself. But I've never physically hurt a woman, nor ever wanted to.'

He looked at her, his face red, and she sensed he was telling her more than he really wanted to.

'What I'm trying to say is that you're safe here, with me.'

Stella felt her eyes brim with hot tears that threatened to escape at any moment.

'Thank you, Joe. You're a good man.' She glanced at his overstuffed bookcase and took a step towards it. 'Even if you do have a bit of an obsession with serial killers.'

He looked horrified and she began to laugh again. 'I'm joking. I love this stuff. I think you and I are two peas in a pod. Just how long have you been coming into the shop to buy these books?'

'Two years, give or take.'

'Oh, my God, I'm so sorry. All that time, all those books, and I've only just realised how amazing you are.'

'You weren't always the one to serve me,' he replied. 'Aden seemed to be there most of the time.'

'That's because Aden has nothing better to do. Well, I'm glad you chose my shop to buy your books from. In fact, I'm really glad.' She turned and crossed the room, kissing his cheek.

He stared at her, a smile spreading across his lips. 'So, what do you fancy to eat? You must be starving. Hospital food is terrible.'

She had to stop herself from saying 'you'. She had no idea

what was wrong with her, but it seemed as if her hormones had gone into overdrive this last week.

'A sandwich would be great. Don't go to any trouble.'

He laughed. 'I'm a chef and I love to cook, but I'm also an excellent sandwich maker. Sit down and I'll rustle something up.'

Stella did as she was told. Sinking down into the world's comfiest sofa, she wondered how her life had gone from disaster to something quite extraordinary in the space of just twenty-four hours. She liked Joe a lot; he was easy to talk to and funny.

When he came back carrying two plates, she jumped, letting out a small squeal.

'Sorry, I didn't mean to scare you.'

'It's me who should be sorry,' she told him. 'I'm a little bit nervy. Thank God you didn't drop the food. That would have been a complete disaster.'

He passed her a plate loaded with soft wholemeal triangles with an assortment of fillings, a leafy green salad with home-made coleslaw, and some hand-cooked crisps on the side. Stella looked up at him.

'Will you marry me?'

He laughed. 'It's only a sandwich.'

'Only? It's my idea of love on a plate.'

'I'd marry you any day.'

It was Stella's turn to blush; her stomach was doing tiny somersaults. Had he really just said that? And had she finally met the man she'd dreamt about spending the rest of her life with?

She looked at him to see if he was being sarcastic, but he was smiling at her. And she knew in her heart that he meant it.

# THIRTY-FOUR

Maddy wiped her sleeve across her forehead. She was perspiring in the most unladylike manner – a thought that made her smile.

'All clear.'

Seth's voice echoing down from the attic had made it sound as if he was far away, not directly above her head. Plucking up courage, she ran up the narrow staircase and stepped inside; unlike the cellar, which had reeked of damp and mould, this smelled different. There was a sweeter scent, which lingered in the air, faint traces of lavender and dust. She'd take this aroma over the dark, scary cellar any day. In fact, it was comforting because it reminded her of the huge, oak wardrobe in her gran's bedroom. The one filled with beautiful dresses and suits from years ago when women wore tea dresses and cocktail dresses most of the time.

Seth smiled at her. 'At least we know the only people in this house are you and me now that we've checked every inch of it.'

She nodded. *What about the ghosts? Or maybe there are secret passages where a person could quite happily live and hide?*

She never said her thoughts out loud, though. She was grateful to him, and she'd already taken up his entire afternoon on what felt like a pointless game of hide-and-seek.

'Thank you, I'm sorry to have wasted your time.'

'You're welcome, and how have you wasted my time? I've had a grand time exploring the house, and with such a beautiful companion.'

Maddy laughed. 'The dust has gone to your head.'

'Don't get me wrong, I'm knackered now. I had no idea exactly how many rooms there were, but it's been lovely spending time with you.'

He crossed the huge space towards her, and for a split second she wondered if he was going to kiss her. Not sure whether she wanted him to or not, she turned away before he could. Beside her was a huge leather chest and a couple of much smaller ones. Bending down, she tried to open the large one, but the lock was rusted shut with years of not being opened.

'I wonder what's inside these. Can you imagine if they were stuffed full of furs, jewels, and beautiful dresses?'

'You have an excellent imagination, no wonder you're a writer. I hate to break it to you, but they're probably empty. This whole house was emptied of most of the personal possessions years ago. Some of it was auctioned off at the sale room in Keswick. It was quite sad, really. A whole lifetime of photographs, letters, and clothes were all sold off to the highest bidder. Rumour has it someone from the BBC bought a lot of it for the props department.'

'Really, wow. That's fascinating and sad. Fancy having no family to leave this beautiful house and all your belongings to. Do you think the wedding dress came from the house?'

He shook his head. 'I doubt it. As far as I know, there's nothing like that left.'

Maddy made up her mind to come back up and open the

trunks when Seth had gone; she wanted to check. It would be amazing if there was something interesting inside them, and she could feel the ideas beginning to spin around in her head for a story. In fact, she wanted to pour herself a huge glass of wine and sit in front of the laptop and write. It had been so long since she'd wanted to do it because it was what she loved, that she immediately turned and went back down the steps.

Scared to lose the momentum while her muse was striking, she led Seth down to the entrance hall.

'Thank you, I really appreciate it.'

A puzzled expression spread across his face and she knew he was thinking she was batshit crazy, but she had no choice. He wouldn't understand that she needed to write, that she'd be terrible company if she tried to ignore the nagging feeling that spread from her brain into her fingertips. If someone asked her to explain it, she couldn't, because she didn't know how to. All Maddy knew was she couldn't afford to ignore this feeling. She'd almost given up the hope of experiencing the itching to create something because she wanted to, and not because her publisher demanded it.

'I'll see you later,' he said, still looking puzzled. 'Maybe you could come to the pub for a bite to eat.'

'I'd love to. I will. Definitely.' She opened the door and all but pushed him out of it.

She felt bad she hadn't even offered him another drink. But before she could change her mind, she shut the door behind him. There was a slight pause and she envisioned him standing on the other side with his hand in the air, debating on whether to knock on the door or not. Then she heard the crunch of the gravel under his feet and released the breath she hadn't realised she'd been holding in. The noisy engine of his car turned over, and she heard the sound of the tyres rolling along the bumpy, gravelly drive.

Almost running down to the kitchen, she tugged open the

fridge, grabbed a bottle of wine and a glass, and ignored the confetti, which was strewn all over the floor. That could wait. She'd clean it up when she'd finished writing.

# THIRTY-FIVE

Seth gave one last glance over his shoulder at the house behind him before it disappeared. *Well, that was weird.* He'd spent all afternoon helping her search for the bogeyman and she'd practically thrown him out of the door. If that was all the thanks he got, she could find someone else next time, although realistically he hoped there wouldn't be a next time.

He liked Maddy much more than he'd liked anyone in a long time, and weren't writers supposed to be a bit strange? He drove back to the village, the windscreen wipers squealing against the glass in sequence. The rain was heavy, much heavier than forecast, and he hoped that didn't mean any unprepared walkers would get lost or stranded on the fells. The weather around here could be brutal and change in an instant.

When he turned into the main street, he saw Maddy's car. He needed to get hold of Martin to take it to his garage and check it out. At least returning her car would give him an excuse to go back and see her; maybe she'd be in a better mood tomorrow. He'd never been particularly good at reading women. He'd had his fair share of girlfriends over the years, but he'd struggled at keeping hold of them. Maybe Maddy was different.

It didn't seem as if she had any better luck with men, judging by the comments she'd made earlier about her last relationship.

The pub was empty; the rain had seen even the diehard customers off. His dad was sat in the armchair near to the fire, which was lit for the first time in months.

'Are you okay, Dad?'

'Fine, just felt a bit chilly. What have you been doing all this time? Although I'm not sure I really want to know the answer. Did you find the owner of the dress?'

'I decided to check the house from top to bottom, to make sure there were no crazy people living in the attic.'

Jacob laughed. 'Oh, there have probably been a few of them in that house over the years, especially in the attic. Did you find anyone? They say the family who originally built it had a daughter who wasn't quite normal and was confined to the attic space.'

Seth grabbed a packet of crisps and sat down opposite his dad.

'No, we didn't, and we searched every room. It's huge. I've been in it before, but I had no idea just how big it really is inside. That's awful, what was wrong with the daughter?'

Jacob shrugged. 'Probably not a lot, I think she had some physical deformities, and back then it was seen as a blight on the family name. They used to hide anyone like that away out of sight, God knows why. The poor girl must have led a miserable life cooped up in there.' He sighed heavily. 'That house is an optical illusion. I used to work in the garden a long time ago, when it was summer and old Samuel the head gardener couldn't manage. It was hard graft for a bit of extra cash, but it was a beautiful place back then. I only went inside a couple of times, but I remember how big it was.

'There were a couple of times when I worked out in the front gardens that I felt as if someone was watching me. I'd turn around and stare up at the house but could never see anyone.

Far too many windows to take in before I'd set my eyes on whoever it was. I used to wonder if it was the poor girl in the attic, watching the world continue outside without her. Then again, I think she died a long time before I even started working there, so it might have been her ghost.' He frowned. 'Not that I'm saying it's haunted, mind. I'm just reminiscing, and there's a chance the morphine is making me a bit nostalgic, for want of a better word.'

Seth laughed. 'I never knew you worked there, why didn't you say?'

He shrugged again. 'I worked all over the place, it's what you did back then. Any odd job to make ends meet; work has never been exactly bountiful around here. It was even worse when I was a lad, although if you could travel, there were plenty of big houses that took staff on. You like her, then, the city girl?'

Seth smiled. 'You don't miss a trick. Yes, I suppose I do. I don't think she quite likes me as much, though. She practically threw me out.'

Jacob laughed. 'She's a feisty one then. I like a woman who can stand her ground and isn't afraid to argue the toss with you. Your mother would disagree with me over almost everything, but it made me love her even more.'

Seth felt a warm glow spread across his heart at the thought of his mum. She'd been the most loving, strong woman he'd ever met.

Jacob's voice broke into his thoughts. 'Your other woman phoned up looking for you.'

'What woman?'

'Purple-haired Glenys from the kooky shop.'

'What did she want? And you have to stop calling her and the shop kooky.'

'How else do you describe the pair of them? She never said. Mind you, she did have the decency to ask if I needed a hand, which was nice of her.'

'She's nice, I've told you that. Maybe just a bit misunderstood.' He stood up. 'I'll ring her back. Thanks.'

As he walked away, Seth realised he didn't have a clue what Glenys's phone number was, so he would have to go and see her. At least it would give him a chance to ask Alfie it was him who'd been playing silly buggers at Lakeview House earlier.

Tugging on his waterproof jacket, he pulled the hood up and stepped out into the rain. Despite it being summer, the sky was almost dark because of the looming rain clouds. He was knocking on Glenys's flat door a few minutes later and heard the ancient window grind against the wood as she pushed it up.

'Oh, it's you.'

'Dad said you rang. Is everything okay?'

'Hang on, I'll come down.'

He stood in the shop doorway wondering what was up. Glenys appeared in a purple, fluffy dressing gown that was the same colour as her hair.

'You could have phoned,' she said, as she opened the shop door and he followed her inside. 'You didn't need to come out in this weather.'

'I don't have your number.'

'Ah, sorry. I did something on my phone and now it comes up as withheld whenever I ring, it's a right pain. It wasn't important. I just wanted to ask you if Alfie had mentioned anything to you about people living under the water. He asked me before, and he seems a bit distant.'

Seth shook his head. 'No, I haven't seen him today, although I do need to speak to him.'

'What about?'

'Lakeview House. Someone put a sodden wedding dress on the front steps and then threw confetti over the kitchen floor. I thought it might have been him.'

'Why would he do that?' Her tone was immediately defensive.

'I don't know, maybe he thought it was funny. The woman living there didn't think it was, it scared her half to death. I wanted to let him know he can't go around doing stuff like that.'

Glenys folded her arms. 'Look, I know he's a pain and he does stupid stuff, but I don't think he'd have the capability to even come up with something like that. He wouldn't connect a wedding dress and confetti together, and besides, where would he get them from? No, it wasn't him, Seth. I know it wasn't.'

'Okay, but if he mentions Lakeview House, can you tell him the lady stopping there on her own doesn't want to be frightened to death?'

Glenys glared at him then nodded. He could tell she was annoyed with him for even suggesting Alfie was responsible, but Seth knew the lad was a lot brighter than she gave him credit for.

'Thank you.'

He turned and began to walk back to the pub. He was hungry, and after today's exertions he wanted to have a hot shower and make something to eat. All thoughts of Alfie, Maddy, and Lakeview House were pushed from his mind as he ran through the contents of the fridge and what to make for tea.

# THIRTY-SIX

Picking up the wine glass, Maddy realised how light it felt. It was empty. She looked at the bottle; that was empty, too. She couldn't remember drinking so much and so fast, then she glanced at the time in the corner of the laptop and blinked. How could it be almost midnight? She hadn't stood up for hours.

Saving her work, she glanced down at the screen. The words were blurred, unfamiliar, and looked foreign to her. A sharp pain in her bladder made her realise she needed to pee, and quick. Rushing into the toilet, she let out a sigh of relief when she'd emptied what felt like the entire bottle of wine into the toilet.

Her head felt muzzy and she wanted to know how she'd been sucked out of this world and into another for such a long time. Yes, she'd had long writing sessions before, but never six hours straight.

After washing her hands, she stripped her clothes off. And pulled on the clean pyjamas she'd left in the bathroom earlier. She felt exhausted, mentally drained. Not even bothering to brush her teeth, she lurched into the bedroom and shut the laptop. It didn't matter what she'd written, now she needed sleep. Tomorrow she'd read through it.

Clambering into the bed, she tugged the duvet under her chin and closed her eyes, then opened them again. The room was spinning, and she felt as if she was going to puke. How did she have room-spin from one bottle of white wine? On a good day she could manage almost two bottles and just be a little tipsy.

Prickles of perspiration began to form on her forehead, and despite the house being cold she felt as if she was on fire. Throwing back the duvet, she kicked one leg off the side of the bed, lying on an angle with a foot pressed down on the bare, wooden floorboards to anchor herself. If she looked up at the ceiling, it was turning around at a spectacular speed. She closed her eyes and prayed she would fall asleep to escape the dizziness. Maddy cursed herself for being greedy. She should have checked the volume on the bottle to make sure it wasn't something ridiculous and eaten something to line her stomach.

Mercifully, sleep must have ascended over her fast, because sometime in the early hours of the morning there was a loud crash from somewhere inside the house. Maddy stirred, murmured something, then turned on her side without opening her eyes. Footsteps echoed around the halls and she didn't hear a thing. They went from room to room, searching for something only they could find.

When she finally woke from the deep slumber, it was to crawl to the bathroom. Her mouth was dry, her throat was parched, and her head was thumping so hard she thought her brain might escape through her ears. Grabbing onto the sink, she ran the cold tap then scooped up handfuls of the icy water; it tasted delicious. When she'd satisfied her thirst, she splashed the water over her face then stumbled back to bed. Her eyes were shut before her head hit the pillow, and she stayed there until the scorching heat of the sun's rays through the full-length glass doors woke her.

She lay for a while, wondering what had happened, afraid to move quickly in case the dizziness came back. *No more alcohol for you. What if you'd fallen down the stairs and broken your neck, or choked on your own vomit? What a way to go. No one would find your body for days, because you were so rude to Seth last night. The builders would have come in and found your rotting corpse. At least, she wouldn't have to worry about this stupid deadline, though, would she?*

Finally, she realised she was going to have to move, and pushed herself up. Her legs still felt wobbly. It was strange, she'd never felt this way in the past no matter how much alcohol she'd consumed, and there had been some times when she'd consumed enough to pickle her own liver.

Pushing the kitchen door open, she saw the pastel-coloured confetti that covered the floor, and felt her heart begin to race a little too fast. She still couldn't figure out how that had got there. She didn't believe in ghosts, and besides, why would a ghost want to throw confetti around? She'd never heard any haunted house stories where the ghost had a tendency to sprinkle that stuff all over the place.

Putting three wedges of bread into the toaster, she switched the kettle on and made herself a large mug of coffee. Then, taking the dustpan and brush from the pantry, she began to sweep up the mess. Talk about adding insult to injury; it was bad enough cleaning up her own mess without having to clean up a mess she had no idea who had made it.

At least she knew the house was secure and there was no crazy person living in a locked room somewhere. She'd watched a film a few weeks before coming here about a nanny who went to live in a big house like this one and had to look after a doll. Maddy had been totally freaked out when the bloody thing had started moving around the house. At least she knew after Seth's search that there were no dolls here either... unless there was one hiding in one of those old trunks in the attic.

She laughed at herself. *Now you're being ridiculous.* Opening the bin, she tipped the confetti from the dustpan into it and slammed the lid down. Seth had to be right; this was someone's idea of a joke. But it didn't make any sense, and no matter how much of a brave face she put on, it didn't mask the terror inside her if she thought about it for too long.

She wished Stella was here with her. God, she missed her so much. Her friend's loud laugh and permanent state of happiness would turn this house into a much cheerier place. Maddy was convinced that was what it was sadly lacking: fun and laughter.

# THIRTY-SEVEN

Stella woke up early. Joe's sofa was comfortable, but she was aware of the prickling guilt in the back of her mind, coupled with the dull ache in her face where Connor had repeatedly punched her. She needed to speak to Maddy and explain what had happened. It didn't matter if she was angry; Stella was worried that if the police hadn't picked Connor up by now, he could be on his way to the Lakes to find Maddy.

Stella had no phone to ring her friend to warn her. She would need to go to the shop and get Maddy's number from Aden; he was like a walking phone directory. If not, she could log on to Facebook and try to get hold of her through Messenger. If all else failed, she could ring the local police where Maddy was staying and ask them to pass a message on, although she didn't know if they would do that.

The sound of Joe's gentle snores filtered through from the bedroom. He was such a nice guy. He hadn't even tried it on with her. As he'd said goodnight, he'd bent down and kissed the top of her head, which had sparked a tingle inside her chest. He'd left her with a warm feeling in her heart and a smile on her face – something no man had done for a very long time.

Creeping quietly into the bathroom, she looked into the mirror and grimaced. *What a state!* There was no amount of make-up that was going to make this face look better anytime soon. Prodding and poking the swollen, bruised mess, she blinked to stop the tears before they could fall. She had no right to feel sorry for herself, because she'd got herself into this. It was karma for wanting to sleep around with her friend's ex.

Squeezing some toothpaste onto her finger, she opened her cracked, swollen lips and rubbed her finger around her teeth. Then, tugging the elasticated hairband from her wrist, she ran her fingers through her hair and tied the mountain of curls up into a messy bun. She left a note for Joe, telling him where she'd gone and that she'd be back later.

First stop was the second-hand shop, next door but one to the bookshop. Stepping out of Joe's flat, she felt the warmth of the sun on her face and it felt good. Things happen for a reason, and she was pretty sure at some point she would find out why the last twenty-four hours had happened. If people asked her about her face, she was going to tell them she'd been in a car accident. It explained the mess and saved her the embarrassment of telling anyone what had really happened.

She reached the tiny street and smiled to see her bookshop. It wasn't much and it wasn't making thousands of pounds' profit a month, but it was surviving. A bit like her. She loved it and was determined to do her best to make it work, whatever it took.

Aden wasn't there yet, and she looked up the steps that led to her flat. There was a large piece of wood across the middle of the door and a shiny new lock. She'd always hated that front door anyway, and as soon as she'd spoken to Maddy she was going to get herself a new one. A pink one, like the one she'd been admiring on Pinterest. She might even put a plant pot outside, filled with pink flowers. It was time to appreciate everything that she had, instead of taking it for granted.

She came out of the second-hand shop with a phone. It was

only a basic Samsung, but it was all she needed, as long as she could contact the police, Maddy, Aden, and Joe. Elsie, who owned the shop, had felt sorry for her and let her have it for free. Stella had argued with her, but she'd insisted, as long as the next time Aden baked a batch of brownies, he'd drop a few off for her.

The world was full of good people, if you took the time to look. Despite her situation, Stella had never felt so much love and kindness. All she needed to do was speak to Maddy and she would feel much better.

Aden was opening the shop, and she tapped him on the shoulder. He turned to look at her and let out a screech. 'Jesus, Stella, take that mask off. You terrified me.'

'Ha ha, funny guy.'

He grabbed her in a bear hug and pulled her close. She let him. Hugging him back, she sighed.

'That's one big sigh, lady. Come on, let's have a coffee and some cake. You can tell your Uncle Aden everything.'

She smiled. 'I don't know what I'd do without you.'

'Me neither. If Waterstones find out I'm such a good book-shop manager and bake the best cakes in Camden, they'll offer me thousands and snatch me away from you.'

'God, I hope not. I couldn't cope without you.'

'I take it I'm forgiven for Zara's poetry reading?' He winked at her and she laughed.

'Just.'

As they went inside, Stella stood for a moment. She inhaled the air, which was filled with the smell of paper and ink; it was her idea of heaven, and it was all hers.

# THIRTY-EIGHT

Seth decided he had to speak to Alfie whether Glenys wanted him to or not. He wasn't angry with the lad, but he needed to explain that he couldn't go around pulling stunts like that. It wasn't funny; poor Maddy had looked terrified yesterday. He really liked her, and it had been so long since he'd felt this way about anyone. The last thing he needed was Alfie scaring her so much that she packed up and went back to London. His last girlfriend had left him without so much as a goodbye, and it had broken his heart.

He opened the pub door and spied Maddy's car. At least he knew she was still at Lakeview House for now; she couldn't go anywhere without the Beetle. He still had her keys in his pocket and would drop them off to Martin, then go and find Alfie.

A loud thud from upstairs filled his heart with fear. He ran back inside and up the stairs.

'Dad!'

He found his dad on the floor outside the bathroom, the skin on his face devoid of all colour and his eyes glazed. Bending down, Seth shook him gently. 'Dad.'

He pulled out his phone and rang for an ambulance, but he knew it was too late. Cradling Jacob in his arms, he held his head on his lap and stroked his hair, as tears streamed from his eyes.

He heard the sirens as the ambulance finally entered the village, the sound piercing the morning air outside, echoing around the empty streets. Finally, voices shouted from below in the pub. 'Hello?'

'Upstairs.' The heavy footsteps pounded up the narrow staircase and he felt relieved to see the familiar red, ruddy face appear at the top step. The paramedic, John, was also a member of the Mountain Rescue Team in his spare time, and Seth had known him for years.

'Oh, mate, I'm so sorry. Is he breathing?'

Seth shook his head.

'Did you do CPR?'

'No. I think he was dead before he hit the floor.'

John didn't question Seth any further. They had both seen enough dead bodies up on the mountains to know. 'I'll have to call the police, mate, it's a sudden death.'

'What? He had terminal cancer. It was going to happen sooner or later.'

'I know, and I'm so sorry, but you know how it is. It's protocol.'

Seth nodded; he did know how it was. He just didn't like the thought of his dad's death being so matter of fact. He'd envisioned Jacob lying in his bed, with Seth holding his hand, when he passed. Not this. It felt so wrong, yet he knew this was what his dad would have wanted. No drama, no lingering on for days, just bam, lights out, Jacob Taylor has left the building.

John knelt next to him and began to unpack the defibrillator.

'I have to run the line and make sure. It's all standard procedure, even though you and I both know he's dead. I'll get a bollocking if I don't.'

Seth nodded again. Tenderly moving his dad's body back onto the floor, he stood up, grabbed a pillow from the bed, and pushed it under his head then took a step back so John could do what he had to.

*Now what?* His whole life was about to change, and he wasn't sure he was ready for the responsibility of running the pub on his own. He'd stayed here because of his dad, but now there was nothing to keep him in the village. He was free to do as he pleased, which was a sobering thought. He was forty-two years old, single, no children... and now he had no family.

Footsteps came running up the stairs and he stared at the red-faced vision standing in front of him.

'Oh no! I heard the ambulance and saw it stop outside and knew it was something bad.'

John shook his head at Seth, confirming what he already knew.

'Glenys, there's nothing we can do. It was so sudden.'

'What do you mean there's nothing you can do? Have you even tried jump-starting his heart?' She was glaring at John, who was talking into his radio.

Seth grabbed hold of her arm, leading her back downstairs. 'Yes, but I knew the moment I heard the thud he was dead. John is just following protocol. Dad died before he hit the floor. And in a way, it would have been exactly what he wanted.'

She let out a sob. 'Oh God, I'm sorry. I'm crap with people dying and stuff like this. Are you okay? Come on, let's have a drink or something to calm our nerves.'

He sank down onto the chair by the fire that had been occupied by his dad less than twenty-four hours ago. The newspaper he'd been reading was still on the table, and Seth reached out to stroke it. Glenys crossed towards him; a glass of amber liquid clenched in each hand. Sitting down opposite him, she passed one glass to him and downed the other herself.

He took it and did the same, grimacing. He wasn't a brandy drinker, but the warmth as it burnt his throat and began to heat his frozen insides, numbing the pain in his chest, was a welcome sensation.

# THIRTY-NINE

Connor stretched out in the double bed, weary after the long drive. He'd taken a detour to Kendal when he'd realised it was getting harder to keep his eyes open, and found a Premier Inn, booking in under a false name. The teenager on the desk had barely made eye contact with him when he'd asked for a credit card, and Connor had passed him his emergency card – the one he'd taken out in Maddy's name, but had so far never used.

The police might have issued an alert of some kind for him, so he was keen to cover all his angles. His main priority was to find the house where she was staying, and until then he'd try anything not to risk getting caught.

Turning on his side, he reached out and picked up the leaflet from the display in the reception area, and a map of the South Lakes printed inside it. He was missing having his all-singing, all-dancing iPhone, which he'd left at home and bought a cheap pay-as-you-go phone from **Waitrose**. Luckily, the hire car had satnav installed, otherwise he would never have made it this far. He knew the police could ping a mobile phone to track a location, so there was no way he wanted to risk that.

He didn't have a clue how strapped for time and money the

police were, and whether they would make much effort to try to find him for GBH. He knew he'd left Stella alive, despite her injuries. He'd only wanted to hurt her enough to make her regret ever letting Maddy leave him like this.

Feeling recharged after a good rest, he decided to have a shower and some breakfast then drive the rest of the way. Judging by this map, it appeared to be a straight run on the A591. When he arrived at the village, he would need to find somewhere to hide. Hopefully, there might be a public car park where he could wait until it got dark. He wanted to surprise Maddy when she was at her most vulnerable; if she ran and it was dark, she wasn't going to get very far over hills and mountains.

The churning in his stomach was a mixture of excitement and nerves; he wanted this to be perfect. If only he had brought his smartphone so that he could capture the look on her face when she opened the front door. He could have recorded it to keep forever.

Connor didn't believe he was going to get caught, but he didn't really care if he was. What mattered most was that he executed his plan in all its bloodthirsty, gory action. It was a shame really that Maddy was going to die. Her story was going to make an excellent book or film for someone else to write one day in the future.

Connor smiled. He might even write it himself and then he could finally have his fifteen minutes of fame.

# FORTY

Maddy opened the fridge door and stared inside; she needed to replenish the wine. It wasn't that she wanted to drink any just yet, but if she was inviting Seth for a picnic, it would be rude not to offer him a glass or two. She also needed fresh bread, cheese, and meat. Did the village have a decent food shop? It must have, or how else would they all survive when the weather got really bad in the winter?

Pulling on her trainers, she walked out of the front door and stopped, sighing heavily. She'd forgotten that she didn't have a car, and it was quite a walk along the main road to the village.

Standing with her hands on her hips, she looked around. It wasn't as if she could phone a cab out here, like she could at home. She supposed it wouldn't hurt to ask Seth if he'd taken her car to the mechanic, and he might even offer to pick her up.

She dialled the number he'd given her, but the call rang out before going to his voicemail. Her heart skipped a beat; she hadn't realised just how smooth and sexy his voice was.

'Sorry to bother you, Seth, it's Maddy. I was just wondering about my car, but I'll ring you later. Bye.'

She ended her message, then tried the number of the pub.

This time the phone was picked up after the fourth ring, and a woman's voice echoed down the line.

'Yes?'

'Sorry, is this the right number for the Horse and Cart?' Maddy asked.

'It is, what do you want?'

*How rude was this woman?* Maddy was shocked. She'd be telling Seth he needed to teach his staff how to answer the phone. You couldn't talk to people like that.

'Is Seth there?' she tried again.

'He's very busy.' And the line went dead.

Maddy stared at her phone then dialled the number again.

'Yes?'

'I need to speak to Seth, please. Can you ask him to answer the phone?'

'Look, I've already told you he's busy. Ring back later.'

'Wait! I don't care how busy he is. Please tell him Maddy would like to speak to him.'

'Is it important? Is it a matter of life and death?'

Maddy was puzzled. 'Well, no. It's not that important or serious.'

'Then you can ring him later. He's with the police. He can't speak now.'

The line went dead again, and Maddy wondered what the hell was happening. *Why was he with the police, and who the fuck was that ogre?*

Shrugging her backpack over her shoulders, she slammed the front door behind her and headed in the direction of the jetty. She'd noticed a worn, narrow path running alongside the lake yesterday, and hoped it might lead to a public footpath and a shortcut to the village.

The sun's rays reflected off the lake, glistening beams of light, as she walked. It was going to be a warm day – perfect for a picnic. She could lay a blanket on the end of the jetty and they could sit there, paddle their feet in the water, chat, and eat. She couldn't think of anything more perfect, and the more she thought about Seth, she realised how much she liked him.

She wasn't looking for another relationship so soon after Connor, but she wasn't going to ignore the signs or the opportunity if one came along. Even if it only turned into a brief, summer fling, maybe that was exactly what she needed – something to give her life purpose, but without the commitment.

A niggling sensation in her stomach made her wonder who the rude woman at the pub was. *What if she was Seth's partner?* They hadn't really discussed if either of them was in a relationship, but she'd just assumed that he was single because there was no wedding ring and no telltale mark where a band might have been worn. And for all she knew, he might have a girlfriend or a fiancée. At least if she turned up at the pub, she could find out what the hell was going on and why he was talking to the police. There were so many questions running through her mind.

She followed the lake until she reached the dry-stone wall bordering the edge of the grounds. There was a dip in the wall where a broken pile of loose stones made it easier to clamber over. She stood on them and scrambled over, slipping and falling over the other side, and landing heavily on her ankle.

'Damn it! Ow, that hurt.' Sitting on the grass, she looked around to see if anyone had seen her spectacular dive, but there wasn't anyone that she could see. She just hoped there wasn't a party of walkers on the fell watching her through binoculars and having a right old laugh at her expense.

She rubbed her ankle. Christ, she was so clumsy. Since she'd arrived in the Lake District, she'd almost severed an artery in her arm and bled to death, and now she might have broken her ankle, miles away from civilisation, stranded on her own.

The laugh that escaped from her lips and filled the air startled her. *Stop it with the drama, girl. You're getting way out of hand.* This made her laugh even louder.

A rustling from behind the huge expanse of bracken behind her made the hair on the back of her neck stand on end and stopped the laughter. 'Who's there?'

It occurred to her how vulnerable she was, sitting on the grass with her legs splayed out in front of her. Pulling herself up, she scanned the bracken, looking for movement. More rustling, as the branches began to stir, filled her heart with cold fear.

'Who's there?' she demanded. 'I can hear you.'

A loud *baa*, as a woolly ewe burst out of the bracken onto the long grass in front of her, almost gave her a heart attack. The relief which flooded through her made her smile until she felt a hand grab her arm, and she shrieked so loud that this time it did echo around the valley.

She turned to see a teenage boy who let go of her sleeve and stumbled backwards in horror at the sound that had come out of her mouth. He had both his hands up, palms facing outwards, as he bent his head away from her.

'Jesus Christ!' she shouted. 'You gave me a heart attack.'

The boy mumbled, 'Sorry, sorry, sorry', over and over.

Maddy realised she'd terrified him even more than he had her and took a small step towards him.

'It's okay, I won't hurt you. I'm Maddy. What's your name?' She smiled at him, holding out her hand towards him.

He looked up at her, not sure what to do with her outstretched hand. After a minute, he grabbed and kissed it, then let it go again.

'Alfie. I'm Alfie.'

She smiled. 'Nice to meet you, Alfie. Do you live around here?'

He nodded frantically.

'That's good. I fell over and twisted my ankle. Do you know how to get to the village?'

He nodded. 'I know you did. That's why I came to see if you were all right. I can take you there. I know a shortcut.'

Maddy's instinct had been right; she'd known someone was watching her. He was tall, but his full lips were parted slightly, and he gave off an air of innocence that suggested he was mentally younger than his age.

Relief flooded her entire body. 'That would be amazing if you could show me. I'm new around here and I don't want to get lost.'

He nodded again. 'I know you are. You live in the house.' He pointed behind them to Lakeview House.

'I do. Have you been inside there lately?' She realised she'd probably found the culprit who had left the wet wedding dress and confetti, but she wasn't mad at him. This must have been who Seth was talking about yesterday.

He shook his head. 'No, sir. I haven't been inside. It might have been the lake people. Come on, I'll show you the way.'

He began walking fast and she hobbled behind him, hoping her ankle wouldn't protest too much. She had no idea who the lake people were, but she didn't care. As far as she could see, there were no other houses this side of the lake, but obviously he wasn't going to admit it was him.

# FORTY-ONE

Aden lifted the mug to his lips and blew the steam away from the tea; Stella mirrored him with her own drink. They were perched on stools behind the small counter, facing each other.

'So, what are you going to do?'

She shrugged. 'I don't know.'

Before she could continue, a man and women – both wearing smart suits – entered the shop. Aden bent towards her and whispered, 'Police, you can spot them a mile off.'

Stella put down her mug, brushed chocolate brownie crumbs from her top, and stood up, smiling at them. 'Can I help you?'

The woman smiled back. 'Stella Sykes?'

'That's me.'

'Detective Constable Emma Sloane, and this is my colleague DC Mike Burns. Can we have a word with you?'

'Does it need to be in private?' Stella was aware of Aden staring open-mouthed at DC Burns as if he'd just set eyes on the long-lost love of his life.

'It's up to you.'

'Come on, we'll go upstairs to my flat.'

Stella led them out of the shop and up to her flat, hoping they were going to tell her they had that prick Connor in the cells and he was crying like a baby. She led them inside and tried to ignore the broken glass and blood still on the floor.

'I'm afraid we're having a bit of trouble tracing Connor,' DC Sloane began. 'Can you give me a list of friends, contacts, addresses where he might be lying low?'

Stella shook her head. 'I'm sorry, I don't know any of his friends or contacts. Have you tried his home address?'

The detective nodded. 'Several times. We have a plain-clothes officer giving it passing attention, and the building security guard has promised to ring should he turn up. How well do you know him?'

Stella tried to stop her cheeks from betraying her, but she could feel the faint redness that always began at the base of her neck begin to burn just below her clavicle.

'Not very well. He's a friend of a friend.'

'Which friend?'

'My girlfriend; his ex-girlfriend.'

DC Sloane took out a notebook. 'I see. And do you think your girlfriend could be hiding him?'

'No, definitely not. She left him. In fact, she's left London, and didn't give him her new address.' A sickness began to spread inside Stella's stomach.

'Has he been in contact with you?'

'No, thank God.'

'Good, that's good.' DC Sloane smiled. 'Well, I just wanted to check with you. If he turns up, you phone in immediately. And don't worry, we're doing all we can to locate him.'

The pounding in Stella's head was making it hard to concentrate.

'Stella, are you okay?'

She looked up, forcing a smile. 'Fine, it's all just been a bit of a shock. I've never been in a situation like this before.'

For the first time, the other detective spoke. 'Are you sure you're okay? If he comes back here, just ring 999. Don't hesitate.'

Stella nodded. 'I'm fine, thanks. I will. I'm not stopping here. I'm staying with a friend, and he doesn't know where they live.'

DC Burns smiled at her. 'That's good, and probably best until we find him and arrest him. Once he's in custody, we can organise bail conditions not to come anywhere near you.'

'We'll leave you to it, Stella.' Emma Sloane passed her a card with her details. 'Here's my number if you need to speak to me.'

Stella watched as they left the flat. Once she heard their footsteps on the concrete steps below, she stood up and ran into the bathroom where she retched and heaved into the toilet. A hot stream of bright yellow bile and chocolate brownie splattered the toilet bowl.

*What have I done?* If the police couldn't find Connor, it could only mean one thing: he'd gone to find Maddy. Stella's legs quivered, threatening to give way as she retched once more. She had to go and tell Maddy what had happened – in person. She needed to warn her and make sure her friend was okay. Maddy was on her own in that huge house, in the middle of the Lake District, with no phone signal. She thought she was safe, that there was no way Connor would be able to find her.

And if it hadn't been for Stella and her stupid hormones, Maddy would be as safe as someone in the witness protection programme. But Stella had blabbed the address to Connor and now Maddy was in danger. She had to get there. She didn't care how, but she was going in the next ten minutes.

Splashing cold water over her face, she brushed her teeth, then ran into the bedroom to throw some things into an overnight bag. Christ, she'd never been to the fucking Lake District, and she wished she'd never bloody seen that advert for a caretaker.

All of this was her fault. Every last detail. And now she had to put it right, or she'd never be able to live with herself.

# FORTY-TWO

Seth relived his dad's final moments for the police officer sitting across from him. Glenys was on her second brandy, but he'd declined another, so she'd brought him a cup of strong, sweet, sugary tea. There were streaky mascara trails down her cheeks where she'd been crying. Coupled with her purple hair, she looked like some teenage Goth.

He knew she was trying to help, and he appreciated it, he really did. But he couldn't be bothered with everyone. He wanted them all to go and leave him alone to have some time to think.

'I've confirmed with the DI that there's nothing suspicious about your father's death,' the officer told him. 'Would you like us to contact the duty undertaker for you, or would you rather do that yourself?'

Seth knew that the duty undertaker was the one his dad had requested to deal with his funeral, because it was the only undertaker in the local area. He nodded. 'Yes please, if you don't mind.' It was one less phone call to make.

The officer excused himself, going outside to speak into his radio. Seth heard voices outside as a couple of the regulars tried to get inside but were turned away by the copper.

Glenys smiled at him, and he smiled back despite the dull ache in his heart. He sipped his tea and grimaced; it was bloody vile. He should have stuck with the brandy.

Standing up, he went outside to see Fred and Tim being ushered away. He called after them; he might as well tell them what had happened. Once the silver van with private ambulance in bold, black letters printed across it pulled up outside the pub, everyone would know anyway. News travelled fast in the small village, so they would spread the word.

The two men shook his hand, offering their condolences. As they turned to walk away, he spotted Maddy's car.

The keys were still in his pocket, so he might as well take them around for Martin. It wasn't fair to leave her stranded out at Lakeview House with no transport when he'd promised to sort it out, despite what was happening to him.

He began to walk away from the pub and the small-scale circus inside, when he heard Glenys shout after him. 'Seth, where are you going?'

He lifted his hand and waved, then carried on walking. He needed to clear his head and get some fresh air – they could manage without him for ten minutes.

Seth turned off the main street and headed for Martin's house on the edge of the village, taking a moment to look up at Helvellyn. The views of the mountain and fells never failed to restore calm in his life; green was such a calming colour, and the entire village was shrouded by the lush verdant fells. Until he was in his late sixties, his dad had been a Mountain Rescue volunteer and his love of the area had rubbed off on Seth from an early age.

Seth felt a sharp pain inside his chest. His dad had been a good man; a much better man than him. He'd married and had a child, but what did he have? At this very moment, a pub he didn't want, a knackered Land Rover, no wife or kids, and a crush on the pretty writer who had moved here in a moment of madness from the big city to write a book and would be leaving the minute it was finished.

Martin was underneath a rusted Ford Focus when Seth arrived at his small cottage.

'Halt, who goes there?'

'Seth.'

Martin slid himself out from underneath the car and stood up. 'Morning, Seth, everything okay?'

He hadn't intended to tell him about his dad, but it all came blurting out, and Martin stood there looking mortified.

'Shit, that's some bad crack that, lad. Is there anything I can do?'

Seth realised the poor guy was probably wondering what the hell he was doing here, and why he'd decided to come to tell him all of this. He cleared his throat. 'Anyway, I came because there's a VW Beetle parked across from the pub. It's broken down and I wondered if you could take a look at it.' He handed the keys to Martin.

'Course I will, no bother. Phew, I was a bit worried there you were going to ask me to do something about your dad.'

Seth frowned. 'Like what?'

He shrugged. 'I don't know. I was panicking in case you wanted me to come and check if he was really dead. Sorry, that sounds terrible, but you know what I mean. A broken-down car I can fix, no problem. I'll give you a lift back and tow the Beetle back here if it can't be sorted out there.'

'Thanks, I appreciate it.' He nodded at the Ford Focus. 'Whose is the rust bucket?'

Martin laughed. 'I'll give you one guess.'

Seth didn't even have to think about it. 'Glenys?'

'Yup. She bought it for two hundred quid. Drove it here a couple of weeks ago in a cloud of black smoke and asked me to sort it out. I've had to go all over Cumbria to get spare parts for it. Best thing she could have done is scrapped it.'

Seth laughed. That was Glenys to a tee. 'It looks even worse than my car, and that's saying something.'

'Mate, your car is like a Jag compared to this.'

They got into Martin's car, which smelled almost as bad as his Land Rover, and Seth stared gloomily out of the window. *God, what a hopeless bunch.* It was a village full of knackered cars and strange people.

He just hoped Maddy didn't realise what a lost cause they all were and leave before he got to know her better.

# FORTY-THREE

Maddy walked behind Alfie, who kept slowing down so she could keep up with him. Her ankle wasn't brilliant. It hurt when she put excess weight on it, but it wasn't as serious as she'd feared, and she had no choice but to carry on walking to the village. Hopefully she would get a lift back.

After what seemed like hours, they arrived at a small play-park on the outskirts of the main street. Alfie turned to her and grinned. 'This is my second favourite place. I hide here a lot. Especially when my mum is mad with me.'

He pointed to a grassy mound that had a tunnel running through the middle of it. Bending down, she looked inside and shuddered; it was creepy. Like one of the storm tunnels that run under Derry, Maine, in the book *It* by Stephen King. Maddy had been reading horror books since her teenage years and that was her particular favourite, though it had scared the shit out of her back then. She'd never really liked clowns and reading about Pennywise had taken her dislike to a whole new level.

'Wow, you hide in there?'

'Yep, all the time. The lake people don't know about it, so

it's safe, and my mum can't get inside it. She has a bad back and can't crawl.'

'Do you have to hide in there much?'

He nodded. 'Yep. Sometimes the other kids are mean to me. Sometimes I do stuff that makes my mum mad at me.'

Maddy felt sorry for the boy. He was obviously a nice lad. He'd scared her earlier, but not on purpose, and he'd shown her the shortcut to the village.

'Well, I think you've been very kind to me today, so I'd like to buy you something as a thank you. Do you like books, magazines?'

She hoped he wouldn't ask her for the latest copy of *Playboy*; how would she explain that to his mum? He was staring at her, smiling. 'Don't read much, but I like chocolate and fizzy pop. Cake I like a lot.'

'Well, you show me where to buy cake and pop from, and I'll buy you some.'

As he led her round the corner onto the main street, Maddy's stomach lurched violently at the ambulance, police car, and crowd of villagers gathered outside Seth's pub.

Immediately, Alfie ran off to see what was happening, leaving her to limp after him. Whatever it was, it didn't look good. She watched as Alfie pushed his way past the copper and paramedic who were chatting outside. Neither of them took a bit of notice of him, which Maddy reckoned was good. At least it couldn't be serious.

A car drove up and parked behind the ambulance, and she saw Seth and a man get out. The man stuck his thumb up at Seth and crossed to where her car was parked. Relief flooded through her. He was okay, and whatever had gone on had nothing to do with him.

She waved at him, but he didn't even look in her direction. He said something to the two men outside then disappeared through the pub doorway. Not wanting to bother him or look like a nosy neighbour, she walked straight past to the general store a bit farther down the street.

It was brightly lit inside and well stocked with an assortment of decent wines; there was even a deli counter. Maddy bought fresh cheeses, meats, bread, olives, crisps, and anything else she thought would make a satisfying picnic, then picked up a couple of bottles of wine. The surly guy behind the counter didn't have much to say, but Maddy didn't care. She was from London, where the shops were full of rude sales assistants. She was tempted to ask him what had happened at the pub, but the fact that he didn't break a smile once while serving put her off. He didn't seem like the sort to gossip. She'd ask Seth herself later.

Putting her supplies in the backpack, she hoisted it onto her back and went to find the guy who had dropped Seth off. But by the time she emerged from the shop, he'd gone – along with her car, the ambulance, and the police van. The pub door was shut, the villagers who'd been loitering outside had gone, and the place was as empty as the *Marie Celeste*.

Maddy frowned in confusion. *Where did they all go?* She hadn't been inside the shop that long. Maybe they were inside the pub. She walked through the small beer garden and knocked on the front door. Then waited. No one answered, so she knocked louder.

When the door eventually opened, she was greeted by a woman with the purplest hair she'd ever seen, mascara smudged down her face.

'Are you the undertaker?'

Maddy shook her head. 'No, is Seth there? Is everything okay?'

The woman whispered, 'He's busy.'

Maddy felt the fine tendrils of black mist fill her veins as anger threatened to explode from her chest. So, this was the rude woman who'd answered the phone earlier.

'I don't care,' she snapped. 'I've walked all the way from Lakeview House to speak to him. It's important.'

'As important as him finding his dad stone dead at the top of the stairs?'

The colour drained from Maddy's face and she felt terrible. 'No, it isn't. Oh God, I'm so sorry. Please accept my condolences, and would you tell Seth I called?'

The woman smiled. 'You're the crazy lady living in Lakeview House?'

'I'm not crazy.'

'Sorry, I didn't mean that how it sounded. It's been a terrible morning, such a shock.' She held out her hand. 'I'm Glenys. I own the kooky shop, or at least that's what the locals call it. They think I'm crazy as well.'

Maddy grinned at her and shook her hand. 'I'm Maddy. Seth has been helping me out. He's been great.' A thought suddenly struck her: *What if Glenys was his girlfriend or partner?* Her heart dropped. She'd been hoping he was single. 'I'll leave you to it. Nice to meet you.'

'Hey, you should come to the shop. Not now, but tomorrow. I'll pull some tarot cards for you and give you a reading.'

'I'd love to.' Maddy turned and walked away. Poor Seth. She wished she could do something for him. He'd been so kind to her since she'd arrived, and now he was going through this.

She hobbled towards the playpark and hoped she'd be able to find the way Alfie had brought her, because he was nowhere in sight to guide her back to Lakeview House.

# FORTY-FOUR

He'd lain on the sofa listening to the local radio station for hours, although he wasn't really listening. What he was waiting for was a mention of a missing walker; he needed the excitement and the thrill of the search. Then the kill. He didn't know which he preferred, if he was honest. Both had their own different kind of attraction for him, though neither of them was right, and, he sure wasn't going to heaven the sins he'd committed. Did he care? Not one little bit. Life was crap at times.

He was only doing what all those millions of inspirational quotes on social media were always telling him to. Was it his fault that doing what he loved was hunting and killing people? He could photograph one of the corpses before he sunk them into the lake, and caption it #doingwhatIlove. He wondered how many likes it would get before the police came looking for him.

He stood up, pacing the floor and staring out of his bedroom window. From here, he could see the village hall where the Mountain Rescue Team had a base, their mud-splattered 4x4 parked outside. If they all began scrambling towards the hall, it would be game on. He realised his fingers were crossed, wishing for some poor bastard to have wandered off and become lost on the fells. But so far, nothing much was happening tonight.

Just then, he saw an unfamiliar car drive into the village main street. Taking out his binoculars, he fixed on the car and the man driving it. He was alone. He'd pulled up outside the shop; he was either lost or hungry. Or both. The guy got out of the car and began to stretch his arms and legs.

This was interesting. It was almost closing time, and he'd be lucky to make it into the shop before Brian shut the door and locked up for the night.

He grinned to see the shop door, which had been propped open, suddenly slam shut. The guy legged it across the road and hammered on the door. Brian wasn't going to like that; he was a miserable sod on a good day.

Sitting on the edge of the sofa, he turned the lamp off and watched to see if the shop door opened again. If he was a betting man, he'd have put twenty quid on it staying shut. He let out a gasp when it opened again. *Well, I never! Brian, you must be feeling charitable tonight. That makes a change. I wonder what he wants?*

He watched as the guy from the car managed to talk Brian into letting him inside, and he wished he knew what the conversation was about. Maybe they knew each other.

But a few minutes later, the guy came out with a carrier bag, and the door shut quickly behind him. The guy looked around the village; the light had faded fast in the short time he'd been inside the shop. It would be fully dark soon.

The mystery man began to walk towards the pub. That was all in darkness, too. After today's tragedy, no one had expected it to be open, and the front door was shut. He wondered if the guy would be cheeky enough to hammer on that door, too. There was a guest house a bit farther along, if he was looking for a room for the night, but when he'd passed earlier the sign outside had said NO VACANCIES.

Still staring out of the window, he was undecided. Should he wait for a missing walker, or should he try to find out about the single guy looking for a room? Maybe he should do the right thing and open his door for him, go out and chat to him then offer him a couch to sleep on for the night. It would be so easy: let him inside, feed him, then kill him. That was one way to satisfy the urge pressing down inside his stomach and making it feel as if there was a lead ball in his gut.

Undecided, he'd just watch for now and play it by ear. Pushing one hand into his pocket, he felt the rough edges of his lucky coin. He could flip it and let fate decide the man's future. Heads he died, tales he lived. It was as simple as that; nothing more to it.

Pulling out the coin, he began to turn it between his fingers. Flipping it into the air, he already knew the outcome. His lucky coin was a double-headed ten-pence piece.

# FORTY-FIVE

Maddy made it back to Lakeview House without getting lost. It was a struggle to climb over the wall, because her ankle was now painful and swollen after all the walking. Taking her time to mount it, she hoped no one was watching her, because right now she was doing a good impression of a fish out of water, and it wasn't very ladylike.

As she limped along the lakeside, the sound of the water lapping against the pebbled edge soothed her troubled mind. She felt awful for Seth, but what would she do to fill her days now, if he was too busy mourning for his dad? *Maddy, you selfish cow*, she told herself. *That's despicable; the man is grieving and all you're bothered about is being bored out of your head.*

She looked across the grounds at the imposing house. It was beautiful, desolate, and quite scary from this angle, with its blacked-out windows and no lights burning inside. She realised just how crazy this idea had been; she was on her own in the middle of nowhere. Her shoulders were aching from carrying the backpack full of food and wine.

As she reached the jetty, she shrugged the bag off and let it fall onto the grass. Kicking off her shoes, she rolled up her leggings and decided to sit and paddle her feet in the icy-cold water. It might help the swelling on her ankle to go down, and perhaps she would be able to get a phone signal. She needed to speak to Stella; anyone, really. She didn't think she'd ever experienced loneliness in her entire life but was pretty sure the way she felt now was quite close.

Lowering herself onto the end of the wooden jetty, she dipped her toes into the water, letting out a small squeal as the cold water numbed them. Counting to three, she pushed her feet in all the way to her calves, screeching even louder. It didn't matter how much noise she made; there was no one to hear her. The coldness enveloped her legs, but it felt so good against the burning sensation in her swollen ankle. She'd been hoping Seth would come to her rescue and strap it up for her, but this was almost as good as the thought of his hands touching her skin.

Despite her reluctance to get involved with another man so soon after Connor, there was something so nice and normal about Seth and the thought of his touch made her skin tingle. He was older than her, pretty laid-back, a real hero who had rescued people from the mountains at all hours of the day and night, yet he didn't think anything of it. She should have insisted on speaking to him today. How would she know if that strange woman would pass her message of condolence on to him? She needed him to know she was sorry and that she cared.

Kicking her legs back and forth in the water, she took her phone from her shirt pocket and searched for Stella's number. It went straight to voicemail again, and Maddy didn't know whether to be angry or worried. She was both, if she was honest. This wasn't like Stella; they'd had minor disagreements in the past and not spoken for a couple of days. But this was different. They hadn't fallen out, but Stella had been a bit odd on the phone the last time they'd spoken.

Maddy had no idea what to do. She supposed she could

phone Aden, but she didn't have his number; she normally spoke to him on the shop phone when Stella wasn't around. She dialled the shop on the off-chance that either one of them might still be there, but the phone rang and rang, cutting off before she got the chance to leave a message. *Fuck, Stella, what's happening?*

Her stomach let out a loud groan, and so did she as she tried to stand, a sharp pain shooting through her ankle. Picking up her trainers and her backpack, she hobbled barefoot across the grass to the entrance of the house.

There was quite a lot she could be doing; she should be writing, and now she had no excuse. Seth was out of the equation and she had no idea what Stella was up to, so she would make herself something to eat then hide away in the bedroom and write. After all, wasn't that the whole point of this turn-your-entire-life-upside-down-and-finish-this-bloody-book upheaval of her lifestyle?

She opened the heavy front door and stepped into the shadow-filled hall. A faint smell of lavender and cinnamon lingered in the air. Inhaling, she wondered where it had come from. It didn't smell anything like the Chanel Chance she'd spritzed herself with before leaving, and anyway, she'd left that in the bedroom upstairs.

Just to be sure it wasn't her mind playing tricks on her, she tugged the collar of the T-shirt she'd put on, and sniffed it. Nope, it definitely wasn't her. So where was the smell emanating from? She supposed she should be grateful it didn't smell of rotting flesh or damp earth, like the cellar.

For such a huge building, inside it was peaceful. Maddy had never really believed in ghosts, but she could imagine the owners who had died here loving the house so much that they might not want to leave. *Is that where the smell had come from?* Maybe the lady of the house was still here, wandering the halls.

*What if she doesn't know she's dead, and is still carrying on with her life, just like always?*

A cold chill settled over Maddy. She was creeping herself out, but not in a Freddy Krueger–kind of way, because she didn't imagine anyone who had lived or died here had been a violent serial killer. More in a was-someone-watching-her kind of way. She shuddered; there she was again, filling her head with stuff she shouldn't be. At this rate, she'd leave here and go straight into a hospital for mental health patients to get her head back together.

Once she'd unpacked her backpack and put the shopping away, Maddy sat at the desk with a huge mug of coffee and half a packet of biscuits. All the walking and fresh air had given her a huge appetite.

She was definitely off alcohol for the time being – or at least until she could share a bottle with Seth. She didn't trust herself. Her head was still a bit muggy despite the walk into the village and her paddle in the lake, and two painkillers had taken the edge off but not completely.

Opening up her laptop, she began to read the last few chapters of what she'd written last night to refresh her memory. She had no recollection of writing any of it, which disturbed her a little. Normally, she could remember the gist of how the story was going, so it wasn't like her to have this complete blank.

Sipping the hot coffee, she dunked the biscuits in; she was nevertheless pleased with how the story was shaping up. Maybe this book was going to be even better than her first one? And she knew the next one was going to be fabulous, because she'd already decided it was going to be set here, among the shadows of Lakeview House.

# FORTY-SIX

Stella hadn't been able to concentrate. She'd tried phoning Maddy numerous times from the shop phone, and each time it had gone to voicemail. When Joe walked into the shop a couple of hours later, she'd been relieved to see him, and she felt a warmth spread through her insides, soothing her fears away.

'How are you?'

'Worried.'

'About that idiot?'

She shook her head. 'No, Maddy – the idiot's ex, and my best friend. I can't get hold of her and the police called earlier. They can't get hold of him. What if he's gone to find her, Joe? He was so angry about her walking out on him. I'd never live with myself if something happened to her because of me.'

She crossed to the shop door, closing it, then turning the key in the lock.

'So, where is she?'

'In a huge, bloody desolate mansion in the middle of the Lake District with little or no phone signal,' she replied. 'I can't get hold of her. I've been trying all day.'

Joe crossed to where Stella was standing. He pulled her

close, and she let him. She needed his warmth; she was freezing, and he was like a hot-water bottle. He bent down, kissing her cheek.

'Then there's only one thing for it.'

'What?'

'We need to go and check she's okay. Warn her about him.'

'How? Plus, she's going to be so disappointed in me when I tell her I let him take me out for a meal then I invited him into my flat.'

Stella didn't know how Joe was going to react, but she needed to be straight with him. She owed him that much.

'None of that matters,' he told her. 'We need to check on her. If she's angry with you, then that's fine. At least you know she's still alive to be angry with you. She won't be angry for long anyway, how could she be? She'd left him, so it wasn't like you went behind her back, and I think she'll know how good he is at manipulating people. She'll know he was only using you to get to her.'

'Ouch.'

He held her tighter. 'I don't mean that in a horrible way, but it's true. He took advantage of you because he's a conniving, slimy, dangerous creep. It wasn't your fault, Stella. And besides, you deserve so much better than him... than me.'

Stella hugged him back. 'No, I don't deserve better than you, Joe. I don't know how I've been so lucky enough to have your friendship and not realise before how amazing you are. You're the best thing that's ever happened to me.'

His lips bent, touching hers, and she pressed her mouth against his so tight she wondered if she'd sucked all the air out of his lungs. Pulling away, she felt her heart racing. She wanted him more than she'd ever wanted anyone in her entire life, but she knew that now was not the time. She'd let Maddy down once; it wouldn't happen again. She could pick up where they'd just left off as soon as she knew her friend wasn't in any danger.

'How are we going to get to the Lake District?'

Joe grinned. 'I'll borrow my grandad's car. He can't drive now his eyes are too bad, but he's too stubborn to admit defeat, so it's in his lock-up, gathering dust. I'll go and get it. You get some things together and arrange for Aden to take care of the shop.' He winked at her. 'I've always wanted to spend a romantic weekend in the English Lake District with a beautiful woman. I'll be back in an hour. Will you be ready to go?'

She nodded, blinking back tears of gratitude. She had no idea what she'd done to deserve this man standing in front of her, but one thing was for sure, he wasn't getting away.

'Thank you.' She didn't know if he'd heard her because he'd unlocked the door and was already striding down the street.

Closing the door behind him, she let out a huge sigh of relief. Thank you, God, Universe, whoever. I promise not to mess this up now. Please, just let Maddy be okay and that arsehole Connor to have driven his car off the side of a mountain, and everything will be back to normal.

* * *

Stella had stuffed some things in her Cath Kidston weekend bag that Maddy had bought her for her birthday, along with some basic make-up essentials. She didn't need a lot; Joe made her feel as if she could be herself.

Glancing in her bedroom mirrors, she did a double take; her face was horrific. The swelling had gone down slightly, but the bruising had darkened. It was a good job Joe had seen her this way, because things could only ever improve.

A car horn beeped from the street below and she rushed to the bedroom window, lifting the blinds. Down below was a burnt orange Ford car of some kind. It wasn't the prettiest or the poshest of cars, but it didn't matter. It would do, as long as it got them to Lakeview House. Slinging the bag over her shoulder, she rushed out of the flat, locking it behind her, and ran towards the car.

Joe jumped out of the driver's side and opened the rear door for her to put her bag in.

'Sorry, the boot doesn't open unless it feels like it. You might put your bag in and it gets stuck in there.'

Stella smiled at him, then rushed around to the passenger side and climbed inside. The car smelled of lemon and pipe smoke. Joe got in and looked at her with a worried expression.

'Do you hate the smell? I'm used to it, but it's not that nice to a non-smoker. My gran won't let him smoke his pipe in the flat, so he sits in the car with the engine running to have a smoke. Then he sprays it with lemon air freshener to get rid of the smell. Only it doesn't. And they both linger on the upholstery like a bad dream.'

She laughed. 'It's fine. It reminds me of my grandad, actually. I like it.'

Joe kept his eyes on her, clearly unsure if she was lying or not.

'Honestly,' she assured him, still grinning. 'Even if it smelled of crap, it would still be okay. It's very good of him to let you use it.'

'Right.' He put the car into gear. 'I'm hopeless at directions, should we use your phone's Google Maps?'

Stella laughed again. 'Have you seen this phone? I don't know if it will even load a map.'

Joe pulled his mobile from his trouser pocket and handed it to her. 'There's a car charger in the glove compartment. If you plug that in, we should be good to go.'

Stella opened it and rooted among the receipts until she found the charger, plugged it in, and waited for Google to load, then typed in the address. The voice began to tell Joe to go north-west then turn right. Stella didn't have a clue what direction that was, so she was glad Joe was driving.

She felt the butterflies in her stomach subside a little. Everything was good; it was going to be okay. They would get to Lakeview House with no problems, Maddy would be pleased to see them and ask them to stay for a couple of nights. They would sink a couple of bottles of wine, she would tell her all about Connor, and then they could all get on with their lives. No guilt hanging over her shoulders, and no worry that he'd found Maddy and hurt her.

# FORTY-SEVEN

Connor hammered on the pub door. The place was in darkness, and he wished he'd come straight here instead of wasting most of the day in Kendal. It seemed odd for a pub to be shut at this time of evening; it wasn't past closing time. He pulled out his phone to see where the nearest guest house or hotel was, but there was no signal. It was a shame his map wouldn't load or he could have gone straight to the place Maddy was staying, then he could have charmed his way in and spent some quality time with her.

'Can I help you?'

He turned to look at the guy who'd almost made him jump. He looked like a local, with his fleecy jacket and walking boots.

'I don't know if you can,' Connor replied politely. 'I'm looking for somewhere to stop for the night. Does everywhere close this early in the summer? I'd have thought it was open for people like me. You know, tourists?'

The man shrugged. 'There's been a bit of bad news at the pub. It's normally open. The nearest place that might have rooms available is Keswick.'

'Is it far? I've been driving for the last couple of days, and I'm tired. I only wanted somewhere to crash for the night.'

'I live behind the pub. You can stop at mine for the night, if you want. My wife's on a shopping trip with her sister. We've got one of those sofa beds. Never used it, to be honest. But as long as it's just the one night, you're welcome to christen it.'

Connor stared at the guy, wondering why he would offer a stranger a bed for the night. *Did these people not worry about killers or thieves taking advantage of them?* Obviously not, if he thought it was acceptable. He didn't look like a nutter. Well, no crazier than he was himself. And he could do with a rest, some time to plan out what his next move was. He wasn't used to driving for long spells and the need for total concentration had given him a terrible headache.

'Do you not mind?' he asked. 'Obviously, I'll pay you the going rate for a B and B. But I'd really appreciate it.'

The guy shrugged. 'Wife is always telling me to be kinder to strangers, so I guess this is a good start.'

Connor guessed the man's wife would go fucking mental with him when she found out, but by that time he'd be long gone. He only needed a few hours' sleep, time to figure out the best route to get to Lakeview House, and he'd be gone before the Good Samaritan woke up for his early morning piss.

The guy turned and began to walk off. Connor followed him; he had nothing to lose.

'You might want to move your car to the small car park behind the pub,' the man advised. 'You don't want it to get towed. The police only turn up once in a while, but they're strict about cars on double yellows on this narrow road. I wouldn't take a chance.'

Connor nodded, and the guy walked around the side of the pub to wait for him. The car park wasn't very big, but he managed to squeeze his car into the last gap between a skip and an overgrown bush. His Good Samaritan was waiting for him.

'Have you eaten?'

'I had a sandwich and a couple of chocolate bars earlier, so I'm okay, thanks.'

'Rubbish, I can make you a fry-up. I was going to make one for myself anyway, so you might as well join me. Got plenty of bacon, sausages, and eggs, it's all the wife buys.'

Connor felt his stomach groan at the thought of a plate of bacon and eggs.

The guy began to walk along the small, cobbled streets, and Connor had to walk fast to keep up with him.

'I don't want to be cheeky, but is it far?' he asked. 'We could take my car if it is?'

The man shook his head. 'It's not far, just in a bit of an awkward place. Your car won't make it along the track. It's only another five minutes up the fell.'

Out of breath, Connor realised they'd been climbing for some time up the side of a steep hill. Looking behind him, the lights of the village were some distance behind them.

A ramshackle building loomed in the distance, and for the first time in his life a feeling of uneasiness fell over him. There were no lights burning in the building, and it looked as if it hadn't been lived in for years.

'Are we nearly there, mate?' he puffed. 'I'm knackered.'

'Just behind the old summerhouse. There's a bit of a dip on the hillside, so you can't see the house from here. It's literally just five minutes.'

Connor stared down the hillside. He could make out the outline of a huge building down below them. It looked a bit like the house Maddy was staying in, when he'd googled it.

'What's that building down there?'

'Which one?'

Connor frowned; it was the only building he could see for miles. Surely there weren't two huge houses which looked the same in this area?

'That house down there, by the lake.'

'Ah, you mean Lakeview House. We don't talk about that around here, it's bad luck. No one bothers about it, we let it be. Always have done. It's best that way.'

'My friend is stopping there; I've come to surprise her with a visit. In fact, I could just head back down there and save messing you around. It looks a bit desolate and run-down.'

'It is. No one has lived there for years. Your friend is either very brave or very foolish to even think about living there on their own.'

A voice spoke directly down his ear, tickling the tiny hairs and making him shudder.

'Your friend is mine now.'

Connor turned in time to see the huge rock that was being brought down in his direction. Before he could register what was happening, it smashed into his skull, bringing a wave of hot bile into his mouth as blackness began to fill his mind. It hit the side of his head again and his knees buckled. But as he tried to lift his hands to protect himself, the third blow crashed down, and he sank into unconsciousness.

Oblivious of being dragged the last few feet to the derelict summerhouse that had once served Lakeview House, he didn't feel the way he was thrown over his attacker's shoulder like a sack of coal and thrown through the broken window. He crumpled to the rubble-filled, dirty floor in a heap, his blood and brain fluid leaking heavily from the open wound in his fractured skull.

# FORTY-EIGHT

The early morning dawn chorus was loud. So loud that Maddy stirred in her sleep. Stretching out, she lay there in that blissful state between being fully awake and still in a dream. Last night, she'd written until her fingers were aching and her eyes could barely stay open. Unsure whether it was the walking, the fresh air, or a combination of both, she'd fallen into bed and slept without stirring.

Opening her eyes, she blinked at how bright the sun was so early, then rolled onto her side and drifted back off. This time, there were dreams, lots of them. The house was restored back to its original splendour and there were a lot of people bustling around. Servants were bringing silver platters of food from the kitchen and laying them out on the huge dining table. Her stomach had grumbled at the sight of it all; it was so vivid she could smell the freshly baked bread and roast hams. In the kitchen, a sideboard filled with cakes made her mouth water. There was a cook, kitchen maids, and several other people chattering loudly while they worked.

Moving on from there, she marvelled at the hallways, which were decked out with the most beautifully scented floral arrangements. They were having a party. How wonderful! This was going to be fun.

She followed a maid rushing up the staircase with a beautiful pale-blue silk dress over her arm. There was a lot of excited chattering from the bedroom that was hers. She floated towards the doors, which were ajar, and saw a cluster of girls all dressed in matching gowns. They were lined up on chairs, with a maid behind each one, rolling their hair up into intricate pin curls.

A tall, dark-haired woman was standing with her back to them. She was staring out of the windows, down at the gardens or the lake. From this angle, Maddy couldn't be too sure, but something had caught her attention.

She stepped closer to the glass, pressing her face against it, then let out the loudest, high-pitched shriek that Maddy had ever heard. It was as if time stood still; each and every girl stood in slow motion then walked across to the picture windows to see what the woman was screaming at. Before long, there were gasps and more screams.

The woman turned around, pushing through the line of girls with both hands, parting them so that she could get through them, then she ran. Maddy tried to step to one side, but the woman ran through her. The feeling was strange, as if she'd been winded and her insides had frozen for a second. She couldn't breathe, then a rush of air filled her lungs as she exhaled and stumbled forwards. Running into the room, she pushed her way to the window to see what all the commotion was about... and that was when she saw her.

There was a woman, floating face down in the lake, her beautiful white wedding dress and jet-black curls billowing around her. Maddy pushed herself away from the window; she knew a bit of first aid. She'd learnt how to do CPR at her last job, so she could help. Turning, she ran for the stairs. The noise behind her was deafening, the girls huddled together sobbing and wailing so loud the floor of the room was vibrating.

Running down the stairs, Maddy raced through the open doors and across the grass, which scratched at her bare feet. There was quite a crowd around the lakeside; she heard thudding footsteps behind her as a man's voice bellowed, 'Ada! Ada!'

Maddy turned to see whose voice it was and felt her heart miss a beat. It was a younger version of Seth, with similar eyes and facial features. Much taller and fitter than her, he raced towards the water's edge where a group of men were trying to reach the woman but her heavy, sodden dress was making it extremely difficult.

She watched the man unbutton his heavy coat, throwing it onto the ground. He kicked off his boots, shrugged off his ruffled shirt, and ran into the water, where he slipped his hands under the woman's armpits and began to drag her out of the icy lake. Maddy found herself praying for Ada to be okay. The other men waded in to help him, and between them they managed to drag her body onto the grass and turn her onto her back.

Maddy stared in horror at the frozen face of the woman lying in front of her. She was beautiful... and looked a lot like her. She stepped closer. Maybe she could help. She tried to get past the men who were all standing around staring in horror, but couldn't push through them.

The Seth guy was kneeling on the floor, cradling his bride-to-be, and crying. The woman's eyes were glazed, her lips parted slightly and tinged blue. No amount of resuscitation could help her; she'd been dead for some time.

Maddy wanted to scream in frustration. This was her wedding day. It wasn't supposed to end like this, here. The woman hadn't even made it to the church. How had she ended up drowning in the lake?

A sob filled her chest and she opened her eyes, relieved to see she was in bed, not standing like a morbid onlooker at the lakeside tragedy. *Thank God, it was a dream! It was just a dream, Maddy.* She lay for a while, breathing deeply, trying to calm her nerves. She'd never before dreamt anything that seemed so real, so horrific, and so sad. She tried to process and store it all before it slipped away, like most dreams do.

Realising she needed to write down what she'd dreamt, she threw the covers back and stood up. Immediately, a shooting pain flared from her ankle up to her thigh, reminding her that she'd injured it yesterday.

Gingerly, she hobbled over to the desk where she took out a notebook and wrote down everything she could remember. She didn't realise her hands were trembling and her heart was racing until she put the pen down and breathed a sigh of relief. *It was just a dream, just a dream.*

Looking out of the window, she could see the exact spot where they'd dragged the dead bride out of the water and laid her on the grass. The dead bride who'd looked remarkably like her, not to mention her fiancé, who had looked like a younger version of Seth. She knew that was frankly ridiculous, because she had no idea what he'd looked like when he was younger. He could have sported a Mohican and wore tartan drainpipes, for all she knew. It was her subconscious taking his image and turning it into a Mark Darcy lookalike, nothing more.

A cold chill settled over her despite the warmth of the breaking sun through the windows. Slipping her boots on to support her swollen ankle, she carefully made her way down-stairs. As she did, she was reliving the whole dream, the images going around inside her mind. It had been so real: she'd smelled the fresh bread and the flowers; she'd heard the laughter and excited chattering – the screams had shaken her to her very core. But the house was still now, and she got the impression it was listening to her, waiting for her to give her opinion out loud on whether she was losing her mind or not.

She walked into the kitchen, expecting to see it full of servants, and was relieved to see it was the same empty, run-down room it had been last night. Flicking the switch on the kettle, she made a mug of tea then hobbled outside to drink it on the front steps. She was frozen.

The warmth of the sun felt good on her face, and she cupped her hands around the mug to warm them until the sun took over. Her eyes scanned the grass for the spot where the bride had been pulled from the water. *Am I going mad, or am I reliving something that had happened here a very long time ago?* She didn't think she was going crazy; it was only one dream. And no one in her family suffered from hallucinations or mental illnesses that she was aware of.

Was the house sharing its secrets with her? Had it decided to show her its past because she was the only one brave enough to stay here on her own? The sodden dress on the front steps and the confetti in the kitchen could have been some villager's idea of a joke, but then they must know the history of the house. Whatever it was, she needed to find out more. She felt as if someone or something was reaching out to her.

Maddy made up her mind to go back to the village and speak to Glenys. If she didn't know, maybe she knew who would. Anyway, she needed to see if her car had been fixed. Once she got it back, she could travel to the nearest library and do some research on the house. And if it turned out that what she'd 'witnessed' had been nothing more than a dream, then at least she had the bare bones to make into a story. That was the trouble with her creative mind; sometimes it took the simplest of things and turned them into a full-blown horror story.

As she turned to go back into the house, her eyes fell on the grassy spot where the woman had been cradled by her grieving fiancé. *Did you go into the lake and take your own life, Ada? Or did someone take it from you?*

# FORTY-NINE

Lost in thought, she glanced up to the fells and stared in wonder at the colourless rainbow that had formed among the mist. The arc appeared white but, squinting her eyes, she could see the slightest hues of colour throughout it. It was the opposite of the colourful rainbows she'd had a fascination with her whole life.

Maddy stared at it in awe, wondering exactly what it was, when a voice mumbled from behind her.

'It's a fog bow.'

'Jesus!' Clutching her chest, she turned to see Alfie standing to the side of her. He'd crept up while she'd been lost in thought. 'A fog bow? What's that? I've never heard of it.'

'It happens when the water droplets in the mist are too small to retract and reflect the light. It makes the rainbow appear white.'

Maddy looked away from him and back towards the fell. The sun was making the fog fizzle away and, along with it, her fog bow.

'They're very rare.'

She looked back at him. 'Yes, they must be. I've never seen anything like it.'

'We get all kinds of weird weather here. I like the weather. Thunderstorms are my favourite. I love watching the lightning and listening to the sky rumble. My ma hates them; she acts all weird before one breaks.'

Maddy smiled. 'I like a good thunderstorm, too. Alfie, why do you keep lying on the jetty and staring down into the lake? I've seen you there a few times now.'

He shrugged and looked down at his feet. 'I told you, I like to watch the lake people. I count them to make sure they don't move.'

'Who are the lake people?'

'Dunno. They just live under the water.'

Maddy didn't know what to say to him. Maybe it was his way of coping with life. Who was she to question him and his imaginary friends? She didn't know who or what the lake people meant to him.

She stood up. 'I'm going into the village. Do you want to walk with me?'

He shook his head. 'Too slow.'

'What is?'

'You. I have to be quick today. Can't hang around. Ma will go mad if I'm late.'

'Oh, okay. You better get going then.' She watched him, then as an afterthought shouted, 'Alfie, how many lake people are there?'

He was walking away but paused briefly to count on his fingers. 'There were three, and now there's four. Next week there might be five. Sometimes they grow. I don't mind it when there's more of them. I get scared when I count, in case there's less of them.'

He began to run towards the dry-stone wall he'd led her over yesterday to show her the shortcut to the village, and she watched him go. She had no idea what he was talking about, but at least he was harmless. And now she knew all about fog bows;

she hadn't known such a thing even existed. He was more intelligent than she'd given him credit for, and she instantly felt bad for judging him. Who was she to form an opinion of the boy? He'd lived here long before she came along, and at least he was happy. He didn't seem to shoulder the worries most teenage boys his age did.

Christ, what she'd give to be that age and innocent again. You thought going to school and falling out with your friends over which band was the coolest was the worst thing in the world. She looked up at the mansion. She couldn't complain. Her life was probably the simplest now it had been in forever – no man; no friends to please; just her and her laptop against the world. Even her agent couldn't get hold of her.

Seth was a welcome distraction; she couldn't deny that. He wasn't like the other guys she usually ended up friends with; he hadn't wanted to drag her into bed. He was nice, funny, different, and very good-looking. It was a wonder he wasn't the prime catch among the local women, but then again, what did she know? He probably was and had a whole string of lovers.

# FIFTY

Stella groaned. She'd never slept in such an uncomfortable position. She turned and came face to face with Joe, who was inches from her face, flat out. The fact that they'd had to recline the front seats in his grandad's Ford Focus and try to get some sleep obviously didn't bother him. They'd come off the motorway late last night when the car had started making a strange hissing noise, but at least they were halfway there.

Joe had asked her if she wanted to find a hotel, but she hadn't wanted to put him out or waste an extortionate amount of money on a room. As she lay there, her neck feeling stiff and an overwhelming urge to pee, she was now regretting that decision. They could have woken up in a luxurious hotel room, had breakfast in bed, then made love until it was time to leave.

She made a promise to herself that as soon as she knew Maddy was okay, that Connor wasn't anywhere near the county, and their friendship was still intact, she would book her and Joe into the closest hotel she could find and show him exactly how grateful she was.

'Joe, are you awake?' She knew he wasn't, but she wanted to get going, and it might take him some time to get his bearings.

He opened one eye, smiled at her, and mouthed, 'Good morning, beautiful.' Then he cupped his hand over his mouth and frowned. 'Oh God, does my breath smell? Sorry, Stella.'

His reaction tickled her, and she began to laugh. 'No worse than what mine does, flower.'

Joe climbed out of the car, and Stella did the same. They both stood at the side of the road, stretching the best they could. She looked around; the lay-by was on the side of a bypass. Traffic wasn't busy, but it was flowing. There were no public toilets, café, or petrol station anywhere in sight. She leaned on the bonnet of the car.

'I really need to pee, and I don't know how long I can hold it for.'

'Me too. Look,' he suggested, 'why don't you climb over that gate and go behind the bush? No one will see you. I'll keep watch.'

Despite her reservations, she knew it was the most sensible option. Grabbing some tissues out of the glove compartment, she walked towards the gate and climbed to the top. With one leg dangling down, she heard Joe's voice.

'Check there's no angry bull in there before you jump down.'

Horrified, she looked around. She couldn't see anything but grass. 'I can't see anything.'

'Then you're good to go.'

She jumped down, glad she was wearing trainers and not her usual heels.

By the time she'd climbed back over the gate, Joe had the car bonnet up and was emptying the last of their bottled water into the radiator. 'I think this should solve the hissing; the radiator was bone dry. We'll pull over the next chance we can, to get some breakfast.'

'Do you think the car will make it to Lakeview House?'

'I hope so, but it's a bit old and knackered. I suppose if it breaks down again, we can leave it and hitch a ride the rest of the way.'

'Hitch, as in stick our thumbs up and hope a total stranger will stop to pick us up?' Stella looked horrified. 'And pray that we haven't just got in a car with the Boston Strangler?'

'Yep, pretty much that.' Joe smiled. 'There's just one thing with that scenario, though. The Boston Strangler lived in Boston, but maybe we could get the Lakeside Strangler.' He began to chuckle at his joke which made Stella roll her eyes then join in.

'You're crazy, but funny.'

He stared at her. 'But you love me, right?'

'I do.' Stella bowed her head so he wouldn't see the redness that had crept up her neck and consumed her entire face.

He pulled her close, kissing her lips. 'Good, because I've loved you for such a long time, you have no idea how it feels to hear you say it back to me. Come on, let's try to see how far we can get. It's like the road trip of fortune: Will we make it, will we not?'

'I think I'll ring the local police and alert them to Connor's possible whereabouts. It's the sensible thing to do in case we break down.'

Joe gave her the thumbs up.

She dialled 101 and heard the voice telling her she was being connected to Cumbria Constabulary. After a few minutes, a man answered.

'Oh, hello. I'm a bit concerned for my friend who's stopping in a property called Lakeview House near Armboth.' She spent the next ten minutes giving her and Maddy's details to the call handler.

When the call finished, Joe asked, 'What did they say?'

'That they'll get a patrol to drive past and speak to her about Connor.'

'Oh, good.'

'Not really. He didn't seem very interested. He said there was no immediate concern for her welfare if Connor lived in London. So, it wouldn't be a priority.'

'Well, at least you've told them. If he turns up and Maddy rings them, they'll be aware of the circumstances. Don't worry, Stella, it will be okay.'

They got back into the car, and she opened the map on his phone and typed the address in once more. She was scared to face Maddy, but she needed to know that she was fine.

Stella pushed the sinking feeling in her stomach to the back of her mind and hoped the guy on the phone was right. That Connor *was* hiding in London somewhere, and not on his way to Lakeview House.

# FIFTY-ONE

Tonight, he would put the body in the lake. He hadn't been back to check, but he was almost certain the guy would be dead. If the head injury hadn't killed him, hypothermia would have. Last night it had been cold on the fells, and although the summerhouse was sheltered, it wouldn't have saved him. Not with an open wound like that. Even if he'd crawled out of there to try to get help, he wouldn't have known where to go or how to get anywhere. He'd have been concussed, disorientated, weak.

He pushed the plate of toast he'd made away from him, his appetite gone. Who had that guy been, anyway? He'd said he was visiting his friend who lived in the big house. The only big house he was aware of was Lakeview House, where the city girl was staying, but if she was expecting that guy, there was a risk that she'd be worried about him and would call the police.

He clenched his fists. He'd been careless; he should have thought this through a lot more. Acting on his impulse could have caused more problems for him than he'd anticipated. There was the guy's car for one thing; he should have taken the keys for it last night. He could have driven it into his garage when it was late, and no one would have been any the wiser. *Fool, you've thrown away a perfect opportunity!* he told himself.

If the guy's friend reported him missing, the police would be all over the village searching for him. He needed to move the car, and now he was going to have to go back up the fell in broad daylight to retrieve the car keys. *How could he have missed such a significant detail?* He'd never done anything so stupid before.

At least no one would question him driving the car. He often drove different cars around, and nobody took a bit of notice. They were used to it and him, which was a good job. He wouldn't mess up like this again; he'd been sloppy. What did sloppy equal? It equalled getting caught.

The police could be on to him right now, breathing down his neck before he knew it. Then what? He hadn't really considered the consequences of the police realising what he was doing then putting a stop to it. The lake was the perfect burial ground for his bodies. They were deep enough not to float, yet he could still visit them whenever he wanted. The thrill of looking down into the water to see their swollen, pale, dead faces, never diminished.

No one had even connected the missing walkers, even though there had been a couple more this year than in the past. They had put it down to the strange weather patterns the fells were renowned for, and the lack of preparation by people who decided to climb a mountain to take a decent Instagram photo. How many had been rescued because they'd been ill-equipped to deal with the sudden changes in weather? Too many to count.

And the ones they didn't find were forgotten about soon enough. Loved ones, with no idea where to even start looking, accepted that their family member had come to a terrible fate as a result of their own foolishness. No one would expect a killer to be lurking on the fells, preying on the vulnerable, the injured. Some of them were dying anyway when he found them.

It was the perfect hunting ground for a game of cat and mouse. Not that he'd had to chase them far. They often thought he'd come to save them, and it was such a shock when they realised his real intention. If they couldn't save themselves, why should he?

Lacing up his boots, he shrugged on his waterproof coat. Despite the warmth of the sun now, the weather was going to change later. A storm was forecast for this afternoon and he didn't want to get caught out in it. He was the hunter, not the hunted.

# FIFTY-TWO

Maddy arrived at the playpark and breathed a sigh of relief to see the village square. She hadn't realised just how unfit she was until yesterday, and her ankle was still painful. Hopefully all the walking back and forth would help to strengthen her lungs a little, because right now she was out of breath and they were on fire.

Today there were actual people walking up and down the main street, thank God. She'd been beginning to think she'd moved into the deadest village in England. The pub door was still shut, but she hadn't really expected Seth to have opened up, as much as she wanted to go and see him.

She let herself out of the playpark gate, bending to check the tunnel and see if Alfie was hiding in there. It was empty. Even Alfie was better company than herself, and she'd never really been into kids. They scared her. Maybe if she hadn't been an only child, she'd know how to interact with them a little better. As it stood, she did her best to avoid them and her friends who'd decided to have them.

She limped along the main street looking for Glenys's kooky shop, although she didn't actually know what a kooky shop was.

There was the village store, which doubled as a post office; a gallery, which sold strange pottery and prints of the Lakeland fells; and a small second-hand shop, which had a hand-carved sign above the door that said ANTIQUES, which made her smile. The crap in the window looked as if it had all come from an Age Concern house clearance, but she supposed people would buy anything.

A couple of battered cardboard boxes contained an assortment of books, and she scanned them to see if she could recognise the black-and-yellow spine of her own book. Not sure whether she was relieved that it wasn't there or not, she walked on towards a shop which had dreamcatchers, crystal balls, and decks of tarot cards in the window, along with some fairy and dragon ornaments. This had to be Glenys's. It certainly looked out of place, and she wondered if it did any business. For all Maddy knew, it could do a roaring trade, because there wasn't much else to buy in the village.

She stepped inside and was instantly overpowered by the heady scent of lavender and something that reminded her of an aging heavy metal rock star. The shop was empty, no sign of Glenys, so she began to look through the books on crystal healing, tarot cards, and teach-yourself-to-be-psychic.

'Morning, what brings you here so early?'

Maddy looked at her watch, it was almost one. 'Erm, I was bored and wanted to come and chat to you.'

Glenys stepped out of the back room, her purple hair piled on the top of her head in a messy bun. She was wearing a black T-shirt and black, ripped jeans. She looked a lot more attractive than Maddy had first given her credit for when they'd met yesterday. Her make-up was amazing, and Maddy had never seen eyeliner with such neat wings.

'Wow, you look incredible.'

The woman began to laugh, a proper gut-wrenching belly

laugh that immediately made Maddy join in, even though she had no idea what they were laughing at.

'I take it I looked dreadful yesterday, then?'

'Yes. Oh God, no, I didn't mean that.' Maddy stumbled for the right words. 'You were obviously upset yesterday. I love your hair, that colour really suits you.'

Glenys laughed even more, then walked across to where she was standing and put her arm around Maddy's shoulders.

'I like you. It's been a long time since anyone gave me a compliment, so for that I'm going to make us a cup of herbal tea and pull some tarot cards for you.'

Maddy grimaced. She hated herbal teas and didn't even want to know what her tarot cards said.

Glenys let go of her. 'I take it you're not a fan of herbal tea? I can make a mean cappuccino, if you prefer. Just don't tell anyone. I'm not being a part-time barista for this ungrateful lot of heathens.'

Maddy smiled. 'Cappuccino sounds great, and I won't tell a soul.'

'Good, they try to make my life a misery, but I don't care. They can all go screw themselves. They get jealous because I make more money than the rest of them.'

Maddy looked around the empty shop and wondered how that could be possible. She followed Glenys through to the back of the shop where a desk dominated the room with a computer so big it could have doubled up as a cinema screen.

'Wow, that's impressive.'

'It is. I can't see on a laptop, because my eyes are terrible,' Glenys explained. 'I need it because this is where I do most of my work.'

'Are you a writer?'

She shook her head. 'God, no. I'm not that clever. Don't get me wrong, I'd love to be one. I just wouldn't know where to start.'

'What do you do with it then?' Maddy's interest was piqued.

'I do a lot of video calls. You know, Skype, Zoom, those kind of things.'

For a brief moment, Maddy wondered if she was some kind of porn queen.

'You wouldn't believe how popular tarot card readings are. I do a lot of personalised readings with people. Sometimes I do a psychic reading; it depends what they're looking for. Sometimes they just need someone to tell them their shitty life is going to get better.' Glenys shrugged. 'It's sad, really, and I feel a bit bad charging some of the clients. Then I remind myself that I have to make a living, to support myself and Alfie. It takes away some of the guilt.'

'Alfie is your son? I didn't know.'

Glenys was immediately defensive. 'Why, what's he done?'

'Nothing, he's a good kid. I mean, he's scared me a couple of times, but not intentionally. I'm just a jumpy person by nature.'

'And a little crazy.' Glenys smiled. 'You'd have to be to think living in Lakeview House by yourself was a good idea. Crazy is good, though; all the best ones are a little, don't you think? I mean, life would be boring if we were all sane.'

Across from the desk was a kitchen worktop with a coffee maker almost as big as the computer screen.

'I live in the poky flat above the shop, so I can drink the kind of coffee that sets my soul on fire.' She winked at Maddy.

'Are you sure you're not a writer? I think you might be missing out on a very suited career.'

'How would you know?'

'I'm a writer. I write crime stories. Well, psychological thrillers. Actually, I've written a psychological thriller, but I'm stuck on the second one, which is why I thought moving from London to live in Lakeview House would be a fabulous idea.'

Glenys was staring at her open-mouthed. 'How is that working out for you?'

Maddy began to laugh and found she laughed so much that tears began to fall from her eyes.

'Honestly? I don't have a clue.'

Her response set them both off again.

# FIFTY-THREE

Seth came back from the funeral home wondering how his dad had managed to organise his funeral, right down to the music and flowers, without any fuss. Everything had been taken care of. His body was being released from the mortuary this afternoon.

The pathologist had confirmed he'd died of natural causes; his heart had simply had enough, and he'd suffered a massive heart attack. It had been sudden, unexpected, and somewhat of a relief.

It was all so matter of fact that Seth didn't know how he felt, if he was honest. He'd expected to be heartbroken, moping around crying, and feeling sorry for himself. The fact that he felt relieved it was all over made him feel guilty, if anything. The last thing he'd wanted was his dad to lay in bed suffering, but he hadn't expected it to be over like this.

He kept wondering if it was his fault: Had he pushed his dad too hard the other day when he'd disappeared to visit Maddy? He'd been helping her search for a phantom confetti-thrower while his dad had worked himself into a frenzy. *Stop it now, Seth, you know that's a load of rubbish. Glenys was here to*

*help him, and he didn't look knackered or complain he was in*
*pain. It was what he wanted, to carry on as normal until the time*
*came when he couldn't.*

Going behind the bar, he poured himself a neat Glenfiddich
– his dad's favourite whisky – and downed it quickly. It burnt
his throat and made his eyes water so much he began to cough.
Wiping his eyes with his sleeve, he decided to stop moping
around feeling sorry for himself. His dad hadn't, and neither
should he.

The pub would be open at three o'clock to serve the regulars. They'd be lost without somewhere to come, drink real ale,
and gossip, so who was he to deprive them of their daily
routine? He could always ask Glenys to help out if it got too
much. But first, he was going to visit Martin and see if he'd
managed to fix Maddy's car.

Even though he'd made up his mind to open up later, he
wasn't quite ready to face anyone just yet, so he slipped out of
the pub's side door and walked along the cobbled streets, cutting
behind the main street to get to Martin's house. Maddy's Beetle
was parked outside, its rear end jacked up. He couldn't spot
Martin anywhere, and the garage seemed empty. He walked up
the path and knocked on the front door, but there was no reply.
Maybe he'd had to go and get some parts for the car.

Seth turned and headed back towards the village. A familiar
voice shouted his name and he turned to see Alfie waving at
him from the path that led up the fell behind Martin's garage.

'Seth! Seth, wait for me.'

Alfie ran towards him, out of breath. 'Are you sad today,
Seth?'

The boy stared at him in earnest and Seth realised he was
asking how he was, in his own way. He nodded his head in
reply.

'Sorry 'bout your dad, Seth. I liked him. He gave me salt and
vinegar crisps.'

Seth smiled. 'I know he did. You're the only person who really eats them; everyone else prefers cheese and onion.'

'Will you miss him a lot?'

'Yes.'

'So will I. Can I have some crisps now? I'm starving.'

Seth began to laugh. 'I suppose so. You don't get if you don't ask. Come on, you can help me get the pub ready to open up and I'll feed you. Where's your mum today? Has she not fed you?'

'Working. She said I had to keep out of the way and would break my fingers if I touch her new computer.'

'I don't think she meant that, but you did mess it up for her.'

Alfie shrugged. 'She had it all the wrong way, I was only trying to help.'

Seth reached out and ruffled his hair. 'I know you were, kid, and so does she.'

The pair of them walked back to the pub, Alfie asking lots of questions and Seth doing his best to answer them.

# FIFTY-FOUR

Glenys passed a huge mug to Maddy. The whole time she'd been here the computer had been pinging away non-stop behind them with notifications. At least, Glenys had Internet, which was good to know.

Sitting opposite her, Glenys inhaled her coffee. 'I don't know what it is about this stuff, but it really is a magic potion.'

Maddy agreed. 'So, you're busy, then?'

'What, that incessant noise from the computer? Yes, it's good. I'm saving up for a decent house for me and Alf. It drives the locals mad, but the shop does okay. It gets plenty of visitors, but they don't realise it's the online stuff keeping it going. I kind of think they want it to bomb so they can say they told me so as they run me out of the village with their burning pitchforks.'

Maddy frowned. 'Are they that bad?'

'No, they're not. I'm being mean. You know Seth, and he's lovely. One of the nicest guys I've ever met, so helpful and thoughtful. He's really good with Alfie as well, which is a bonus. God knows, he needs a bit of male company in his life.'

Maddy felt her heart crush; Glenys obviously had a thing

for Seth. Who was she to interfere when she'd only been around a couple of days? Talk about awkward.

'I like Alfie.'

'Has he been bothering you?' Glenys asked. 'I've told him to keep away, but I can't watch him. He won't stay inside. He loves being out on the fells and exploring and would go stir-crazy if I didn't let him wander. That's another thing the locals don't agree with.'

'Why?'

'Well, he's got a few learning difficulties, and he hates school. They think I should keep him cooped up in the flat. If I thought that he was in any danger, I would. But the worst he can do is get lost on the fells, and he hasn't up to now. He follows Seth around like a lapdog and he knows the area like the back of his hands.'

'What about you and Seth?' Maddy asked tentatively. 'Are you a couple?'

Glenys laughed. 'Oh no, he's really not my type. Too male for a start. Do I need to go on?'

Maddy smiled back, a feeling of relief washing over her. So, Seth was fair play. She needed to go and talk to him when she left here.

'Alfie talks a lot about the lake people, do you know who they are?'

Glenys shook her head. 'No, I don't, but he did ask me if people could live underwater the other day. I've been meaning to ask him what he means, although he clams up whenever I ask him anything. He probably talks to you and Seth more than me.' She paused briefly to sip from her mug. 'So, how is it inside Lakeview House?'

'What do you mean?'

'I don't know... the atmosphere? Is it scary being there on your own? A lot of the locals won't even acknowledge that it exists.'

'Why?'

'I don't know if I should be telling you this, especially when you're living there.' Glenys frowned in concern. 'It's a bit mean and I don't want to scare you.'

'I need to know. I was going to go to the library and do some research on the property, see who lived there and find out the history. It's such a gorgeous house, I can't believe it's been left empty for so long.'

Glenys sighed. 'They say it's haunted and knows nothing but tragedy and sadness. Sir John Rowland built it for his wife and daughter in the 1800s. As far as I know, he only had one child and she was found drowned in the lake on her wedding morning. From what I can gather, she was wearing her wedding dress, her hair was loose around her shoulders, and she looked as if she was sleeping. They dragged her out of the lake, but it was too late, she was dead. Her fiancé never got over it, neither did her parents. There were rumours that she'd been killed by a jealous servant who'd fallen in love with her and couldn't bear to see her marry another man.'

Maddy hadn't realised she'd been sitting open-mouthed until she let out a gasp. She felt as if she'd stumbled into some kind of déjà vu.

'No way!' she said. 'I can't believe that. It's just like my dream. I found myself in the house and it was full of servants and people bustling around. There were girls being dressed by servants in the bedroom I use, and they were all getting ready for a wedding. Then one of them screamed and I saw a man running towards the lake. There was a group of men standing around and they fished the most beautiful dead woman, in a wedding dress, out onto the bank. It was heartbreaking and so real.'

It was Glenys's turn to stare open-mouthed. 'You're winding me up?'

Maddy shook her head. 'I swear, I'm not.'

'Shit, that's a bit too freaky. Are you psychic?'

'No, definitely not. I've never experienced anything like that in my life. I felt as if I was there with them, only they couldn't see me. I could even smell the food in the kitchen.'

Glenys frowned. 'It must be a residual haunting, it's the only explanation.'

'What's one of those?'

'When something tragic happens in life, it can imprint itself in its surroundings. Lakeview House, like many of the houses around here, is built from local limestone, which is known to be a conduit for storing such memories.'

Maddy studied Glenys carefully; no wonder the villagers thought she was kooky. She sipped her coffee and wondered what to do about the whole living-in-a-haunted-house situation. She didn't believe it, *but what about the sodden wedding dress and the confetti?*

'There's something else,' she told Glenys eventually. 'I've heard loud noises, and the other morning I found a sopping wet wedding dress on the front steps outside the entrance. When I went back inside, there was confetti strewn all over the kitchen floor. Seth thinks it was someone playing a trick on me, maybe one of the locals trying to scare me away. He wasn't sure if it was Alfie. Did he mention it to you?'

Glenys nodded. 'He did. In fact, I saw my arse with him over that. There's no way Alfie would know about the history of the house, and even if he did, he isn't bright enough to leave a wet wedding dress and sprinkle confetti around without getting caught. It's just not him. And if someone put him up to it, he'd be so proud that he'd managed to do it right, he'd have come home and told me or Seth all about it.'

'Then who do you think did?'

Glenys shrugged. 'I don't know, but we need to find out who and why pretty quick. That's a real lowlife thing to do to someone living there alone. Don't tell anyone about it,' she advised. 'I'll ask around and see if I can find anything out.'

'What should I do?'

'Keep doing what you've been doing. Are you scared to stay there? I have a sofa you can sleep on, or Seth has plenty of rooms in the pub.'

Maddy thought for a few moments. She didn't believe in ghosts, although in the past few days she had begun to think there could be something to the phenomena. She did, however, think someone was trying to scare her off. The dream was probably just one of life's odd occurrences. They happened, for some reason, without any sense to them.

She wasn't about to be scared away so easily, despite her reservations. She'd survived living in London her entire life and Connor's abusive relationship. No, she was staying put, but she resolved to be a lot more vigilant.

'I'm okay,' she assured Glenys. 'I don't feel scared of the house. I kind of feel as if I've been there before, even though I know for sure I haven't. In fact, I'm more annoyed that someone thinks they can play such mean tricks on a single woman trying to get on with her life. I'll stay at the house, unless it gets too much. But I really want to know more about the woman who drowned. I feel as if she has a story that needs to be told.'

'Maybe you lived there in a past life. Leave it with me. I'll do some research and speak to some of the oldies who love to gossip. If you do get a bit freaked out, you can come here anytime. You're always welcome.'

'Thank you, that's very kind but I'm not leaving without a fight. Besides, if I don't finish this book, my agent when she hunts me down will be scarier than any ghost that might be living in Lakeview House.'

Glenys laughed. 'Good. You're tough, I like that. Don't take any bullshit.'

Maddy stood up and was shocked when Glenys rushed towards her and pulled her close, hugging her tight.

'We're like Velma and Daphne from *Scooby-Doo*,' she said with a chuckle. 'We'll find out what the mystery is all about.'

Maddy hugged her back, smiling. 'I always did love that dog.'

As she walked out of the shop, her mind was a whirl of possibilities as she tried to make sense of what the hell was going on.

# FIFTY-FIVE

Maddy had a lot to think about: murdered brides, haunted houses, bitter locals... and Seth. Walking towards the pub, she was relieved to see the front door wedged open and she paused before stepping out of the glorious sunshine into the dark, gloomy pub.

Inside, it took her eyes a few seconds to adjust to the darkness. Her stomach was churning with nerves at the prospect of facing Seth. It was difficult to know what to say to someone in the throes of grief without sounding like a fool.

She spotted Alfie perched on a bar stool, one hand propping his head up while his other hand dipped in and out of a bag of crisps. Seth wasn't anywhere to be seen.

Crossing the room, she perched on the stool next to the boy. 'Give us a crisp, I'm starving.'

He turned to stare at her. 'They're salt and vinegar.'

'I know, my favourite.'

Reluctantly, he passed the bag to her, watching as she took a couple of crisps out and shoved them in her mouth. She winced; they were very vinegary but tasted divine. When Alfie snatched the bag back, she laughed. 'Don't worry, I'll buy my own. I'm not going to eat them all.'

'No, you won't,' said a deep voice. 'They're short-dated and you'll be saving Alfie from severe dehydration. He's on his fifth packet.' Seth smiled at her, passing her an unopened packet of crisps.

As his hand brushed against hers, she felt as though an electric current had run through her body.

'Thank you. Seth... I'm so sorry to hear about your dad.'

He smiled at her, but this time it didn't reach his eyes, and she noticed him blink several times as though to stop unshed tears from falling.

'It's what he would have wanted. It was sudden. I suppose if you're going to go, that's the way.'

'It is,' she agreed. 'Is there anything I can do for you? I could man the pub for a few hours if you need a break, you know, a bit of breathing space.'

'No thanks. To be honest, it takes my mind off it. Glenys has offered to come and help out at teatime when she's shut up shop.'

Maddy smiled. 'Oh, she's very kind and nice.'

'You've met her then?'

'Yesterday, and I've just had coffee with her.' Maddy left out how rude her new friend had been yesterday. It had been a bad day for them all, so it was understandable.

'Coffee? She must like you. It took me three months to get invited over for coffee, didn't it, Alfie?'

The boy, who'd just crammed a handful of crisps in his mouth, nodded.

'I wanted to thank you for the other day,' Maddy went on. 'You were so kind spending all afternoon searching the house, and then I shoved you out with no explanation. I'm afraid I had to start writing; when I get an idea and it hits, I have to do it there and then, otherwise it goes and I've lost it again. But rudeness is inexcusable.' She paused for a minute. 'I was wondering if you'd like to come to the house for some supper? Nothing too fancy. Maybe a picnic by the lake and a bottle of wine, as a thank you.'

She held her breath, scared he was about to say no.

'I'd love to,' he said, smiling. 'It sounds like my kind of supper, and I love picnics. I love wine as well.' He winked at her, and she breathed a sigh of relief.

'Great, that's amazing. I'll see you around six, then.'

Alfie looked at her. 'I like picnics. Hate wine, though. It tastes funny.'

She laughed. 'You can come another day, Alfie, is that okay?'

He nodded. 'Yep, tomorrow is good for me.'

Seth winked at her again. 'You'll be feeding the entire village at this rate. Can I get you a drink?'

'No thank you. I'm full of coffee and will be in bed before you arrive if I start drinking now.'

'Maybe that wouldn't be such a bad thing.'

Shaking her head, she got off the stool. 'It wouldn't be very ladylike, though, would it? See you later, Seth. Alfie, I'll see you tomorrow.'

She walked back out into the warmth and sighed. It didn't matter what was happening at the house; she was going to go back and prepare a picnic fit for a king. She wanted Seth to be able to relax and talk to her. No, what she really wanted was for Seth to take her to bed and spend all night with her, their bodies entwined around each other.

She didn't think she'd ever wanted a man the way she wanted him, and for once she didn't care. She was going to do what made her happy, not what she should do.

# FIFTY-SIX

He stared down the side of the mountain at Lakeview House. The jetty, his jetty, was lit up with a hundred flickering candles. His hands were clenching into tight fists then unclenching; angry was an understatement. Who the hell was that woman to move into the house and take over his lake? No one had used that jetty for years, except for him. Yet here she was, after a couple of days, acting as if she owned the place. Well, he had a surprise for her, because she didn't. The jetty and this part of the lake were his.

It was his dumping ground, but he couldn't exactly dispose of the body from last night now, could he? Not when she was lighting it up like a gaudy fairground ride. What if she took a moment and stared down into the water when it was calm? He knew she'd see his bodies, all standing upright in a row, swaying against the swell of the water, weighted so they stayed in that position. Their hands were pressed together in prayer, secured with fishing line to keep them that way.

The first time he'd thrown one in, it had sunk to the bottom. But for some reason, because of the rocks he'd used to weigh it down, it had righted itself by the next time he came to visit.

That had both terrified and thrilled him at the same time. And he'd followed the same process with the others.

If anyone was to stare into the depths of the lake for more than a moment, they might see the bodies, so it was risky. But it was also wonderful, because he could still see them clearly any time he wished to look and relive those last special moments again.

The locals never came near the lake, anyway. The only one who ventured into the overgrown grounds of Lakeview House was that dopey kid. He wasn't a problem, though. No one listened to him, and if the lad became too inquisitive, he would quite happily add him to his collection.

However, he hadn't bargained on the woman turning up and staying around this long. She was becoming a problem.

He turned away, walking towards the summerhouse. The breeze carried the underlying smell of rotting decomposition his way. It was mild now, but with this heat it wouldn't take many hours before it was a tangible, distinguishable scent. He might have to kill a sheep and drag its body nearby to rot, in case any passing walkers got too near.

For some reason, he didn't like killing animals. Apparently, most serial killers either hated their parents or killed the family pets, but he had done neither. His parents had been wonderful, caring, supportive, loving, and kind, and he'd loved them deeply. He was also really fond of animals. Their innocence and loyalty were much better traits than those most humans possessed.

It turned his stomach and made his hands tremble at the thought of hurting an innocent animal, but for some reason he didn't feel that way about humans. Surely it should be the other way around? Shouldn't he have an aversion to taking away an innocent human life? He knew he wasn't normal; he didn't feel what most people felt. He lived his life under a disguise and hid his true self well.

Reaching the broken window, he climbed through and lifted his hand to his nose. The smell was much stronger in here, but at least it answered one question. The guy was definitely dead and hadn't managed to escape. But now what was he going to do? The longer he left the body in here, the less chance there was of him being preserved by the cold water, because the flies and mice would eat away his best features.

He realised he should have brought a sleeping bag with him. He shook his head angrily; he wasn't thinking straight. That bloody woman had thrown his mind into a jumbled mess, and his rational thoughts were slipping. He knew that meant he was more likely to be slipping in every other aspect. He needed to be careful that his mask didn't fall and expose him. He didn't want to get caught, but he was putting everything on the line.

He kicked the body on the floor. You, my friend, have fucked this up big time. Why did you turn up last night and think I was a Good Samaritan? If you'd have said no, I wouldn't be in this mess now, would I? You might have to be buried on the fell if I can't get you to the lake soon. And that is hard work. Do you realise how stony the ground is up here? No, you don't, you bloody arsehole. Why didn't you stay in a hotel, or better still, why didn't you stay in London? I bet you wished you had after that rock hit the side of your head.

Unable to stop himself, he began to laugh so loud the sound echoed around the crumbling stone walls and out onto the fells.

# FIFTY-SEVEN

Maddy had found a box filled with dusty glass jars in the pantry, and she washed them all in the cracked, white Belfast sink, leaving them to dry on the draining board. She had a bag of tea lights so decided to pop one in each jar and light up the whole length of the wooden jetty.

In the empty library, she'd found an ancient radio, which she also dusted off, plugged into the mains, and prayed it wouldn't blow up. Normally she'd play music on her phone, but with no Internet connection that was a definite no. The radio crackled to life in a blast of static, making her jump; the sound was so loud in the empty kitchen, it echoed around the walls.

Turning the volume down, she slowly turned the dial, not really expecting to get anything, and was surprised when music began to play. She recognised the sweet, ageless voice of Ella Fitzgerald singing 'Night and Day', one of her gran's all-time favourite songs. Maddy immediately felt her heart strings tug at the thought of her gran. She hadn't spoken to her since she'd arrived. Tomorrow, she vowed to make a call her top priority.

Humming along, she began to prepare the food, her hips

swaying in time to the music. She smiled. That was what this whole house needed, something to lift the oppressive atmosphere and lighten the feeling of loneliness that was seeping from the walls in waves.

Satisfied with her various dishes that she'd carefully wrapped in foil and placed in a box, she looked at her watch. It was quarter to six. By the time she'd set the candles up and spread the blanket out, hopefully Seth would have arrived. Leaving the radio playing an assortment of jazz and swing music, she carefully packed the jars into another box, along with some matches, and headed out to the lake.

By the time she'd reached the jetty and lit the candles, she was breathing a little too heavy; she hadn't done this much exercise in years. Her back aching, she stood on the bank of the lake, her hands on her hips, and nodded. It looked magical. Even though it wasn't yet dusk, the flickering lights looked so romantic that she pulled out her phone and snapped some photos. This would go on her blog, although she wouldn't mention who she'd gone to all the effort for. Seth might not be the least bit interested in her, but the dramatic backdrop of the jetty over the lake against the mountains was stunning.

A vision of the dead bride being dragged out of the freezing cold water broke her trance, and she shivered. *Stop it, Maddy, that was over a hundred years ago. Don't let your imagination ruin this.*

Shaking her head firmly to wipe the vision of her dream from her mind, she headed back to the house to collect the box of food. The music from the kitchen filtered through; the pleasant sound was a real game-changer.

Suddenly the loud rumble of Seth's Land Rover as it crunched along the drive made her heart skip a beat. She felt like some lovesick teenager, but she didn't care. By the time she emerged from the kitchen carrying the box, Seth was standing at the open front door.

'Evening.'

'I wasn't sure if you'd come,' she told him.

'Why?'

'Well, you know. You have a lot on at the moment.'

He stepped inside the gloomy entrance, his smile making her hormones race. 'I definitely wouldn't miss this for the world. It's very kind of you and exactly what I need to take my mind off my dad. He'd go mad if he thought I was moping around when I could be on a date with a beautiful woman.'

Maddy felt heat explode from her chest and up her cheeks, leaving her speechless.

He rushed towards her, taking the box from her hands. 'What's in this?'

'Cake and wine. You know, life's essentials. I hope you're hungry.'

He nodded. 'I think I probably am. I haven't really eaten since yesterday.'

'Good, because otherwise I'd end up eating it all and not being able to get into my jeans when I finally leave here and go back to civilisation.'

They headed outside towards the lake. Seth glanced towards her. 'Are you leaving soon?'

She shook her head. 'Oh no, not unless I have to. I'm falling in love with Lakeview House, despite its unloved appearance and mysterious happenings, which kind of add to its appeal. I've always been a sucker for a bit of mystery.' She aimed a smile in his direction. 'I also really like the locals I've met so far; they've all been so nice and friendly. Not at all what I expected, if I'm honest.'

Seth laughed. 'What did you expect? That we'd all be angry, pitchfork-wielding inbreds?'

'Oh God, not at all. You hear these horror stories of small villages and their residents not being very welcoming, that's all. Look at *An American Werewolf in London*. Those guys got stared out of the pub and ended up being chased by a werewolf.'

'Well, that wouldn't happen in my pub. I treat everyone the same. It doesn't matter if they've turned up on a coach or lived here sixty years. My dad's favourite saying was "treat folk as you'd like to be treated".'

'Your dad was a wise man.'

They reached the jetty and Maddy stepped onto it, thinking he was behind her. But when she reached the edge, she turned to see him standing at the water's edge staring in horror at her.

'What's the matter?'

'I can't come on there, I'm sorry. I'm not very good on water. That thing's really old, you know. It could collapse any time.'

She began to laugh. 'It's okay. I've been sitting on it and paddling my feet in the lake since the day I arrived.'

She began to jump up and down, but Seth dropped the box of food and shouted at her, his hands waving in the air.

Realising he wasn't joking, she stopped. 'Oh God, I'm sorry. I didn't think you meant it. You're being serious?'

He nodded. 'I am. I can climb mountains and I'm not scared of heights, but I can't sail on water or stand on bridges. It makes me feel sick, and my knees do this whole turning to jelly and giving way thing, which is really not very manly at all.'

She bent down, grabbed the blanket she'd spread out, and walked back towards him.

'Then we'll sit here, at the water's edge. I'm sorry, Seth. I didn't mean to scare you.'

He grabbed her hand, tugging her off the end of the jetty. Maddy tripped and fell into him; he caught her and held her close. He smelled so good; his arms felt safe wrapped around her. She lay her head against his chest, then wondered if he thought she was too forward and pulled away.

Taking the blanket from her, he spread it out a few feet away from the edge of the lake.

'Now you know my darkest secret. I guess I'm not such a tough guy after all.'

'If being afraid of open waters is your darkest secret, I'll take it. Everyone's afraid of something.'

They sat down onto the blanket. 'What about you? What are you afraid of, Maddy?'

She shrugged. 'At the moment, my agent getting hold of me to see if I've finished this damn book.'

He laughed. 'That doesn't count. Is there anything that really scares you? I'm guessing not a lot, because you've moved from the busiest city in England to live on your own in what looks like a haunted mansion in the middle of nowhere. So, it's not the dark, spiders, or being alone.'

'Very funny,' she replied with a smile. 'I don't suppose those things do scare me. Being trapped in a relationship with someone you thought you knew scares me the most.'

'Bad experience?'

She nodded and began to take the different plates of food out of the box, setting them down on the blanket.

'It could have been worse, I suppose. My ex-boyfriend Connor, he had it all, you know. Amazing job, loads of money, luxury penthouse with views of the River Thames, fancy car, everything.'

'Yet he's still your ex? He can't have been that wonderful.'

'He wasn't. Well, he was at first. Then when I moved in, he began to show his true colours, the jealous rages, the punches, smashing things, threatening me. He scared me so much I knew I had to get out before he did something serious.'

Seth reached out his hand, his fingers brushing against the side of her cheek. 'Well, I'd like to meet him one day. I've never hit a woman in my life, but I'm not averse to hitting a man who deserves it. Did he hurt you?'

Maddy blinked away the tears, not wanting to ruin their evening. 'Only because I was stupid enough to let him. It won't ever happen again. Anyway, enough of this feeling sorry for myself. I'm putting you off your food.'

Seth laughed. 'Nothing puts me off my food.'

As they ate, Seth began to tell her the tale of woe about Alfie ruining Glenys's new computer programme, and the mood soon lifted.

# FIFTY-EIGHT

Glenys watched Alfie lying on the sofa flicking through the pages of a magazine. Although she didn't for one moment think it was him who'd been playing tricks on Maddy, it was playing on her mind.

'Alf?'

He didn't hear her; he was concentrating too hard on the pictures in the magazine about the sky at night, staring at the photographs of the constellations. She had no idea why they interested him so much.

'Alfie.' She crossed the room and shook his shoulder.

He jumped, shocked at her sudden touch. 'What?'

'Have you been going to the old house?'

He looked at her, then nodded.

'Have you been messing around up there? Did you leave a wedding dress on the steps?'

A look of confusion spread across his face as he tried to digest what she was asking him, then his head began to shake from side to side. Glenys knew by the expression on his face he didn't have a clue what she was talking about – proof enough for her that whatever was going on, it had nothing to do with her son.

'What for?'

She smiled at him. 'Nothing, it's okay. Don't worry about it. Is your magazine good?'

He smiled, nodding. His attention was drawn back to the glossy pages; she was forgotten about.

Glenys walked over to the window where she could see the very tip of the roof of Lakeview House over the trees. A shudder wracked her entire body and she wrapped her arms tightly around herself as she continued to stare at it. Something was wrong, but she had no idea what. She'd avoided the house ever since she'd moved here because of the bad feelings she got whenever she thought about it. But she couldn't ignore her feelings any longer; she liked Maddy, and the woman was living there all alone.

Regardless of its history or the atmospherics, it was time for her to pay Lakeview House a visit. She would open herself to it and let its history seep into her mind. If there were any ghosts that walked the desolate corridors, she would talk to them and find out if they were intelligent or residual. For some reason, she felt fiercely protective of her new friend and she had no idea why. But no matter the consequences to herself, she knew she needed to find out what was going on before things got out of hand, and the last thing she could do was ignore it.

Little things were happening; small occurrences that might very well be some village idiot trying to scare Maddy away. Somehow, though, she didn't think that was the case. It was as if the house was being roused from a deep sleep and was slowly waking up.

Glenys had no idea what it was capable of, but tomorrow she would try to find out.

# FIFTY-NINE

Seth lay on the blanket staring up at the inky blue sky. The clouds were rolling in and the breeze had picked up, blowing the edges of the blanket and extinguishing most of the flames on the tea lights. Maddy, who was packing away the plates and leftover food, shivered.

'The weather around here has a mind of its own,' she commented. 'It changes so fast, from one extreme to the other. One minute you're baking in the sun, the next, well, it's like winter.'

'You noticed that? It does, and that's often why walkers get lost or stranded on the fells. They set off and the sun is burning so brightly they don't take the right equipment with them. There's a shift in the weather pattern, and suddenly they're dressed for an afternoon sunbathing by the pool when a torrential downpour begins. Soaked to the bone, high up a mountain, and with no sense of direction, it isn't long before hyperthermia can set in.'

'Does it happen often?'

'Too often. You'd be amazed how many people get caught out.'

'You and the other rescue guys are real heroes.'

Seth laughed. 'No, definitely not. I don't wear my underpants on the outside.' He winked at her. 'Come on, I'll help you get this stuff into the house. You can blow the rest of the candles out, though. As brave as I am, I still don't want to go onto that rotting wooden jetty when it's almost dark.'

Maddy shook her head. 'Deal.'

Seth watched as she walked along it, his heart racing a little too fast. He knew it was ridiculous; she'd walked on it lots of times and it hadn't collapsed. Yet he still had this irrational fear that it would, and he'd be buggered if she plunged into the lake. He'd have to go in after her; he couldn't stand by watching and let her drown. That wouldn't be very heroic, would it?

She bent down, blowing out the last few flames, then stood up. 'Should I leave these on here? Do you think they'll blow into the lake?'

He shrugged. 'I doubt it. I'd leave them until tomorrow when it's light. That way, if you fall in, you'll be able to see to drag yourself out.'

'Very funny.'

She walked back onto the grass and he felt his shoulders relax. She looked so cute with her hair in a messy bun. Strands of it had come loose where she'd been lying on the grass, and he wanted to pull her close and kiss her, pick her up in his arms and carry her back into the house. But he wasn't sure if it was the right thing to do. He got the impression that she liked him as much as he did her, but he didn't want to make a move and upset her.

And if he was honest, he didn't know if he wanted to make love to her in the dark, inside Lakeview House. Whenever he was inside the building, he got the uncomfortable feeling he was being watched. By whom, he had no idea. No doubt it was his imagination, fuelled by the rumours many of the villagers had spread over the years. *Definitely not much of a hero,* he thought, *if you're afraid to sleep in an empty house*. And he couldn't admit that to Maddy, because she'd been here almost a week and didn't seem in the least bit bothered about staying there on her own.

They walked back towards the house, which seemed to have doubled in size as the light had faded, looming now against the backdrop of the fells. The shadows cloaking the building gave it a sinister edge.

Maddy, who'd been in front, paused as she glanced up at it. 'I've never looked at it from the outside in the dark. It's something else, isn't it?'

Seth nodded.

'Have you ever read *The Haunting of Hill House* by Shirley Jackson?' she asked.

'No, I haven't.'

'What about *Hell House* by Richard Matheson?'

'God no, definitely not. I'm far too much of a wimp to read haunted house stories. I take it you have?'

'Yes, both, several times when I was a teenager. They're fabulous books; you should read them. Every time I look at the house, it reminds me of them. The stories were set in sprawling mansions built by rich, mad men.'

'Yet still you don't mind staying here, on your own? Are you like some kind of crazy woman who hides it really well?'

A snort escaped her mouth, followed by loud laughter that echoed around the valley.

'Who knows? I suppose I must be. This sounds mad, but the minute I set my eyes on Lakeview House, I felt drawn towards its abandoned beauty. I fell in love with it and, yes, I suppose that makes me a bit crazy, because how can you fall in love with something so desolate yet hauntingly beautiful?'

She carried on walking up the steps while he followed. There was no answer to her question because he didn't know at all. He'd never felt that way about anything, except maybe for her. If he had to describe Madison Hart, then hauntingly beautiful was a pretty apt description.

As he followed her inside the house, the faint sound of jazz music was carried towards them.

'Where's that coming from?' he asked.

'I found an ancient radio in the library, so I plugged it in and got what seems like a 1940s station, which plays swing music and jazz. I like it.' She smiled at him. 'The music makes the house seem more...'

When she paused, he knew she was searching for the right word, and wondered if she was going to say 'homely'.

'It makes it seem more alive,' she finished eventually.

Seth's entire body shivered. That was a terrible description. Could a house come alive?

# SIXTY

Maddy wanted Seth to stay with her so badly, but she wouldn't ask or beg him. When he followed her to the kitchen where the radio filled the air with music, it was dark inside, so she grabbed the torch she kept by the door on the worktop and flicked the switch. The beam illuminated only a small part of the huge room.

Maddy shone it at the pine table. 'Just put the box on there,' she said. 'I'll sort it out in the morning.'

She stood with her back against the door, holding it open for Seth, who obliged then scurried back towards her. Maddy hid a smile. He really didn't like being in here in the dark, but she couldn't really blame him. She was kind of used to it now, so it didn't scare her as much as it had the first couple of nights.

'I'll just turn the radio off.'

It was his turn to prop open the door while she crossed the expanse of terracotta-tiled flooring and pulled out the plug. The silence was deafening, the blackness became suffocating, and she heard Seth let out a gasp.

When she reached the door and stepped into the hallway,

he followed, letting it slam shut behind him. The sound echoed throughout the house.

'Shit! Maybe you should leave the radio on,' he told her. 'I see what you mean, it makes it sound so much better.'

Maddy nodded. An overwhelming rush of tiredness took over her body, the urge to curl up under the duvet and sleep until the morning filling her mind. She let out a huge yawn, which she tried to stifle unsuccessfully with her hand.

'I should leave it on, really,' she admitted. 'It does seem much lighter in here with music playing, but I'm just scared because of the dodgy electrics and how old it is, in case it's a fire hazard. The last thing I want is to fall asleep and burn the house down with an ancient radio. There are no smoke alarms, so I might get stuck in here and burn to death.'

Seth stared at her, wide-eyed. 'Your imagination is really something else.'

Maddy smiled. 'I know. It's my downfall.'

'Why don't you come back to the pub with me?' he suggested. 'I have plenty of spare rooms; you can take your pick. If you don't want to be on your own, I have a king-size bed I'm more than happy to share.'

She thought about it, then shook her head. 'That's a very kind offer, but I like it here. And I'm getting paid to stay here. I don't want to wimp out at the first chance and lose my job.'

'Who would know? I'm not going to say anything; you could sneak out in the morning before any of the villagers saw you. Even if they did, they wouldn't know who you were or what you were doing there.'

She shook her head again. 'Sorry, I can't. It wouldn't be right. You're welcome to stop here, though. You'd have an easier time sneaking out of here than I would at your pub. There are no neighbours for miles that I know about.'

Seth half smiled at her. 'I would, that's true. I'm sorry,

Maddy, but I can't. I think I'd be a bag of nerves, and I have a lot to do tomorrow.'

He reached down and kissed her, but she turned at the last moment, so his lips brushed her cheek. He stepped back.

'Thank you for supper, it was lovely.'

'You're very welcome. Thanks for coming.'

The conversation had become strained, both of them too stubborn to give in, despite it being obvious that what they both wanted was each other.

Seth turned and headed towards the front door, and an irrational anger filled Maddy's chest as she watched him turn one last time to shout goodnight. Lifting her hand, she waved, not sure she should reply in case she said something she regretted.

The front door shut behind him and she felt sad that he'd had the chance and turned her down. Just like that, he'd wimped out at the thought of spending the night here, and it upset her beyond belief. What sort of man said no to the chance of a night of passionate sex because they were scared to be inside a house in the dark?

That was it, she determined. He could go and find someone else to wine and dine. He obviously didn't find her that attractive.

Maddy stomped her way along the hall and up the stairs to the bedroom, slamming the door shut behind her. A flurry of emotions ran through her head and her heart that she'd never felt before, and she really wasn't sure what to do about it.

# SIXTY-ONE

Glenys lay in bed. She'd tossed and turned most of the night, unable to settle into her usual deep sleep. It was that damn house; she was becoming obsessed. Bad enough she hadn't stopped thinking about it all evening, now she was lying awake worrying if Maddy was okay there on her own. She had no idea why she had this terrible sense of foreboding, but it was a dark cloud that clung to every shred of her being.

Kicking the duvet off, she lay in her pyjamas, wondering what she should do. She closed her eyes and began to breathe deeply in through her nose, releasing the breath out of her mouth. It was a silent meditation, which could go one of two ways: she would either relax herself enough that sleep came and took her once more; or, she would make contact with her spirit guides who would tell her what she needed to know. In all fairness, she was hoping it would be sleep that came to her and not a visitor from the other side.

A loud thump from Alfie's room made her jump up. Throwing open her bedroom door, she ran across the hallway and knocked on his door.

His groggy voice answered, 'Dropped my book. Sorry.'

'As long as you're okay. Are you okay?'

'Yes.'

'Good. Get to sleep, Alfie, it's early.'

Wide awake now, she decided she might as well make herself a coffee and do a bit of work. Or she could do some research on Lakeview House; she'd promised Maddy she would. Damn! That house was taking over her mind. She hated when that happened. Thankfully, it wasn't often, but now and again a person or a place would make such a strong connection with her that she couldn't ignore it. Whoever or whatever it was would lodge itself firmly inside her head, spinning around, gathering speed like a tornado.

The puzzling thing was that until she'd met Maddy, she'd never really given the house much thought. So, was it the house or Maddy that was messing with her mind? Slipping on her dressing gown and a pair of slippers, she let herself out of the flat and went down to the shop where her all-singing, all-dancing new computer was.

The moon was almost full. The clouds kept dancing across it, blocking out the glow which illuminated the village. Glenys shook her head; this wasn't looking good. The moon would be full tomorrow or the next night. Some shit was going down with either Maddy or Lakeview House, and she was caught up in the middle of it.

Unlocking the shop door, she entered, the smell of incense filling her nostrils and making her retch. God, she hated that smell, but it was what customers expected from these kinds of shops. It was what the villagers expected as well, and she'd always felt a sense of duty towards them. They'd labelled her as kooky and she'd felt it was her place to make sure she lived up to the label. What a load of rubbish.

Turning on the shop light, she grabbed the bin from behind the counter. It was time to make a stand and bollocks to conforming to other people's expectations. Who said her shop couldn't smell of lemon drizzle cake or vanilla cupcakes, which was the fragrance of the expensive wax-warmers in the flat? Gathering all the incense sticks, candles, and anything else which offended her sense of smell, she threw them all into the bin, tied the bag, then carried it outside and dumped it into the wheelie bin.

When she went back into the shop, the smell still lingered in the air, but it wasn't as strong. In the morning she'd open the windows and wedge the door wide to clear it completely, but already she felt much better. All this time she'd put up with that smell: For what, or who?

She grabbed her mug and went into the back room where she sat at the computer and powered it up. The tarot deck on the table was drawing her in, but she didn't want to pull any cards from it until she knew what was going on. As she logged onto the computer, she ignored the cards and sipped her coffee.

Today was going to be a long one.

# SIXTY-TWO

Maddy opened her eyes; it was still dark outside. A gentle, silvery, shimmering glow from the moon cast its light inside the room. She turned and grabbed her phone off the bedside table. It was just after 3 a.m. She lay there with a queasy feeling in the pit of her stomach as the soft sounds of Ella Fitzgerald's voice filtered up the stairs.

She blinked several times before pushing herself up onto her elbows. Getting out of bed, she crept towards the door and listened to make sure she wasn't imagining it or dreaming. Nope, she wasn't. She could faintly hear the words: 'Night and day, you are the one. Only you beneath the moon and under the sun.'

Cold fingers of fear wrapped themselves around the back of her neck and she shivered. Maddy knew one hundred per cent that she'd unplugged the radio power cord from the socket on the wall. Seth had been there; he'd watched her.

Not for the first time, she wondered what the hell she was thinking agreeing to live in this house on her own. It was okay pretending you weren't scared during the day to put on a brave face. But this was different. She hadn't ever felt terror like it.

There were two explanations: the house was haunted; or whoever was playing these stupid mind games with her had upped their game. *Who would be so mean as to try to scare her this much?*

Last night, Seth had offered her a nice, warm, cosy bed at the pub. A lovely king-size bed, with him to keep her warm, and she'd refused flat out. In fact, she'd been offended by his offer, as if he was doubting her sanity in wanting to stay in this mausoleum alone. But right now, she doubted her own sanity and wished she hadn't been so bloody stubborn. *Why were you so adamant that you had to stay here alone, Maddy? That was plain stupid and now look: The radio is playing the same song as when you first turned it on hours ago. Even though you removed it from the socket. How do you explain that one?*

She grabbed hold of the heavy-duty torch from the dresser and turned it on. The weight of it afforded her some comfort; at least she could use it as a weapon if she came face to face with an intruder. She didn't want to consider the possibility of anyone apart from her being in the house.

Her limited options weren't exceptionally good. She should phone the police and say... what? 'Hello, the radio is playing the same song on repeat, despite me turning it off?' Christ, they'd probably have her sectioned and carted off to the nearest hospital. She could keep the bedroom door shut and barricade herself inside, wait for the sun to break through the clouds, and then go for help. Then she could leave this place, forget the sense of belonging and duty she felt towards the house, and go back to her gran's tiny London flat and finish her book there. But the rhythm of the dull thud of the football, as it bounced against the wall below on a continual loop, would mess with her mind, disrupting her creative flow and taking away all possibility of her finishing this book on time.

She knew she couldn't go back there, despite the love she had for her gran. It just wasn't the right place for her to be. And you think that Lakeview House is? Have you lost your mind, Maddy? What about Stella? You could stay with her for a few days until you sort out your own place to live. Stop running away and being so pathetic!

The last line from her inner critic shook her to the core; she hadn't realised that she'd been running away. She was, though. She'd run from Connor, from London, from her life, and now she was stuck here in the middle of nowhere with no one to turn that bloody radio off.

Her feet felt as if they were glued to the floor and didn't want to move. But she knew she had to go down and face whatever it was, because she wasn't going to be chased out of this house without a fight. If it was a ghost, then it could bugger off. It would just have to accept that she was here and live alongside her in harmony. This thought made her giggle. As if she were brave enough to live with a ghost! Before coming here, she didn't even believe in them, so what was wrong with her? It must be a bloody amazing one if it could plug a radio in.

If someone was out there, then it was time for a showdown, and she had the advantage. She knew the layout of the house, so she could find somewhere to hide if she needed to until the police got here.

Stepping onto the landing, the beam from the torch was wavering all over the place and she realised it was because her hands were shaking. Taking a deep breath, she ran down the staircase towards the kitchen and the offending music. As she reached the bottom of the stairs, she realised the music had stopped. Silence filled the air, making it heavy and oppressive once more. In a way, she preferred listening to the sweet sounds of Ella Fitzgerald.

She pushed open the kitchen door, shining the light around. 'Who's in here?' she demanded. 'Who is messing around with me? Because I'm not standing for it. You better show yourself now and we can come to some kind of agreement, because I'm telling you now that you won't scare me away. I'm here to stay. This is my home now. So, you either crack on with what you're doing and leave me the fuck alone, or you get out. It's up to you.'

She stood still, her stomach a mass of churning knots, but she felt better for saying what was on her mind. If someone replied to her, she'd be out of there like a shot, straight out of the front door and all the way to Seth's pub.

Her temples throbbing and pulse racing, she listened. There was no answer; Maddy was greeted by silence, which made her feel a little braver. The kitchen didn't feel cold like she'd expected it to; it felt empty – a bit like her. She slowly crossed the room towards the worktop where the radio stood. It wasn't plugged in!

Maddy stepped away, shaking her head. You're losing the plot, hearing things. It must have been in your dream and you can't have been fully awake. Either that, or someone is messing with your head, and who would really want to do that? One name flashed into her mind... Connor. What if he'd found out where she was? He would enjoy this game of cat and mouse, but how would he know where to find her? Only Stella knew where she was, which could explain her friend's strange behaviour. Maddy whispered, 'Stella, what did you do?'

# SIXTY-THREE

Seth lay in bed, staring at the ceiling, wondering just what had happened again between him and Maddy. Twice now they'd spend a pleasurable couple of hours in each other's company, then it had ended on a sour note.

He turned on his side. He wasn't tired. He kept thinking he could hear his dad, which was stupid because his dad was in the funeral home, laid out in a pine coffin that was going to take him to his final resting place in a few days' time. Maybe he should go and say goodbye tomorrow. Seth didn't like the thought of him being there alone, with no one popping in to see him.

It was strange being here alone for the first time in forever; his dad or guests normally kept him company. Thankfully, they'd taken no bookings for this week. He wasn't sure how the Tripadvisor reviews would have gone down if guests had to witness the landlord's dad dropping dead on the landing. The thought made him smile. Who really cared about all that crap, anyway? When did the world get so hung up on reviewing anything and everything?

He closed his eyes again, begging sleep to come and take him away for a couple of hours. But his mind switched between images of his dad's body and Maddy. Lakeview House was a thing of desolate beauty that he appreciated even more now he'd spent time in it, and he could see the attraction for Maddy. It truly was magnificent, though lonely, but something about it made you want to spend more time there. Maybe not after dark, though.

He wondered what to do about their situation. Were they friends or could it be more? He'd like it to be a lot more; he'd like to take her out on a date, get to know her better, read her books, and become her number one fan. *Christ, Seth, you sound like Annie Wilkes out of* Misery, *you little cockadoodie brat.* His laugh filled the room and he opened his eyes again.

He might as well get up and do something useful if sleep wasn't going to come. He had a copy of her book in the bar, which the bookshop had ordered for him; he would go and get it. He could make himself a hot chocolate and read until his eyes had no excuse to give in and close for a couple of hours.

He picked up the book, tucking it under his arm, then went into the kitchen where he warmed up a mug of milk in the microwave. Years ago, his mum would take a heavy metal pan from the rack and put it on the stove. Then she'd pour in a mixture of milk and fresh cream from the dairy, stirring it while it warmed through. If they had chocolate in the house, she'd break a couple of squares and drop them into the warm milk, stirring until they melted. She'd add a couple of spoonfuls of drinking chocolate and a sprinkling of sugar, then pour it into the large stone mugs she kept for best, and pass him one. It was truly the most indulgent and probably the most calorific hot chocolate the world knew, but it had been divine. These fancy coffee shops had nothing on her secret hot chocolate recipe.

Nowadays, he stirred a large spoon of hot chocolate powder into the microwaved milk and hoped for the best. Maybe he could lure Maddy here with the offer of the best hot chocolate she'd ever tasted and make one for her. It was worth a shot; who could resist?

As he walked back into the bedroom, he crossed to the window and glanced out. He couldn't see Lakeview House from here, which was probably just as well. He could see Glenys's shop, though, and wondered why the light was on at this time in the morning. As much as she drove him mad, he cared for her a lot and was happy to help if she needed anything.

He propped himself up on the bed, lay back, and opened the book. At first, it was hard to stop reading the words in Maddy's voice. She was all he could imagine as he read each line, but after a while it got easier. Pretty soon, as the story and the characters drew him in, he forgot all about the author. It was good, and he could understand why the book had become so popular.

Sipping his drink, he read page after page until his eyes finally began to blur at the small print in front of him. Yawning, he put the book down on the bedside table and went to turn off the light. Glenys's shop was still lit up. *Glenys! Did you forget to turn off the light, or is there a problem?* He couldn't ignore it. What if something was wrong and he'd stayed in his warm, cosy bed, his belly full of hot chocolate? He'd feel terrible if he went to sleep when she needed his help? For God's sake, being a Good Samaritan was a pain in the arse at times.

He dressed quickly, ran downstairs, and slipped on his trainers. Shrugging a hoodie over his head, he left the pub unlocked and rushed down the street towards the shop. He wasn't worried about anyone going in and burgling it at this time of night; he had nothing worth stealing in there. What money there was, his dad kept locked in an old-fashioned safe at the back of the storeroom behind countless empty beer crates. Even Seth was too lazy to move them all to check what was in it, so he doubted a sneak-in burglar would be bothered.

# SIXTY-FOUR

Glenys rubbed her eyes and stared at the spread of tarot cards in front of her. It didn't make sense: Death, the Nine of Swords, and the Eight of Cups were all face up in front of her. Glenys felt uncomfortable even staring at them.

The Death card didn't necessarily mean someone was going to die, because it was usually about symbolic endings of a major phase in life that might bring about the beginning of something more important. But the Nine of Swords was one of the most negative cards she'd pulled in a spread for quite some time, and she didn't like it. This one foretold of powerful mental anguish and was symbolic of worry and grief. The Eight of Cups symbolised abandonment, leaving, a time to move on. So, what did this mean?

The whole time she'd been pulling the cards, she'd had Maddy's name spinning around in her head like a whirlwind. *Christ, I wouldn't share these cards with her worst enemy! So what am I supposed to do about this mess?* Did it mean that Maddy was going through some kind of mental anguish that would result in her abandoning Lakeview House and start a new beginning somewhere else? Glenys didn't know. Chewing on her thumbnail, she picked the cards up. It was late and she was tired. Too damn tired, and now these cards were freaking her out.

She really liked Maddy and wanted her to stay, but if these cards were for her, they appeared to be telling some kind of warning. Maybe she should go and visit Maddy tomorrow and tell her about the cards. She could ask her if she was okay, at least let her know to be aware of what could be around the corner for her, and offer a friendly warning to be careful.

Glenys opened the shop door and walked out, straight into the man standing outside. The scream that left her lips pierced the air and echoed around the deserted street as he reached out and grabbed her.

'Jesus, Glenys, you've woken the dead.'

'What the fuck are you doing sneaking around at this time in the morning, Seth?' she snapped, slapping his arm as if he was a naughty boy.

'Ouch, you're too rough. As a matter of fact, I was coming to check that you were okay, I couldn't sleep and saw the shop light on. I was worried something was wrong with either you or Alfie.'

Glenys felt her cheeks begin to burn and a warm, fuzzy feeling wrap itself around her heart.

'Really? You came to check on us both? Aw, that's so sweet of you. Thank you, but we're good. I couldn't sleep either.'

'Why?'

She shrugged. 'You tell me. Actually, I can't stop thinking about Maddy being on her own in that house. It's mad. She's mad, if you ask me, and there's something not right.'

'She's mad, all right,' he agreed. 'What do you mean something's not right?'

'I don't know exactly, but I keep getting bad vibes. Then I pulled some tarot cards and, well, let's just say they're grim.' She looked more closely at him. 'Why can't you sleep? Is it your dad?'

He shook his head. 'No, I'm the same, it's Maddy. I don't know what's wrong with me, but I'm worried about her being on her own there. It's so desolate and secluded, but she's more stubborn than you. I offered her a room at the pub earlier and she turned me down.'

Glenys grinned. 'You're losing your touch, Seth, if she turned you down.'

'Yep, but I wish she hadn't.'

'I bet you do.'

'Not like that. I'm honestly concerned about her being there, especially after the wedding dress episode. We don't know who left it there or why.'

'I can tell you why. Someone is trying to scare her away, and she's too stubborn to leave.'

'Which is all very good,' he agreed, 'but what if there's more to it?'

Glenys shivered. 'It's nippy. Are you coming upstairs?'

'No, I better get back. I've left the pub unlocked.'

'What do you mean there's more to it?' she asked.

'She left London and a violent ex-boyfriend behind, so what if it's him? What if he's followed her and is trying to scare her?'

Glenys clutched the cards in her fingers tight. 'It might explain this awful spread of cards,' she mused. 'You need to ask her about it tomorrow. See if she thinks it's a possibility, and maybe she should tell the police so they're forewarned if something happens and she has to ring them for help.'

'Yes, that's a good idea, but it's a bit awkward. Can you not ask her?'

Glenys chuckled. 'Seth, you're such a wimp at times. But yes, I suppose I can. I need to speak to her about these cards and warn her, so I'll ask her if there's a possibility this ex could be here. It's a huge house. He could be hiding out in there trying to scare her and she'd never know.'

Seth sighed. 'That's a very reassuring thought to go to bed on. As if I wasn't having trouble enough sleeping. Thanks for that, Glenys.'

'Sorry, just thinking out loud.'

'I'm sure it's fine. We checked it from top to bottom the other day. The only living person inside there is Maddy, I'm positive of that.'

'What if it's not a living person then? What if it's a ghost?'

Seth frowned. 'Quit while you're ahead, Glenys. I wanted at least a couple of hours sleep. Do you think I should go back and check on her?'

'In the morning, yes. If you turn up now, you'll scare the shit out of her, like you just did me. In all honesty, I don't think her ex is likely to be stalking around the village or Lakeview House. You know what this lot are like; they don't miss a trick. Someone would have mentioned some Londoner snooping around asking questions.'

'You're right. What a pair of regular Miss Marples we are. Night, Glenys. Glad everything's okay.'

'Thanks. Night, Seth. Tomorrow we'll go and see Maddy, talk some sense into her, and get her to stop at the pub for a couple of nights so we can all get some sleep.' She winked at him, then turned to lock the shop door.

She heard his footsteps as he turned and began to walk back along the cobbled street towards the pub. Damn, he was a good-looking bloke and a pretty decent one as well. They were so hard to find in such a small community.

It was nice to know that someone in the village cared about her and Alfie, even if there wasn't a chance of them ever being more than friends.

# SIXTY-FIVE

He wondered if he should go and move the body now. The only problem was that when he'd looked out of the window earlier, it seemed as if half of the village was awake.

It would take him fifteen minutes to get to the summer-house, then he had to wrap the body up well and get it down to the lake before it got too light. He stood up and stared out of the window again. It was still dark, but not as black as before, which meant he didn't have enough time.

He was in a bit of a conundrum: he didn't have the time to dispose of the body, yet he couldn't leave it there much longer. He was taking a huge risk. Maybe he should get rid of the car first. That would buy him a little more time. If he didn't, someone was bound to notice the car sooner rather than later.

He could drive it to Keswick, leave it in the main car park, then walk back. It was at least five miles, but that didn't bother him. He was used to walking and scrambling around the hills, and he would feel much better knowing that car wasn't there. It was like a beacon and it could be his downfall, so he needed to get rid of it.

Dressing all in black, he pulled on his walking boots and

took the keys from the bottom of the wood basket where he'd hidden them. Tugging on a black beanie hat, he caught a glimpse of himself in the mirror and smiled; he looked as if he'd joined the SAS and was about to go out on a top-secret mission. To be fair, he was on a mission – it just wasn't a government one. Although, it was definitely a classified one.

He stepped outside and locked his door. He liked the village at this time of night when most people were sleeping. It was a beautiful place, the air was always fresh, the grass green, and the lake icy cold.

He walked briskly towards the car park at the rear of the pub, checking there was no one around before he approached the car. No point in making awkward conversations for himself just yet; it would be better if he could drive it away with minimal fuss. He got in the car and started the engine, making sure to drive slowly out of the village to avoid attracting attention.

He drove as casually as a killer with a victim's stolen car could drive and doubted his pulse had raised a single beat. He was methodical and cautious, which was why up until now no one had even figured out that the number of missing walkers had increased this year. This made him happy; he liked a challenge, and this would definitely count as one.

This one had been the most unplanned, unorganised killing that he'd carried out, yet it wouldn't happen again. He just needed to clean up the mess he'd made for himself, without getting caught. If he was arrested, he doubted he could cope with being locked up twenty-four hours a day. He'd always lived a life of freedom, following his own rules, doing his own thing, and there was no doubt he would struggle if he was put into confinement.

Then there was the media circus, if he was discovered. He had always been shy, worked hard, did his own thing; he'd never liked attention. If it came out what he'd been doing, there would be a news explosion and the village would be turned into a hive of camera crews and reporters. Everything would be turned upside down.

But the worst part would be that he wouldn't be able to visit the bodies that lay below the lake, to watch them swaying gently in the underwater current. Who would watch over them if he was incarcerated? Anything could happen. They might get loose, drift off, and surface. That would be terrible! At the moment, they were at peace, and he didn't want them disturbed.

The fresh water preserved them like nothing else could, and when he got them in the water not long after death, they looked as if they were perfect.

He wasn't sure what the body in the summerhouse was going to look like, because it was a mess and had possibly lain too long. In fact, it would ruin his others.

That thought made up his mind. Tonight, he would have to bury it on the fell.

# SIXTY-SIX

Maddy sat on her bed, her knees tucked under her chin, staring at the door. She'd dragged the heavy chest of drawers in front of it to give her time to call for help if anyone tried to get in. *Call who exactly? Your phone only works every other day, if it feels like it.*

She shivered and tugged the duvet around her. How much was she regretting not going back to the pub with Seth now? She tutted in disgust at herself. It was all very well being brave and putting on a tough front in public, but it was quite a different matter in the middle of the night inside this huge house. She kept listening for any telltale noises that there was an intruder inside, creeping around.

Surely, there was no way Connor could know she was here, though? And even if he'd managed to get Stella to tell him, how would he get here? He'd be in a car; he wasn't the outdoor type like Seth. He wouldn't be able to scale fells and mountains, or sail over a huge lake to find the exact house that she was living in. This wasn't some Hollywood movie; she wasn't Julia Roberts and hadn't had to fake her own death to get away from him.

*So, what is going on then? Is the house haunted?* She didn't know, and who was she to say that it wasn't? She really didn't know enough about the paranormal to rule it out, though. She hadn't ever thought about ghosts and spooks, and there certainly hadn't been any room for any when she was growing up in her gran's cramped flat.

It was different here. The house was full of empty rooms and memories, with enough space for several ghosts to wander the hallways and corridors without even bumping into each other.

As she sat chewing on her thumbnail, she tried to clear her mind of thoughts of anything supernatural. But she was struggling. Her blood felt as if it was turning to iced slush as it pumped around her body. That dream the other night had felt so real. Was the bride who'd been pulled from the lake trying to tell her something? It was pretty corny, though. Did this stuff happen in real life? And where had the wedding dress come from? She didn't think that was down to paranormal activity.

Her thoughts brought her back to the present and the possibility that someone was trying to scare the crap out of her. Why, though? She didn't know anyone here well enough to have upset them. She'd got friendly with Seth... and would like to get even friendlier. Glenys seemed lovely, even if they'd got off to a rough start. And then there was Alfie. He was a bit slower than other boys his age but seemed innocent and not the type to try to scare her to death when he knew she was living here on her own. What would be the point?

She climbed off the bed and grabbed her notebook and pen off the desk. It was like some complicated book plot, so she should be able to suss it out. This is what she loved doing. Her gran had always said she should have joined the police force and become a detective, but she hadn't wanted to work her way through the ranks or deal with pesky criminals. Instead, she'd put her heart and soul into becoming a crime writer, which, even if she said so herself, she was pretty good at. Or she had been, until it came down to writing this sequel, and then every fear she'd known, plus more, had hit her like a tram with no brakes on Blackpool prom.

She began to scribble her list of names down.

Seth – good guy, I like him a lot and I think he likes me. Just lost his dad, so could be a little mentally unstable, but I don't think so and not enough to try to scare me away. He wouldn't have spent hours helping me search the house the other day if he knew it had been him. And what would he get out of scaring me away? It doesn't make any sense.

Glenys – bit angry, bit strange, nice once you get to know her. Lives on her own with Alfie and is busy running the shop, so wouldn't really have time to dunk a wedding dress in the lake and drape it on the front steps for effect. I can't see her doing it either.

Alfie – hangs around a lot, sneaks up on me – a lot. Knows more than I'd given him credit for, has a strange thing about the lake and the people who live in it. God knows who or what this is, or if it has any relevance, but who are the lake people? Maybe it's them! *Get a grip, Maddy, next you'll be saying it's aliens from out of space.* What are *lake people*, anyway? Better ask him to explain what he means to you next time he scares you half to death.

Connor – control freak, abusive ex, will be furious I walked out on him. Sneaky and stalkerish, or I could imagine him being a stalker. He would get a thrill out of scaring me to death, much more than any of the others who have no partic-ular reason to even want to waste their time or effort trying to scare me.

She knew in her heart everything pointed towards Connor, but where was he and how had he got here? If she could speak to Stella, she'd be able to confirm whether he'd managed to find out where she was. But it was far too late to even try to call her.

Maddy typed out a text message and sent it, hoping that for once the signal was just strong enough to allow it to get through. She really missed her friend and decided that in the morning her priority was to go to the village and try to make contact with Stella. Then she would know whether to report the strange incidents to the police.

As a wave of tiredness washed over her, she placed the notebook and pen on the floor, lay back and closed her eyes. She felt herself begin to drift off. A part of her was battling to stay awake and listen, but exhaustion won, and she slipped into a deep sleep.

# SIXTY-SEVEN

Stella snuggled up to Joe. The car had broken down again in a magnificent cloud of steam and the AA had come and towed it to a garage in Kendal, leaving them with no choice but to book a hotel room for the night. The mechanic had said he'd fix the car first thing in the morning so they could be on their way by lunchtime, which was fine by her.

She'd had the longest, hottest shower of her life when they'd checked in. Smothering herself in the complimentary lemon-and-rosemary-scented body lotion, she'd had to sit on the chair waiting for it to soak in while it was Joe's turn. He'd come out of the shower with the smallest towel known to man wrapped around his waist, and she'd had to stop herself from lunging at him. He'd crossed towards her and she'd stood, falling into his open arms.

The pair of them spent the next hour kissing and making love. Still basking in a happy, warm glow, Joe had whispered, 'I love you, Stella, but I need food. A man can't survive off hot sex alone.'

The comment had cracked her up and she'd doubled over laughing, then they'd ordered room service, which they ate in silence. Joe had lain on the bed watching some crappy documentary about catching a killer, and she'd cuddled up next to him. They must have drifted off at some point, because Stella had wakened up to the television crackling because the signal had been lost.

Needing the loo, she crept from the bed, trying not to wake him. She still couldn't believe how, after everything, she'd found pretty much the perfect man. In the bathroom, she stared at her reflection in the mirror; her face was a swollen, bruised mess. The young girl behind the reception desk had given her a sympathetic look when they'd checked in, then glared at Joe in disgust.

Stella had wanted to tell her not to be so presumptuous, but Joe had softly squeezed her hand as a gentle warning. She supposed she did look as if he'd battered her, bless him. But Stella was sure he didn't have a violent bone in his body. He was the sweetest, kindest man she'd ever met.

Unlike Connor. Just thinking his name made her shudder. She needed to get to Maddy tomorrow, no matter what, and tell her what a complete mess she'd made. If she had to walk or hitchhike the rest of the way to Lakeview House, she would, because she needed to make things right. This sinking feeling of despair inside her stomach was taking away what should be the happiest time of her life.

As she climbed back into the bed, Joe murmured in his sleep and she snuggled close to him, his body heat offering her some comfort. She needed to warm up the block of ice that had settled inside the pit of her stomach, freezing her to the core. She couldn't bear to think of Maddy being stranded, alone, in need of help in the middle of nowhere, in a place where Stella had sent her like an innocent lamb to be slaughtered.

Squeezing her eyes shut, she tried to block out the images that were filling her mind, but all she could see was that empty, bleak house and the fresh, red blood that splattered the walls. The blood that Connor had spilt without a second thought.

Enough, Stella, she told herself angrily. Christ, maybe you should offer to write Maddy's next book. Your imagination is even worse than hers and that's saying something. Tomorrow you will find her knee-deep in sheets of paper, empty coffee mugs, and chocolate bar wrappers. She'll be engrossed in her writing and won't even know what you're talking about. Everything is going to be fine. You're fine, Maddy's fine – get some sleep.

# SIXTY-EIGHT

Maddy woke with a start. She could hear loud knocking echoing throughout the house. Jumping out of bed, she rushed to the windows, pressing her face against the glass, and let out a squeal of relief to see Glenys standing on the drive waving up at her.

Dragging the chest of drawers away from the door, she threw it open and ran down in her pyjamas.

When she opened the front door, Glenys took one look at her and enquired, 'Bad night?'

Maddy laughed, nodded, then laughed even louder. 'You could say that. To what do I owe the pleasure at this time in the morning?'

'I was worried about you. And it's almost eleven; it's practically dinnertime.'

Maddy was shocked. 'No way.'

'Yes way. So, you're okay then? I had no reason to be worried? Are you on your own?'

Maddy liked her perceptiveness. 'I'm okay, but there's some stuff going on that I can't explain. And yes, I'm definitely on my own.'

She walked towards the kitchen with Glenys following behind her.

'Wowee, this is some fucking house. It's amazing, I love it. Maddy, you didn't have to be on your own. I know Seth offered you a room at the pub.'

Maddy frowned. *Just how much did Seth share with Glenys?* Considering they weren't in a relationship, they seemed to spend an awful lot of time together.

'When did he tell you that?'

'About three this morning.'

Maddy turned to look at her, doing her best not to snap... and failing. 'Do you two often have conversations about other people in the middle of the night?' Realising she was standing with her arms crossed and being defensive, she quickly uncrossed them.

'Hey, I came here to see if you were okay,' Glenys told her calmly. 'Seth was worried about you. I couldn't sleep because I was worried about you, and he saw my shop light on and came to check everything was okay. That's it. We're friends and nothing else, so you don't have to get all protective over your man. Bloody hell, you're a bit feisty this morning.'

Glenys walked past her, picked up the kettle, and took it over to the kitchen sink where she ran the tap and began to fill it with water. Switching it on, she began opening cupboard doors, looking for the one that contained the ingredients to make a coffee.

Maddy dragged a chair out from underneath the table and sat down. Yawning, she rubbed her eyes and took some deep breaths to calm herself down. She had no idea what was wrong with her; she didn't normally feel so exhausted.

Glenys made two mugs of coffee, opened the fridge door, and sniffed the milk before pouring it into the cups, stirring them briskly and handing one to Maddy. She sat down opposite her.

'Sorry and thank you,' Maddy began. 'I guess I'm tired and snappy. I think things are getting to me and I'm too stubborn to admit there might be a teeny problem with the house or me. Or the house and me.'

'I knew it.' Glenys looked triumphant. 'I pulled some cards last night, and I'm telling you I stopped at three because it was the worst spread I've pulled in forever.'

Maddy sipped the hot coffee, savouring the aroma as if filled her nostrils, the liquid warming her insides.

'What cards and what's a spread?'

Glenys bit her lip. 'Tarot cards. A spread is when you pull cards to do a reading. I didn't technically know it was going to be about you, although your name wouldn't get out of my head. Did you mind? It was a bit naughty not to ask your permission first, but I had to know why you were on my mind so much.'

Maddy didn't know whether she minded or not. It wasn't something she'd ever had experience with. 'When you say it was the worst spread you've pulled, what does that mean?'

Glenys shifted in her seat and Maddy decided that her discomfort suggested it definitely wasn't good.

'Look, something is going on,' she admitted. 'I found a radio yesterday in the library. I didn't expect it to work, but I plugged it in, and it began to play Ella Fitzgerald and other swing music. Last night, before Seth left, I unplugged it and went to bed. At some point in the night, I woke up to the sound of Ella Fitzgerald filtering up the stairs. It was the exact same song, and it freaked me out. I went downstairs and it wasn't plugged in, so either I have a magic radio, or someone is messing around with me.'

Glenys looked over at the huge radio on the worktop. 'That radio?'

Maddy nodded, and Glenys walked over to it. She plugged it into the socket and a loud burst of static filled the air, making them both jump. Maddy crossed the room towards her.

'It was fine yesterday; it was playing all afternoon.' She began to twiddle the knob, but there was only static. 'Radios repeat songs all the time, so it was probably nothing.'

Unplugging it, she went back to her chair and picked up her mug of coffee.

'Yes, they do,' Glenys agreed. 'It's old, so you might have got its last bit of life from it before it died a death. It's strange, though, isn't it? Do you think it turned itself on, or do you believe that someone of the humankind might have done it?'

Maddy shrugged. 'You tell me.'

'Well, from a professional point of view, I think there's something going on.' Glenys's serious tone made Maddy erupt with laughter.

'No shit, Sherlock.'

Glenys grinned and began to laugh with her.

'Give me a guided tour and let me get a feel for the place, then I'll tell you exactly what. Throw in some lunch and I'll give you an expert opinion all free of charge, because I like you.'

'How could I refuse? Let me get dressed first. I kind of feel a bit underdressed for the occasion.' Maddy drained the last of her coffee and stood up. 'I'll be back in a minute. You can have a look around yourself while you're waiting, if you want.'

Glenys shook her head. 'No, I'd rather wait for you. I want a full guided tour.'

Wondering if Glenys was scared of the house, Maddy ran upstairs to get dressed and brush her teeth.

# SIXTY-NINE

Glenys was in the library when Maddy came back downstairs.

'This must have been some room,' she said. 'All these book-shelves. I wonder what happened to the books.'

'I wish I knew,' Maddy agreed. 'It's like a dream come true. Ever since I was a child, I've dreamt about having my own library. This is where I found the radio yesterday; I like this room. It doesn't feel strange or scary, it just feels sad and empty.'

As Maddy led her into the various rooms downstairs, Glenys found herself falling in love with the house despite her initial reservations about it. She didn't say anything out of the ordinary, but she knew Maddy was watching her expressions in case a look of horror flashed across her face. So far so good.

But when they reached the foot of the huge staircase and Maddy stepped up, Glenys paused. Reaching out, she clasped her fingers around the bannister, gripping the wood until her knuckles went white.

Maddy whispered, 'What's the matter?'

Glenys didn't answer. Instead, she closed her eyes, standing still as if they were playing a game of musical statues and the music had stopped.

Maddy felt a cold chill begin to spread over her shoulders, but then Glenys nodded her head once, opened her eyes, and smiled at her.

'Are you okay?'

'Yes, just getting to know the place. Downstairs was for happy times – dancing, family life, parties, friends, celebrating, and living life to the full.'

'And upstairs?' Maddy asked warily.

'I don't know yet, I need to go up there.'

Maddy led the way, not stopping until she reached the landing and turned to see Glenys only halfway up. It looked as if she had to force her legs to move, then she was moving, running up the last few steps to catch her up.

'I'll show you my room,' Maddy said. 'I want to know what you think about it.'

She opened the door, forgetting she hadn't made the bed, and dashed towards it to straighten the duvet. 'Oops, sorry. I've forgotten what it's like to have guests.' She winked at Glenys, who was looking around the room, her fingers trailing over the furniture.

'This is a good room. There's a little sadness in here but nothing too bad. You chose wisely.'

One by one, Maddy opened the upstairs doors and let Glenys look around the assortment of bedrooms, which ranged from even bigger than the one she was sleeping in to smaller, compact guest rooms.

When they reached the last room at the end of the corridor, nearest to the attic, Glenys paused.

'That room's locked,' Maddy explained. 'It won't open. Me and Seth tried the other day.'

Reaching out, Glenys touched the wooden door with her fingertips, then pressed her ear against the wood. Maddy stepped back, horrified. *Does she think there was someone inside?* Before she could ask, Glenys lifted a finger to her lips, silently shushing her. Maddy was totally freaked out. *What was going on?*

Finally, Glenys clasped the brass knob in her fingers and turned it, pushing the door wide open. Maddy, who hadn't realised she'd been holding her breath, released it to see an empty, dusty bedroom, which had clearly once been a nursery. There was a rusted, spring-mounted rocking horse, a dust-covered, wooden crib filled with dolls and ancient teddies, toy cars, a tiny pram with a cracked porcelain doll tucked up inside it, and various books and puzzles.

'Why is this stuff still here when all the other rooms have been emptied?' she wondered aloud.

'Maybe they couldn't bear to remove the toys.' Glenys walked around the room, picking up a stuffed bear, which only had one button for an eye, and clutching it to her chest.

Maddy felt a wave of sadness wash over her; she didn't like this room. She watched as the woman in front of her placed the bear back inside the crib, nodded her head once, then turned and walked out of the room. She followed, closing the door behind her.

'I don't understand,' she said. 'Seth and I tried that door a couple of times. It wouldn't open.'

Glenys continued walking towards the last door. 'Is this the attic?'

'Yes.'

'There's nothing up there except sadness and memories. Come on, I'm hungry. I hope you have something nice to eat for lunch.'

She turned and headed back downstairs, an intrigued Maddy following closely behind.

# SEVENTY

Seth watched Alfie kicking a stone along the street past the pub. He wondered if he should ask him about the house again, see if he caved in and admitted to messing around in there.

He opened the front door and shouted, 'Alfie!'

The teenager turned around, realised it was Seth, and grinned at him. He wandered back to the pub.

'Have you seen my mum?'

Seth shook his head. He hadn't set eyes on her since their conversation in the early hours of this morning.

'Think she's gone to the house to see Maddy,' the boy said. 'I'm hungry.'

'Come in, then. Do you want some toast?'

'Yes, please. Or can I have a crisp sandwich?'

'You can have whatever you want.' Seth led him inside and they went upstairs to the kitchen where he made a salt and vinegar crisp sandwich and put the plate on the table in front of him.

'Have you been to the house lately?' Seth asked.

Alfie screwed up his forehead while he contemplated the question, then shrugged.

'Sort of.' He took a bite of his sandwich.

'What does that mean?'

'Well, I was there yesterday, but I didn't go inside. I never go inside. I stay outside.'

'Why don't you want to go inside?'

'For real? You don't think it's scary in there? I do. Too big, too dark, and empty for too long.'

Seth sat opposite him. 'I'm going to ask you a question, man to man. Did you put the wedding dress on the steps to scare Maddy? I won't be cross.'

He shook his head. 'What wedding dress? What's one of those? Why would I do that? Not me. It might be the lake people.'

'Who are the lake people?'

Alfie shook his head. 'No one, I dunno. Wasn't me.' He took a bite of his sandwich. 'Do you think my mum will be there long?'

'I don't know. Should we go there and see?'

Alfie glanced up in surprise. 'What, you want to walk with me?'

'No, I was thinking about going in my car. I'm too lazy to walk.'

Alfie laughed. 'Car's good. I like cars.' He stuffed the remainder of the sandwich into his mouth and wiped his arm across it.

They walked out of the pub and Seth locked the door behind him. A voice shouted, 'Seth!' He turned around to see Martin crossing the road towards him.

Alfie put his head down and scurried towards Seth's Land Rover, where he opened the passenger door and clambered inside, slamming it shut.

'Wonder what's got into him?' Seth muttered.

Martin laughed. 'He doesn't like me. I told him off because I caught him snooping around in the garage one day. He didn't appreciate my lecture on it being a dangerous place for him to be, especially when he was messing with things he shouldn't be touching. You're far too soft on him, Seth. He's always hanging around you like a pet dog. You keep feeding him scraps, he's never going to leave you alone.'

Seth shook his head. 'He's all right. I like him.'

'It would help if his weird mother kept an eye on him. It's not right the way she lets him wander all over.'

Seth found himself irritated by Martin's condescending attitude. The man didn't know Glenys or Alfie well enough to be judging them; this was the kind of small mindedness that drove him mad in the village.

'I should have your friend's car ready later today,' Martin went on. 'I only need to fit the part and it should be good to go.'

'Thanks, mate, that's brilliant. I'll come and sort you out if you let me know what time to pick it up.'

Martin waved his hand at him. 'I'll bring it to the pub, and you can buy me a couple of pints.' He walked off in the direction of the post office and Seth made his way to his car.

Alfie was staring at the rear-view mirror, watching Martin walk away. 'Don't like him, he's mean.'

Seth laughed. 'Is that a general observation, or is that because he shouted at you?'

Alfie shrugged. 'Both.'

# SEVENTY-ONE

Stella handed over her credit card and did her best not to grimace when the girl at the reception desk said, 'That will be two hundred and forty-eight pounds, forty-seven pence.' *Where the hell did the forty-seven pence come from?*

Joe smiled at her, mouthing the word 'sorry'. She shook her head. He'd been good enough to drive her to find Maddy, so the least she could do was foot the repair bill for the car, and he'd insisted on going halves with the hotel room.

When they got into the car, he turned the key and smiled when the ignition burst into life.

'So far so good.'

'Yep,' she agreed, 'but we haven't gone anywhere yet.'

He snorted. 'Positive vibes only the rest of the way, please. Don't bring the car down before it's time.'

As they set off, Stella felt her stomach begin to churn at the thought of seeing Maddy again and having to confess every-thing, but she knew she had to. For her own peace of mind, she needed to come clean and face the consequences. She couldn't wait to hug her friend; she'd missed her so much.

She reached out and squeezed Joe's arm. 'Thank you. I don't know what I'd have done without you the last few days.'

He smiled at her. 'It's all my pleasure. Literally. I'm the one having a great time. I've dreamt about dating you for so long, it's amazing. I'll pay you back the money for the car when we get back, I've got some spare cash stashed away. I can't believe I didn't think to bring it with me.'

'No, you won't,' she told him firmly, then paused and spoke more hesitantly. 'Do you think she's okay? It's not like her not to be in touch.'

'I'm sure she's fine. And aren't you forgetting something? She won't have your new phone number, and I can almost guarantee that judging by where that house is situated at the bottom of a valley, there won't be any decent Internet or phone signal.'

She let out a huge sigh of relief. 'You always know the right thing to say. Thank you.'

'Right, now load those instructions in again, and let's get to that house before the car dies a permanent death.'

According to the directions, they weren't too far away. As long as they didn't get lost, they should be there in the next hour or so.

# SEVENTY-TWO

Maddy put the food on the table and watched Glenys pile her plate high with cheese, crackers, grapes, and a couple of the sandwiches. She didn't tell her it was leftovers from last night's picnic with Seth. It still looked fresh and, judging by the look in Glenys's eyes, she didn't care anyway; she was eating it without complaint.

Picking at the corner of a sandwich, Maddy realised she wasn't really hungry. She was waiting for a run-down on the house from the village psychic and feeling a bit tense. She didn't know what she was going to do if Glenys said it was haunted.

Unable to wait any longer, she piped up, 'Well, what do think? Did you pick up anything ghosty?'

Glenys smiled. 'Ghosty, as in ghostly?'

'Yes, you know what I mean. Things that go bump in the night, restless spirits that are wandering the halls for the rest of eternity.'

'Nope, nothing like that.'

'Nothing?' Her answer shocked Maddy. She'd expected to hear some scary advice about how she needed to go and get a local vicar to come and exorcise the house.

'Don't get me wrong,' Glenys replied through a mouthful of sandwich, 'there's a lot of residual stuff going on. Lots of trapped memories that replay over and over again. But that's what you would expect in a house of this age and size. It's quite refreshing, actually.'

'Yes, I suppose it is. Well, it is for me. Are these residual things dangerous?'

'No, they're just memories, and nothing to be scared of.'

Maddy still felt troubled. 'Then how do you explain the wedding dress, the bangs, the confetti, and the radio being turned on and off?'

'That is the worrying part, and I think that's why your spread of cards was so crap,' Glenys replied. 'Someone is trying to scare you.'

'Someone? You mean a person?'

'Yep, a living, breathing, dirty, rotten bastard. Someone is getting their kicks out of scaring you. Someone like an ex-boyfriend maybe, or an angry villager.'

There was a brief pause before Maddy asked, 'What should I do?'

'Phone the police or go and speak to them. You need to report it.'

Maddy sat back in her chair. She wasn't sure whether she was relieved or even more worried than before.

'And before you suggest it,' Glenys went on, 'Alfie has nothing to do with it. I know he wouldn't intentionally scare anyone like this, and he was fast asleep last night at home when your radio was being turned on and off.'

'I didn't think it was him,' Maddy assured her. 'And thank you. I guess I should report it. I need to find out where Connor, my ex, is because I walked out on him. He was abusive, not to mention violent. He's the only person I can think of that would be mean enough to do something like this.' She sighed heavily. 'I wish I could get hold of Stella.'

'Who's Stella?'

'My best friend who suggested I come here in the first place to get away from him. She's the only person I know who knows that I'm here. My gran does as well, but I never gave her the address; I only showed her the pictures. She's never been farther than Brighton so she wouldn't have a clue where this is.'

'Right, so this Connor is the number one suspect. Is he dangerous?'

Maddy nodded. 'Yes, he's violent. I don't know about this, though. It just seems a lot of work for him.'

Glenys shook her head, still nibbling at the food on her plate. 'You can't underestimate someone like that, darling, you don't know what ends they'll go to. Please will you consider stopping at Seth's or mine until we get this mess sorted out?'

Maddy nodded. 'I suppose so. Do you think he'll mind?'

'No, he won't. He's as worried as I am. He'll be relieved, and if it makes you feel better, give him a few quid for the room,' Glenys suggested. 'Not that he'll take it; he's too much of a gentleman. Why don't you pack some things and I'll drop you off at the pub?'

They heard a car pull into the drive, the tyres crunching along the gravel, and both women stared at each other.

Glenys stood up and rushed towards the front door. 'It's okay,' she called back, 'it's just Seth and Alfie.'

Maddy breathed a sigh of relief. She needed to speak to the police. Maybe Seth could take her to the local station.

# SEVENTY-THREE

Seth got out of the car. Alfie clambered out of the passenger side, took one look at his mum standing on the steps with her hands on her hips, and ran off.

'Alfie, come back here! Where are you going?' Glenys shouted after him, but he waved and carried on running towards the jetty.

Seth walked up the steps to the front entrance and turned to see the boy heading for the rickety wooden pier. He felt his legs turn to jelly and he turned away. If the lad fell into the lake, Glenys could go after him. He was her son, not his.

When Maddy joined Glenys at the front door, he felt his heart sink. *Christ, I hope they aren't going to try to fill my head with some bollocks about the house being haunted.* He could believe in many things, and had an open mind, but he didn't believe in stuff like that.

As he followed them inside, he turned to take one last look at Alfie, and felt his stomach lurch. The kid was kneeling down at the edge, staring down into the water.

'Glenys, what the hell is he doing?'

She shrugged. 'No idea. Leave him to it. He's okay.'

'No, he's not. What if he falls in?'

'Serve him right, won't it? He won't drown, Seth, he's a good swimmer.'

He shook his head but couldn't erase the image of Alfie kneeling on the rotting jetty. The boy looked as if he was praying. But praying to what? A voice whispered in his head, *The lake people*.

'Seth.' Glenys was shaking his arm.

'What?'

'I think someone is trying to scare the shit out of Maddy,' she told him. 'I've been through the entire house and there's nothing here apart from some residual memories. No intelligent activity or haunting.'

His head was pounding. He was worried about the kid falling in the lake and drowning, and now she was telling him there was some nutter trying to scare Maddy.

'Tell him about the radio last night,' Glenys urged.

As Maddy began to relay the tale about the radio, he listened to her talking while keeping an eye on the view of the lake from the entrance hall window. When he saw Alfie stand up and run back onto the grass, relief filled his body.

'Are you even listening?' Glenys snapped.

He stared at her and nodded. 'Yes, I am. You can't stay here on your own, Maddy. We need to sort it out.'

'She knows that,' Glenys said, 'and she's agreed to come and stay at the pub with you.'

'Good. That's good.' A sharp pain suddenly shot across the side of his head, causing him to squeeze his eyes shut as he lurched forwards.

'Seth, what's the matter?' Maddy asked.

'Headache. I get migraines every now and again.'

She looked horrified. 'Oh my God, I'm sorry. It's all this stress, isn't it? I'm such a pain in the arse. Honestly, I'm fine, I'll be okay. Don't worry about me, you go home.'

Glenys shook her head. 'It's not you, it's me. I get on his last nerve, don't I, Seth?'

He tried to shake his head, but the movement sent a fresh wave of pain through his mind. 'I'm fine,' he assured them. 'Your car is almost ready, Maddy, so if you get your stuff together, I'll go home, get my tablets, and come back for you. I won't be more than an hour. Will you be okay?'

'Yes, it only ever happens at night. Whoever it is isn't brave enough to do anything in broad daylight.'

Glenys agreed. 'There's too much going on here today for anyone to try to do anything. I'll go back with Seth. If he's no good to drive, I'll bring your car then I can drive mine back and you can drive yours.'

Maddy smiled at them. She felt terrible at all this fuss she was causing, but she needed to make sure she'd saved her work and pack her case.

Glenys took hold of Seth's arm and led him out to the car, and Maddy could hear them bickering about who was driving. Seth gave in, she helped him into the car, then went around to the driver's side.

Turning to wave, Glenys shouted, 'Get your stuff and wait on the front steps if you're worried. Alfie's around somewhere, so you're not alone.'

Maddy lifted her hand and waved back, an uneasy feeling in the pit of her stomach. Good job she didn't have much to pack. She would grab her stuff and wait on the steps. Somehow it felt safer outside. She hurried back inside, not bothering to lock the door behind her.

# SEVENTY-FOUR

Alfie decided to climb the fell and get away from everyone. He needed to think about stuff. The lake people were still there. He'd counted them; no more had appeared, and none of them had left. He'd been worried it was them who were trying to scare Maddy away, but at least he knew now that it wasn't.

He didn't like it when there were too many people around, especially when they were talking too loud and shouting, like his mum was doing at Seth. He didn't want to listen to it, because she spent enough time shouting at him. He would get away before they noticed and made him get in the car.

He decided to go and visit the old summerhouse; he hadn't been there for weeks. Last time, he'd left his pack of football cards tucked behind one of the loose bricks, and he wanted to get it back before they got all wet and ruined. His legs ached a little from the steep climb, but it wasn't that far away. He used to play in there a lot before it started to smell bad. Sometimes it smelled really bad, as if an animal had died in there. It turned his stomach when it smelled like that and put him off his food.

As he got nearer, his nose wrinkled at the smell being carried towards him by the breeze. It smelled worse than ever and Alfie lifted his T-shirt over his mouth and nose, wondering what could be causing it. If the adults weren't being so noisy and if he didn't want his football cards, he'd have turned around and gone back home.

Then a thought struck him: *Maybe someone needs help, and I could be a hero like Seth.* He'd like it if people were patting his back and telling him well done. Although that smell suggested it was a bit too late to help anyone. It smelled like the sheep did when they died out on the fell and the farmer left them outside to rot away in the sun.

As he reached the broken window, the smell made him retch and he lifted his arm to his nose. He needed his stuff and he wanted to make sure no one was hurt. Clambering through, he lost his balance and landed on his knees. His hand touched something hard but squishy, covered in something soft.

He looked down and screamed. When he landed, he'd managed to push down a bit of a sleeping bag, and there were two dead eyes staring back at him.

Alfie had never felt such fear in his life, and he scrambled to his feet and threw himself back out of the window. Afraid to turn around in case it was one of the lake people, he began to run back towards Lakeview House to tell Seth, his mum, and Maddy. Seth could be the hero this time; he didn't want to.

Those eyes made him shiver. They were covered in white stuff, and he'd seen maggots crawling along them. Halfway down the fell, he stumbled and fell to his knees. Alfie began to throw up the contents of his stomach, which included the salt and vinegar crisp sandwich Seth had made him earlier.

When he'd finished retching and there was nothing left to come up, he stood up on legs that were a lot wobblier than when he'd set off, and carried on. He was too scared to turn around in case the thing in the sleeping bag was following him. *What if it was a zombie?* He'd watched a zombie film a couple of weeks ago when his mum had fallen asleep. He had to get back to

Lakeview House. The grown-ups wouldn't let a dead zombie get him.

As he stumbled towards the front of the house, he was glad to see his mum's car still there. Seth's car had gone, but his mum or Maddy could phone him to come back.

Alfie ran straight up the steps and turned the handle, then stepped inside the gloomy entrance hall.

# SEVENTY-FIVE

Maddy had packed her laptop, washbag, all her clean underwear, and as many clothes as she could fit into the small suitcase. The whole time she was packing she felt as if she was being watched, and she wondered briefly if there might be secret passages in the walls. How many horror films had she watched where the occupant of the mansion was crazy and hid in the walls, or they were being stalked by someone hiding in their walls? Quite a few.

The thought terrified her beyond belief. Connor could be inside the wall right now, watching her through a mirror or one of the pictures. A cold shiver made her entire body tremble, and she grabbed the small suitcase and ran out into the hall... straight into Alfie. Not realising it was him, she let out a blood-curdling scream, which terrified him more than her. He put his hands to his ears, turned, and ran back downstairs.

Maddy recognised him and shouted, 'Alfie! I'm sorry. You scared me. Are you okay? Is everything all right?'

He paused on the stairs, turning to look back at her. 'Is my mum still here? I need her.'

'She's driven Seth back to the pub because he isn't very well. Can I help?'

Maddy dragged her case down the stairs, and he began to run down the last few steps to get away from her. When he reached the bottom, he looked at her case. 'Are you leaving?'

'Not really. I'm going to stop at the pub for a bit. It's too cold here and I can't get any Internet.' There was no way she was going to tell him they had to leave because a maniac could be hiding in the walls watching their every move. There was no point in scaring the boy even more than she already had.

He nodded. 'I need to show you something. I was going to show Seth, but if he's not here, then I better show you.'

He looked solemn and she wondered what it could be. She reached the bottom step and wheeled her case to the front door where he was now standing, shifting from foot to foot.

'Where is it or what is it?' she asked. She was praying he wasn't going to say it was the lake people, because right now she was already a bag of nerves and feeling on edge.

'It's in the old summerhouse, up the fell.'

She frowned. 'Can it wait until later?'

He shook his head vehemently.

Maddy sighed and let go of her case. 'Well, I guess you better show me then. Is it far?'

'Not too far, but a bit of a climb.' He looked down at the shoes she was wearing. 'Wear your boots.'

Trying not to swear out loud, she turned back to the kitchen where she'd kicked her boots off the last time she'd worn them. All she wanted was to get out of this house until she knew where the fuck Connor was and that he wasn't about to jump out on her and scare her to death. She kicked off her dolly shoes and slipped her feet into her Uggs. If they got all muddy and covered in grass stains, she'd be well annoyed.

When she returned, Alfie was now standing outside on the front step, watching or looking into the distance. He nodded to see her boots then began to walk off, leaving Maddy to jog to catch-up with him.

'Slow down,' she said. 'You're far too fast for me. I'm not used to this. I told you I'm from a city where we don't have many mountains to climb up.'

'Fell,' he replied. 'This one's a fell. It's not a mountain.'

She laughed. 'You could be a tour guide when you're older. You know an awful lot about stuff I don't have a clue about.'

'What's a tour guide?'

'Someone like you, who knows an area well and can show people around.'

He grinned. 'I could do that.'

'Yes, you could. You would be very good at it.'

As they began to climb higher up the fell, the breeze carried the most awful, gut-wrenching smell towards them.

Maddy stopped, her face wrinkled in disgust. 'Alfie, what's that smell?'

He shrugged. 'Smells like a dead sheep, but much worse.'

Her stomach was already a mass of churning knots and this wasn't helping; it was making her want to retch. He lifted his T-shirt over his mouth and nose, so she did the same. A crumbling, decrepit stone building came into sight.

'What's that?' she asked.

'The old summerhouse. It's a wreck now. It belongs to the house. The people used to sit in it and look at the view of the lake and the mountains.'

'How do you know that?'

'Seth told me a long time ago when I asked him about it.'

She smiled. Seth knew everything.

She hoped he was okay; she didn't like to see him unwell. When she got to the pub, she'd make a fuss of him and tell him to take it easy for a bit. He'd been through so much the last few days, yet he had still been happy to help her out.

# SEVENTY-SIX

He reached the house and waited to see if anyone was around. She'd had to call in help, so things must have been getting to her. *He* must have been getting to her, which was exactly what he wanted. She was a nuisance, a liability, not to mention a pain in the arse. Her being here was stopping him from visiting his bodies in the lake and preventing him from disposing of any more bodies.

He noticed the front door was ajar. Standing still, he strained to listen for any sounds but couldn't hear a thing. Then again, the house was vast inside, so he didn't expect to hear much.

Stepping slowly inside, he began to look around. He didn't want to hurt her, but she wasn't leaving him with very much choice. If she stayed here, then she had to die. It was that simple. He'd tried his best to scare her off, but she was stubborn, and he liked the thought of having her pretty face as an addition to his collection. It would be the first time he'd killed someone so beautiful that his heart might regret it, but she'd be forever frozen in time. He'd always be able to visit her whenever he wanted, and she'd belong to him, so it would be worth it.

The house was empty. There were no voices or sounds carrying through the deserted corridors, and he noticed a small suitcase sitting by the door. Running upstairs to the room he knew she slept in, he pushed the door open and looked around. The bed was unmade, as if she'd left in a hurry, but there were still clothes around, a couple of pairs of shoes, and a pair of jeans was slung over the back of a chair. If she was leaving for good, wouldn't she have packed all her belongings?

He crossed to the bed, picked up a corner of the duvet, and saw an open notebook on the floor. Bending down, he picked it up and saw a list of names. Oh, she was good; much better than he'd given her credit for. She'd listed the people she'd met and what little she knew about them.

Sudden movement out on the fell caught his eye, and he dropped the book as he looked out of the window and saw two figures almost at the summerhouse. One was the kid – he'd recognise that walk anywhere. Pressing his face to the glass, he felt his heart begin to hammer in his chest. She was limping along beside the lad, and they were very shortly going to come face to face with her dead ex-boyfriend.

'Fuck, fuck, fuck!'

An anguished cry left his mouth as he slammed his palms against the glass. He had no choice but to get up there before they left and went for help. Panic filling his chest, he ran out of the room, down the stairs, and out onto the overgrown gardens. He kept a steady pace, not wanting to use every last bit of his energy before he'd even reached them. He didn't know how strong that kid was, but he should imagine he wouldn't go down without a fight.

The same went for her. If she was cornered and her life was in danger, he didn't imagine she would go down without a struggle either. She didn't look like much of a fighter, but the quiet ones never did. It was always the most unassuming people who were likely to take you by surprise. Despite the mixed emotions of anger and fear that were bubbling inside his chest, he grinned. It was all about to come down to survival of the fittest, and despite being outnumbered, he wasn't about to let anyone get the better of him.

# SEVENTY-SEVEN

'Ouch.' Maddy felt her ankle give way as she misjudged her footing and stumbled over a rock jutting out of the hillside. She landed on the ground in a heap.

Alfie turned to look at her. 'You okay?'

She smiled at him while desperately rubbing her ankle. It was the same one she'd sprained a couple of days ago, and it hurt like a bitch. She was tired and terrified of what the hell was making that smell. She just wanted to forget about it, go back to the house, wait for Glenys, then tell Seth about the smell. He and the Mountain Rescue guys would know what to do.

She was out of her depth here, and for the first time since she'd arrived, she was wholly regretting the decision to move her life out of the city and into the middle of fucking nowhere without so much as a phone signal.

But she never voiced any of her angry thoughts. She didn't want to scare Alfie, who was watching her with a worried look on his face. The poor kid was probably panicking in case he had to carry her back down.

'I'm fine,' she told him. 'My ankle gave way. It's still a bit sore from the other day.'

He was shaking his head. 'You're too slow, I told you that.'

She agreed with him; compared to him, she was like a snail. She looked back down the hillside in despair. *Oh crap, it's too far*, she thought. *I'm not going to be able to make it back down.*

A loud crack of thunder made the pair of them jump. She'd been so worried about her current predicament that she hadn't noticed the ominous dark clouds brewing in the sky above the lake. The smell of ozone clung heavily to the air, along with the stench of decomposition.

Neither of them had a coat, and the sky was getting blacker by the minute.

'We're going to have to take shelter in the summerhouse,' she told him.

He shook his head. 'No! Can't do that.'

'Why? I can't walk fast enough to get back down before the rain starts to hammer it down. It won't be for long. It's only a passing storm.'

He kept shaking his head from side to side. 'No. There's a zombie in there.'

She tried her best not to roll her eyes. *Christ, this kid should be the one writing the books.* What with lake people and zombies, he seemed to have a far better imagination than she did.

A huge flash of fork lightning lit the entire sky above their heads, and Alfie cowered.

'Need to take cover,' he mumbled. 'Dangerous out here.'

When Maddy stood up, her damaged ankle sent shooting pains up her calf and into her thigh, taking her breath away. Another crash above them made Alfie lift both hands to his ears, and she saw the look of panic on his face.

'Alfie, it's okay. You go back to the house and shelter there. Seth will be back soon. I'll stay up here and wait for the storm to pass. I'll be okay.'

He looked surprised. 'What about the zombie?'

'I'm okay,' she assured him. 'I like zombies. Go on, before the rain starts. There's no point in us both getting hypothermia. When the storm passes, you could go and see Seth if he hasn't turned up and ask him if he can help me to get back down.'

'Yep, Seth can help you.' Alfie nodded. 'Don't want no hypothermia; it can make you die. Bye. I'll come back soon.'

He turned and began to run down the side of the fell without so much as turning his head to see if she was still okay. To be honest, she didn't blame him; this was her own stupid fault. She should have worn some proper boots and watched where she was walking.

She began to limp as fast as she could towards the ramshackle building, and just hoped it was waterproof or, better still, thunderstorm-proof.

# SEVENTY-EIGHT

Maddy reached the building as the first of the heavy raindrops began to fall, landing with a splat on the top of her head. If she didn't take shelter, she would be soaked through in seconds.

The stench was emanating from inside the building, and she didn't know what to do. Something had died inside there, and it looked dark and even more creepy than the house. What if Alfie was right and there was a zombie inside? There was definitely something.

As the rain grew heavier, she clambered up and through the open windowsill. The smell inside was so overpowering it took her breath away. Standing still, she waited for her eyes to adjust to the gloominess. There were several holes in the roof, allowing a little light to come through.

Her eyes scanned the building. There were some broken shelves hanging down, a fireplace at one end of the room, and a couple of broken stools. As her gaze dropped to the floor, she squealed. There was a sleeping bag on the floor with what clearly looked like a person inside of it.

'Sorry... h-h-hello...' she stammered. 'Are you okay in there?'

The figure in the sleeping bag didn't move, and a lead ball

began to form in her gut. Oh God. Someone had taken shelter in here and died in their sleeping bag. Maddy tugged her phone out of her pocket. There were no bars on the signal, but she turned on the torch and shone it in the direction of the sleeping bag. This must have been what Alfie had meant when he'd said there was a zombie inside. The poor kid must have been bloody traumatised, because she was shaking and felt as if she was going to throw up.

She could see dark hair poking out of the top of the sleeping bag. Forcing herself to reach out, she bent down and gently shook the shoulder of whoever was inside it, in case they were in a deep sleep. But her hand recoiled at the stiffness, and she knew without a doubt that whoever was in there was dead and had been for some time.

Maddy tried to slow her breathing down; there was no use panicking. The storm was now raging noisily above the fells and a loud boom directly above the summerhouse, followed by a brilliant white flash of lightning, confirmed what she already knew. She was going have to stay here with a dead body for company until Alfie came back with Seth to rescue her.

Maddy wondered whether she should see if there was any ID on the body. Or should she leave it to the police? She pushed herself away from the wall towards the body and slowly knelt. Breathing through her mouth, she reached out with her shaking left hand and grabbed hold of the sleeping bag's soft, silky material. Jerking it down, she stared in horror at the familiar face that was looking straight at her, the eyes crawling with maggots.

The side of his head was completely crushed, and there were big, fat bluebottles crawling all over the bloodied mess. Dropping the material, she stood up and screamed. She had to get out of here! No longer caring about the raging storm outside, she threw herself out of the broken window and fell heavily onto the ground, hot, salty tears falling down her cheeks.

Despite the fact that she'd run to get away from him, the

shock of seeing Connor's dead body, and in that state, turned her stomach. Sobbing, she dragged herself to her feet and began to hobble as fast as she could away from the summerhouse, her heart racing. She didn't care about anything except getting to safety and phoning the police. The grass was slippy, the soles of her boots turning them into ice skates.

She felt herself losing her balance and was sliding down the hillside until a strong pair of arms caught her and stopped her descent. She let out a blood-curdling scream.

'Jesus Christ, Maddy, what's the matter? Are you trying to kill me?'

'Seth! Oh, thank God it's you. I've hurt my ankle and there's a body in that building.' Her words were rushing out in her desperation to explain. 'It-it-it's Connor. He's dead.'

A sob erupted from her throat and he pulled her close, holding her while the rain lashed down on the pair of them. As she clung to him, she didn't think she'd ever let go. What a mess.

He kissed the side of her cheek gently and whispered, 'Up until twenty minutes ago, I liked you, Maddy. In fact, I really liked you.'

She pulled away and looked into his face. It didn't even look like the Seth she'd got to know in the last few days. His eyes stared at her; he didn't break a smile.

She pulled away from him, confused. 'Seth, what do you mean?'

He shrugged. 'You should have come to the pub the first time I asked you, then we wouldn't be here now. Too stubborn for your own good. It's a shame it's going to have to end this way. It's been lovely getting to know you. We could have had something special.'

He took a step towards her and she threw herself at him. Her weight knocked him off balance and he began to slide backwards on the slippy surface, landing on the ground with a loud thud.

Without waiting to see his reaction, Maddy ran the other way as fast as her stupid ankle would let her, pain screaming through her entire body. Never had she prayed so hard to be able to run against the odds.

Too scared to turn around, she heard him groan, 'My head. Maddy, I'm bleeding. I'm sorry, please come back. I'm bleeding so bad, come back and help me. It hurts so much. I didn't mean to scare you.'

For a split second she almost turned around, almost went back to help him. Her heart was pulling her to make the decision; her mind was screaming, *Get the fuck away from him, Maddy! Don't go back!*

She listened to her head and carried on slipping and sliding, leaving long, muddy trails in the wet grass. If she could just reach the house, she could lock herself in and find something to protect herself with.

## SEVENTY-NINE

The steam billowing out from underneath the car bonnet was, in Stella's words, *'impressive as fuck'*. They'd finally found the turn-off for Lakeview House and were halfway along the drive when the car stopped dead amidst a hot, steaming bath. When Joe threw his door open, there was a smell of burning rubber and engine oil wisps of orange flames peered through the gap in the bonnet.

'Get out, it's going to blow!' he yelled.

Stella did as she was told and ran onto the grass verge, into the trees, to stand next to him. Minutes later, there was a huge explosion, and more smoke and steam erupted from underneath the bonnet. She let out a scream so loud it made him jump.

'Jesus, Joe,' she told him. 'Don't get a job working undercover for MI5. Chitty-bloody-bang-bang wouldn't have made that much noise. There goes our discreet entrance. We've probably scared Maddy into having a heart attack.'

She glanced at him and smiled at the look of horror etched across his face, then she started to laugh. Really laugh. And he couldn't help but join in.

'Shit,' he said, trying to control his giggles, 'my grandad is going to kill me. I've blown the fucker to pieces.'

This made them both laugh even harder, and she was clutching at her sides as tears rolled down her face.

'Come on,' she managed eventually. 'We'll have to walk the rest of the way. I hope it's not far. I've had enough adventure for one day.'

Joe bent down and kissed her cheek. 'What a waste of money. Sorry.'

'Don't be daft. Once we've talked to Maddy, I'll be phoning that garage. They can come and get the bloody car and tow it back; it's the least they can do. It would need to explode in the middle of a bloody thunderstorm, though. I'm going to get my hair wet now as well.'

As they began to pick their way carefully along the overgrown drive, Joe pulled her away from the canopy of trees she'd been walking under.

'It's too dangerous to go under there,' he explained. 'You could get struck by lightning. Hasn't anyone ever told you not to stand under a tree in a thunderstorm?'

She nodded. 'Let's be honest, I don't really do walking at the best of times. Especially not in the rain, or in the country, where there are so many trees. I'm a city girl born and bred, so I kind of forgot about that.'

He grinned. 'Survival 101, Stella. Good job you're not in the army.'

'Listen to who's talking, the guy with the exploding car. I bet Maddy is huddled in that big, old house, thinking someone has dropped a bomb on the drive.'

She couldn't wait to see her friend, to hug her tight and explain this whole sorry mess to her. Then they could share a couple of bottles of wine and have a good laugh over it.

# EIGHTY

The burning hot pain shooting up Maddy's leg was unbearable, but she carried on, gritting her teeth, slip-sliding towards the lake. He'd told her he was scared of the water, so even if she got onto the jetty she might be safe. *Or had that been a lie as well?* she wondered.

She was almost at the bottom of the fell. Her lungs were on fire, and she was exhausted, but she had to keep going; the alternative wasn't appealing.

A loud crash behind her made her turn, and she screamed again. Losing her balance, she sprawled onto the grass and felt a huge weight fall on top of her. The dirty bastard had rugby-tackled her to the ground, knocking the wind out of her. Maddy felt defeat fill her body, as all the fight left her.

He was sitting on her back, pressing his full weight onto her, making it hard for her to breathe. She tried one last time to wriggle free, but he gripped her head and slammed her face-first onto the wet grass. The sky above her was a fuzzy, black mess as she struggled to focus.

'Keep still,' he snarled, 'you're not getting away a second time. It's over, so stop fighting. You can't win.'

Maddy had never felt so betrayed in her life. She'd told him everything, shared her dark secrets with him, had wanted to sleep with him. In return, what had he wanted from her? Nothing. He'd just wanted her out of the house, but she still didn't understand why.

Rope bit into her soft skin as he tied her arms behind her back and her feet together. Getting slowly to his feet, he towered over her, then bent down and scooped her up like she was nothing more than a sack of potatoes. He threw her roughly over his shoulder and began walking towards the pier.

Maddy could only stare in despair at the water. The dirty, lying, murdering bastard wasn't afraid of the water at all.

As he stood at the end of the pier, Maddy turned her head to the side and saw two figures appearing around the bend on the driveway. It looked like Stella and the onion guy. *Was she hallucinating?* There was only one way to find out. Sucking in a deep breath, she screamed, 'Helppp!' as loud as she could.

The two figures began to run, and she prayed that, whoever they were, they were here to help her and not him.

She felt Seth's entire body tense in anger at her scream, and he turned to see the two figures heading towards them. Maddy braced herself to be dropped to the ground so that he could run to save himself. But instead, he bent his knees and launched her towards the black, ice-cold surface of the lake.

She hit the water with a huge splash and sank straight down into the murky depths. Maddy, her arms and legs bound, took a mouthful of water and began to choke as the cold sucked the air from her lungs. Unable to move her hands or feet enough to power her back up to the surface, she felt her feet touch something. The light was getting dimmer as she carried on moving down, and it was then that she came face to face with the row of bodies, all lined up, standing on the bottom.

In her head, she heard Alfie's voice: the lake people. Of course.

Struggling to breathe, her lungs burning as the water filled them, it seemed she was now going to be joining them.

* * *

Stella hadn't run since she'd been at school, but when she heard Maddy scream and saw the guy standing at the end of the pier with her over his shoulder, she'd started moving her legs as fast as she could. Joe was much quicker than her; his longer legs were pumping fast towards the pier and Maddy.

When she saw him launch her friend into the lake, Stella screamed and ran as fast as she could to the lakeside. Kicking off her shoes, she waded into the cold water.

'Fuck! Holy fuck, it's freezing!' she squealed.

Ignoring the scuffle taking place between Joe and the crazy guy on the rickety wooden pier, she swam towards where she'd seen Maddy go under the water. She had no idea what the hell was going on, but she knew she needed to get to her friend quickly. Thankfully, she swam much better than she ran.

Gulping in a deep breath, Stella pushed herself under the water, searching for her friend. It was murky and she couldn't see much, and she had to keep surfacing for air then going back under.

Ahead of her, she spotted a figure and reached out for it. Grabbing hold of it, she tried to pull it to the surface, but it wouldn't move. When she went back down and looked again, she realised it was a dead man she was trying to drag up, and quickly let go.

Looking frantically around her, she suddenly saw Maddy, her eyes closed, floating towards the bottom. Giving it her all, Stella pushed herself forwards and, grabbing her by the neck, dragged her friend to the surface of the lake. As they broke through the water, she heard the rotting wooden pier let out a crack that echoed around the valley, then it collapsed, sending both Joe and the guy he was fighting with plunging into the lake.

Stella prayed Joe could swim as she put her arm under Maddy's chin and half swam, half dragged her to the side of the lake. Exhausted, she reached the lakeside where a woman with bright purple hair and a teenage boy were standing. They immediately grabbed Maddy, dragging her body along the bank of the lake onto the wet grass. The woman turned back and offered her hand to Stella, but she shook her head, gasping for air and relieved to be out of the water.

The woman turned around and dropped to the ground where she began to perform CPR on Maddy, while the boy untied the ropes binding her legs and arms. Stella didn't know where to look; she was scared for her friend and terrified for Joe. *Joe! Where was he?*

She turned back to see him swimming towards her, but there was no sign of the crazy guy he'd been tussling with. Stella waded back in, grabbed Joe's hand, and tugged him out. He stared in horror at the sight of Maddy's lifeless body. Sirens somewhere in the distance made Stella breathe a sigh of relief, and she was aware of the teenage boy running towards the driveway as the sounds grew louder.

Maddy began to cough and splutter as the woman straddling her chest pumped her heart, forcing the water out of her lungs. Then Maddy's eyes opened, and the strange-looking woman whooped with delight, clambered off her, and grinned at Stella and Joe.

'Bloody hell! I knew that spread of cards spelt disaster, but I didn't realise just how much.' She turned back to Maddy. 'You'll be fine now. The police are here and an ambulance should be following.'

Maddy turned slowly on her side, then tried to push herself up. 'Where is he? Where's Seth?'

Stella shrugged. 'Who's Seth?'

'The guy who tried to kill me,' Maddy croaked. 'He's killed Connor. I found his body in a summerhouse on the fell.'

Glenys turned to Stella. 'I'm Glenys. I live in the village.'

Stella nodded. 'Stella, Maddy's friend. This is my boyfriend, Joe. We came to see if she was okay and to warn her about Connor.'

Just then, two police officers came running towards them, and Glenys began to explain what had happened. While they were shouting down their radios for back-up, Alfie bent down to Maddy.

'Are you okay?' he asked.

She nodded. 'Thank you, Alfie, yes. And I know now what you meant. I saw the lake people.'

'You did? Is Seth with them? He hurt you.'

She gulped. 'I don't think he is, and yes, he did.'

Glenys put her arm around her son and hugged him. 'He's a proper hero, aren't you, Alfie? He came to the shop and told me you'd hurt yourself on the fell. I went back to tell Seth, but he wasn't there so I rang the police because I wasn't sure what to do.'

Maddy smiled weakly. 'Thank you.'

She looked up at Stella. 'I don't know how or why you're here, but I'm so glad to see you. I thought I was hallucinating when I saw you both.' She studied her friend's face more closely and frowned. 'What happened to your face, Stella?'

Stella bent down and hugged her friend. 'It's a long story. I'll tell you after you've been checked out at the hospital. You almost...' The words stuck in her throat; she couldn't get them out.

Two paramedics came running across the grass towards them, out of breath.

'Some bloody idiot has blocked the driveway,' one explained.

Joe mumbled. 'Sorry, the car broke down and then went on fire.'

The paramedics began handing out foil blankets to Maddy, Stella, and Joe.

'Right, are we walking wounded? Because if you are, I need you to walk back to the ambulance with me?'

All three of them nodded.

'Good, come on then. We need to get you to the hospital and get you checked out.'

Glenys grabbed one of Maddy's arms, the paramedic took the other, and they helped her slowly to her feet.

'I'll wait here and see if there's any news on Seth,' she told Maddy. 'Then I'll lock up and bring your stuff to the hospital.'

'Thank you.' She looked around wildly. 'Do you think he's dead? He killed those people, Glenys. He put them in the lake.' Maddy sobbed, 'He was going to leave me to die in there.'

She nodded. 'I know, sweetie. I can hardly believe it.'

Maddy, her teeth chattering loudly, put her head down and limped towards the waiting ambulance.

# EIGHTY-ONE

Maddy, Stella, and Joe sat in the small side room. All three of them were dressed in washed-out blue hospital scrubs. The two detectives standing opposite them were furiously writing everything down; they had been there for the last thirty minutes. It was Maddy they were questioning now.

'Did you see where Seth went?'

Stella interrupted. 'No, sorry. She was a bit dead, lying there having her chest pumped while the rest of us were praying she was going to make it.'

The young female detective who'd asked blushed.

Maddy glared at Stella, who was guarding her like a pit bull, and reached out to grip her friend's arm. 'It's okay, Stella, I can answer, thank you.' She smiled wearily at the detectives. 'I have no idea. Did you not find him?'

Joe spoke. 'He was definitely in the water. We both fell in when the wooden jetty collapsed.'

'We haven't found him yet, but we have divers out searching the lake. They'll be recovering the bodies and doing a thorough search.'

'What am I supposed to do?' Maddy asked. 'Where do I go? Is it safe to go back to Lakevview House?'

Stella folded her arms across her chest. 'You are not seriously considering going back there after everything?'

Maddy nodded. 'I love it there, and Seth's gone. The whole area is crawling with the police who will arrest him when they find him, so I don't think he's going to get anywhere near the house or me. Besides, the builders are due to start on Monday, so it's going to be full of people. I won't be on my own. Or, not much. I also need to finish this book, and' – she managed a tired smile – 'there's another I have an idea for and want to write as soon as possible.'

Stella shook her head. 'You're crazy.'

Maddy grinned but nodded.

'The grounds are out of bounds, they're a crime scene now,' the older detective explained. 'But I don't suppose we can stop you going into the house after our people have done a sweep to make sure there are no bodies inside.'

Maddy shook her head. 'There are definitely none inside. We checked every single room the day after I moved in.'

The detective nodded. 'Okay, then I'm sure you can. We'll let you know as soon as we have an update on Mr Taylor.'

* * *

A few hours later, Glenys turned into the drive of Lakeview House, nervously stealing glances at her passengers. Maddy was sitting next to her, Stella and Joe were squashed in the back next to Alfie. The broken-down car had been towed away, allowing the police access to the grounds, which were marked off with blue-and-white police tape. A huge police truck was parked on the grass near to the lake, with the words UNDER-WATER SEARCH TEAM emblazoned across the front of it.

The mood in the car was sombre, to say the least. Never had so many people spoken so few words.

She parked in front of the steps. Maddy got out first, walked up to the front door and pushed it open. Inside were lots of dusty footprints where the police officers had been in and out, searching the house from top to bottom – every cupboard, nook, and cranny, the attics and the cellars.

Seth hadn't been back inside, she'd been told; no one had seen him since he'd fallen into the lake.

Maddy was sad, shocked, and disappointed that the man she'd found herself falling in love with had led the kind of double life that would have made a Russian KGB agent proud.

She led the other down to the dining room where she set about tugging the dust sheets off the remaining tables and chairs.

'If I'm going to have guests, I may as well use the place,' she said. 'Sit down and I'll make us all a hot drink. There're some packets of biscuits in the cupboards. I'll bring them in, and we can stuff our faces.'

Glenys smiled. 'I'll help you. And I can do better than that. Alfie and I baked some fairy cakes for you. They're in the kitchen.'

Stella crossed to the window to look at the police activity outside. Joe stood behind her and they watched as the police dragged a black body bag from the edge of the lake, then picked it up and carried it to the waiting private ambulance.

'All those people,' she murmured, 'it gives me the creeps. I wish she'd come back with us, Joe, and forget about this place.'

He put his arms around her and held her from behind. 'I kind of understand why she wants to stay, though. It's a beautiful old house, and Seth won't come back here, it's too risky. If I'm honest, I think he's dead, unless he's one hell of a strong swimmer and crossed the lake underwater.' He kissed her ear. 'At least we can stay and keep her company for a few days. The garage doesn't know if or how long it's going to take to fix my grandad's car, so we might be stranded here.'

Stella laughed. 'Oh God, that poor car. I'd forgotten all about it.'

They stood that way, watching the police activity by the lake, and waiting for Maddy to bring their drinks in. Stella couldn't wait to tell her they weren't leaving for a few days.

\* \* \*

Maddy leaned onto the kitchen side. Picking up the plug from the radio, she pushed it into the socket and smiled at the sound of the sweet jazz music that filled the air. It wasn't Ella Fitzgerald, not that it would have mattered. She knew now that it had been Seth all along, trying to scare her to leave the house. He didn't want her living here because it meant he couldn't carry on killing and he was scared she might find his lake people. It was a good job he hadn't realised that Alfie had found them; it scared her to think that he might have hurt the boy to keep him quiet.

She felt sad about Connor, because she was a decent human being. But after hearing from Stella what had happened back in London, Maddy wondered what he would have done to her if he had found her.

Glenys put the mugs on a tray and grabbed the plate of cakes. Smothered in chocolate buttercream with an assortment of sweets stuck to the top of them, they looked delicious. Exactly the sort of thing you should be eating after almost being murdered by a serial killer.

As they sat around the huge table, sipping their drinks and nibbling cake, Maddy tried to ignore the activity out on the front lawn. She was so happy for Stella. She and Joe made a great couple, so at least something good had come out of this whole disaster.

Alfie had gone outside to watch the police, and one of the divers was chatting to him. If it hadn't been for Alfie going to get help, she didn't know what would have happened. Someone had definitely been watching over her.

Maddy sighed. She wanted nothing more than to finish the book she was writing, because she was desperate to start a new one. And this one already had a title: *Lakeview House*.

# A LETTER FROM HELEN

Dear reader,

I want to say a huge thank you all, my amazing readers, for choosing to read *Lakeview House*. If you did enjoy it, and want to keep up to date with all my latest releases, just sign up at the following link. Your email address will never be shared and you can unsubscribe at any time.

*www.bookouture.com/helen-phifer*

I hope you loved *Lakeview House* and if you did I would be very grateful if you could write a review. I'd love to hear what you think, and it makes such a difference helping new readers to discover one of my books for the first time.

I love hearing from my readers – you can get in touch on my Facebook page, through Twitter, Goodreads or my website.

Thanks,

Helen x

# KEEP IN TOUCH WITH HELEN

www.helenphifer.com

facebook.com/Helenphifer1

twitter.com/helenphifer1

instagram.com/helenphifer

# ACKNOWLEDGEMENTS

If you're reading this, I thank you from the bottom of my heart—you are the reason I write my stories. Your support means the world to me, and if anyone hasn't told you this today you are wonderful, loved, appreciated, and make the world a much better place.

I'd like to thank Jo Bartlett for her unwavering support. She read this story and gave me the encouragement I needed to carry on. The same applies as above, Jo; you are wonderful, loved, very much appreciated, and definitely make the world a much better place.

I have to thank Steve because if it wasn't for his encouragement, I probably wouldn't ever finish any of my books. He's the one pushing me to go write when I want to lie on the sofa binge-watching *Ghost Adventures*.

Much love to my wonderful, crazy, fun-loving family for being so amazing (most of the time, you all have your moments). I love you all so much.

I'd like to thank my book club members Sam, Joanne, Debbie, Wendy, Sam, Debbie, Zena, Anna, Krog, Jenni, Helen, Margaret, and Jackie for brightening up our Monday evenings and sharing my love of all things literary.

A huge debt of gratitude to Paul O'Neill for his fabulous surveyor's reports.

Helen xx

Made in the USA
Monee, IL
24 October 2022

16498409R00184